# EACH TO THEIR OWN

## A MAGS MUNROE STORY

## JEAN GRAINGER

*Mags has a lovely husband, and so do I.*

# CHAPTER 1

*S*taring into the bathroom mirror, I force my eyes open as wide as possible, trying to stretch out the wrinkled bags into which they are sinking. It doesn't work. I swear my eyebrows are where my eyelids used to be. Hooded, that's the word.

Believe it or not, I did not know I had turned into the evil hag from *Snow White* until I saw the picture Kate took yesterday on her new phone and shared to the family group on WhatsApp, saying, *Mam xxx*. She's only twelve, bless her, and she wasn't trying to be cruel, but honestly, I look around a hundred. My nana had a face like one of those old maps, all wrinkled and sun damaged, and I'm not far behind her.

As soon as it pinged up on my screen, I rushed to ask Kieran if I look that bad in real life. He told me I was mad and hadn't a clue what I was on about, that I looked grand and exactly the same as I always did, but he was watching some bit of the World Cup on television, men in green and purple playing other men in blue and pink, so he was being even more unobservant than usual. That's as close as you'll get to a compliment from an Irish fella anyway. One time I got a spray tan for a wedding, and he told me that it 'took the raw look off me'. So not exactly a silver-tongued devil, my husband, but still.

Stupidly, I then went to ask the same question of Ellie. She said that the picture was absolutely accurate and that was exactly how I looked and it was fine. I think she knew it wasn't what I wanted to hear, but she's fifteen and doesn't see why she has to be nice to the woman who gave birth to her.

Turning fifty hasn't bothered me that much up to now, and anyway, fifty is the new forty they say. Or people of my age say. It's funny how your perception of old keeps changing. When I was Ellie's age, anyone over fifty was over the hill and there was no difference between sixty and ninety. But that's changed. Mam told me about a woman in her dancing class who died at seventy-eight. 'Ah, she was no age,' I heard myself say. Mad.

I give up trying to flatten my eye bags. The towel I have wrapped around me is gaping at my middle. Towels can't shrink, I don't think, so I must be getting broader as well as saggier. Which would explain why I'm having a bit of a struggle with my garda uniform. The seam at the top of my thigh split the other day, and I had to get Mam to fix it. I noticed when she returned the trousers, she'd let the waist of them out a bit, the way she quietly does with the mother-of-the-bride dresses when the mother in question has failed to stick to her faithful promise to lose a stone before the big day.

So that was depressing, even though it was kind of Mam.

A meme that popped up on Facebook says people see themselves as four times better looking than they actually are, though how that can be quantified, I've no idea. But there is probably a grain of truth in it, because up until yesterday I thought I looked grand. Not a Kardashian, obviously, but just fine. A middle-aged Irishwoman, with a body that created two human beings who now run around wreaking havoc on the planet, or at least on our house. And though Kieran isn't a man for flowery compliments, he says I look nice, and, well, he fancies me. So there's that, I suppose. But Kate's picture has rattled me, and now all I can think is, *I have to do something.*

Gerry the hairdresser already convinced me to put in a few blond highlights to soften up the greys that insist on sprouting from my head, but I'm not doing that again. I'm a brunette, naturally so for years and in recent years with a little help. He'd said the blond would look much better, and he summoned a gaggle of juniors to crowd around me when it was done, all of them oohing and aahing, which I took as a sure sign that Gerry knew it was desperate on me too. The juniors never got called over when I had my roots touched up warm chestnut. I've held this theory for years: If the young hairdressers crowd around making complimentary noises on your new hairdo, it's time to buy a hat; if they don't make a peep, it's probably fine.

Kate and Ellie had exchanged a silent conversation when I walked in that day with the new hair, and my worst fears were confirmed. Kieran didn't notice, of course. That man is half blind, I'm convinced of it, and when I pointed it out, he said it was nice, easier to keep. Whatever that meant. I doubt that anyone ever told Kim Kardashian that her hair is easy to keep.

Getting old isn't fair on us women. Kieran looks better now than he did as a young fella. His hair is going silvery grey, and even the slight paunch of his belly serves to make him look cuddly and handsome. He is going all silver fox, and I am turning frumpy, soft and distinctly middle-aged. I'm not vain, I swear, but honest to God, this is hard to bear.

In the bedroom, I blow-dry my hair as best I can and apply some make-up, trying to avoid the increasing number of lines on my face where foundation, instead of enhancing my looks, seems to settle in the cracks like one of those old medieval paintings.

Maybe I should get Botox. Everyone is doing it nowadays apparently.

Sharon tells me not to bother going to a fancy place, that there is a woman doing it in her garage out the Headford road. The idea of injecting a form of botulism into my face in a swish clinic in Galway already fills me with terror, so the prospect of a discount service by a woman who's done a one-day training course, wielding a syringe in a space carved out from old pots of paint and stepladders, doesn't fill me with confidence. But it is tempting to let nature be enhanced.

If I start that, though, where will it end? Suck some fat from my tummy, sharpen up my softened jaw, perk up the boobs that are succumbing to gravity more and more with every passing year? Well, if I don't, soon my bra will be around my waist. Honestly, time is a cruel thing.

Kieran and I are going out with Sharon and Trevor tonight. It's Trevor's birthday, and Sharon's present to him is a night off from her cooking. Sharon's my best friend since junior infants, and she's the worst cook known to man. She, Trevor and her son, Sean, live mostly on Pot Noodles and sandwiches as far as I can see. They don't seem to mind, though, and Sharon is as thin as a rail despite it, the lucky wagon. No wonder she can wear the most fashionable clothes known to woman and not look like mutton dressed as lamb.

I had been planning to wear my new orange top and black jeans, but now all I can see about my body is lumps and bumps, so I'll have to come up with something more concealing.

I rummage in the wardrobe and pull out a dress, a wine wrap-around that Mam gave me last Christmas, and which she assured me would hide a multitude of sins. Mam has a great eye for clothes, which is just as well, as she owns the shop that dresses the female population of Ballycarrick.

I extract a shapewear slip from my drawer and wriggle into the wretched flesh-coloured thing. By the way, if your flesh is that colour, you've bigger problems than a lumpy dress, but I digress. The straps dig into my shoulders, but needs must, and I slip the dress over it. I don't look too bad, but then I realise my milk bottle–white legs would frighten the dogs. I need tights. More rummaging in the sock drawer, and under a pile of Kieran's big work socks, which he wears inside his steel-capped boots, and a random pink ankle sock with frills that must have been Kate's when she was in nursery, I find a pair of inexplicably named 'rose quartz' coloured tights. I give a sigh of relief.

But in my haste to pull them on, I stick my finger through the delicate fabric.

'AAARRGGHH!'

My throat tightens. Things are not going my way today. The station was crazy busy all day, so I was late getting home from work, we're due in the restaurant in an hour, and I have to drive because

Kieran is meeting me there. He's always working late; he's so busy with his roofing business these days. He's desperate to recruit more help, but qualified roofers are hard to find and he hasn't time to train an apprentice. And he had to call to his mother after work as well, some crisis apparently. Knowing my monster-in-law, the crisis will be nothing, but she does like her power games. She likes to show me that Kieran might be my husband but he was her son first. Nora Munroe was put on this earth to test me; of that I have no doubt.

I can't resort to spray tan. I can't get back into the shower, as I've done my hair and make-up, so I'll have to run out to the chemist for more tights.

I drag the dress over my head and throw it on the bed, pull down the slip that allegedly sucks everything in – what on earth do they make those things of? Titanium? I pull on a hoodie and a pair of leggings and hurry downstairs, grabbing my car keys from where I left them on the hall table.

I can see Ellie sitting in the kitchen, on her phone that she never lets out of her hand.

I stick my head around the door. 'I've to get tights. I'll be back in twenty minutes.'

'Don't get those disgusting brown ones you always get.' She never takes her eyes off the phone.

I bite back a sharp response. Ellie is the final arbiter, according to herself, on what is cool and what is not. But I can't just let her rudeness slide. 'It shouldn't matter to you what kind I get –'

'"The apparel oft proclaims the man",' she quotes superciliously. She is involved in youth theatre, and to hear her, you'd swear she is the next Kenneth Branagh. She's quoting things at us all the time. It drives me daft.

I decide to let it slide after all. A teenage hissy fit or me fuming at her isn't going to help this situation. 'There's a fish pie in the fridge. Pop it in the oven for yourself and Kate – she'll be starving when she comes in after running around for two hours at camogie training.'

Ellie doesn't answer.

'Ellie?' I repeat, with a hint of exasperation.

She chuckles at something on the screen.

'Ellie, the pie!' I snap. I could give in and do it myself, but I'm sick of this.

'All right, all right,' she snaps back, like I've not had to ask several times. 'The pie, I know. I'll do it.' She gives a truly theatrical sigh, as if she is the most put-upon victim of child labour ever imagined.

I leave before I scream and drive to the chemist for tights. It's the only place that sells them that will still be open at six.

Julie Dullea is behind the counter; the chemist's was her father's before hers, and I often wonder why she never went further afield. Although look who's talking.

'Hi, Mags, can I help you?' she asks.

'Not unless you have a magic wand and a time machine to make me look twenty-one again. How do you do it, Julie?' She was in my class at school, but she looks way younger than me. She has all the creams for anti-ageing at her fingertips; that must be it. She never had kids either. That could also be it. She is fit and always groomed to perfection, her short blond hair in a cute pixie style that makes her look even younger.

'Mags, you're a beautiful woman,' Julie says encouragingly. 'And doesn't your husband adore you. I see the way he smiles at you.'

I feel guilty then for being so caught up about my looks. Julie is such a lovely person as well as being gorgeous, but she is single. It is a sad story. She was engaged years ago to a lad from Barna, but he was killed in a motorbike accident. Her heart was broken, and that was it for her. Some women are like that; they can only love once. Maybe she'll move on one day. It took my mam years after my father died. She was in her seventies before she finally fell in love again and married her longtime friend – and owner of Dillon's Menswear in Ballycarrick – Joe Dillon. Apparently, Joe had been admiring Marie from a distance for donkey's years but could never drum up the guts to say anything during their weekly lunches in the Samovar. It wasn't until Mam took up dancing with a very distinguished Filipino doctor that Joe decided he'd better strike or forever keep his peace. He did, and Mam had a dilemma between the pair of them, but in the end, Joe won.

I examine the display of what Ellie calls 'disgusting brown' tights. They are in fact skin coloured – not the colour of my skin, you understand, or the skin of anyone from Ballycarrick, hence the need for them, but the much more attractive smooth tanned skin of people in Barbados or Spain or somewhere.

'How is your mother, Mags?' Julie asks. Maybe she's been thinking the same as me, about Mam getting married last year.

I smile as I go up with my tights. 'Happier than she's been for years.'

'Still not planning to retire from the boutique?'

'Not a bit of it.' I pay by tapping my card. 'Sure she's only young yet, or so she says if Joe dares suggest calling it a day.'

Julie laughs. 'I suppose you're as young as you feel.'

Which makes me about eighty, older than my own mother. OK. I'm clearly just in a mood, I know. Nothing is right. Don't mind me.

# CHAPTER 2

*W*e've decided to go local instead of to the Carrick Arms Hotel, as Sharon and I usually do for the big occasions. Tatiana, who owns the Samovar, has just turned the back room of the pub into a restaurant, and the word on the street is that the food is as good as her coffee.

Plus we love Tatiana and want to show her our support. She is a hilarious character and such an addition to Ballycarrick. She's stunningly gorgeous in a kind of terrifying way. She basically took this pub, McLoughlin's as it was known, from her then husband 'Leery Benny' and gave him the high road. Benny thought he was getting some docile little Russian bride on the internet who'd be eternally grateful to him for rescuing her, but Tatiana was nobody's victim, and she soon had the measure of her new lecherous husband. So not long after her arrival, Benny moved to England, leaving Tatiana the pub, and that was that. Why he did it, or what hold she had over him to make him up sticks like that, has been the source of much Ballycarrick speculation, but nobody knows the truth.

I arrive outside the pub at the same time as Kieran, and he hugs me and tells me how great I look, disgusting brown tights and all. In fact he squeezes me so hard that between that and the shapewear, my head nearly pops off like a cork.

He releases me, I gasp for breath, and we walk hand in hand into the magnificent lounge bar. On the outside the Samovar looks like any pub you'll find in any street in Ireland, but inside, it's like nothing you'd expect. Tatiana has completely overhauled the tired dark wood and sticky carpet décor of Benny's time and turned the place into sort of a mixture of industrial chic, with brick walls and exposed iron girders, and 1920s speakeasy, with luxurious but really comfortable domestic furniture and some truly quirky pieces. A scarlet velvet chaise longue here, a tasselled standard lamp there, and all around the walls are pictures in gold frames, depicting the scenes and people of Vladivostok, where Tatiana is from, and also photos of the regulars. It makes me smile every time I go to the ladies to see a picture of Joe Dillon and his daughter, Clare, and then in the next frame is Yul Brynner the actor, who was apparently a friend of Tatiana's dad. So you see, it's a bit of a mad old place, but everyone loves it now.

'Is everything OK, love?' I ask as we take two stools at the bar. It's not that he's not usually affectionate, but I sensed something else in that mighty hug – a craving for comfort maybe.

'Yeah...I think so.'

'Think?'

He looks worried. 'Mam and Dad are having a bit of a spat, but they won't say what it's about. You know Dad. He doesn't say much at the best of times.'

'Mm.' Understatement of the century. Kieran's father is nice enough, I suppose, but he never speaks, like almost not a word. I've heard about twenty sentences out of his mouth in the sixteen years we've been married.

'And Mam always wants to make out everything is perfect in the House of Munroe. It was strange, though. She kept showing me this picture of her holding me when I was a baby and telling me how glad she is she had me, because I've turned out so well, with my family and my roofing business and everything.'

9

That *is* strange. Nora doesn't usually praise Kieran's life. To be honest she is still annoyed at him for marrying 'beneath him', to a mere sergeant in the guards; she'd hoped he'd marry a bit higher up the social ladder, like his three sisters. Nora isn't capable of saying her son-in-law Fergus's name without adding 'very high up in the Bank of Ireland', and Seamus, her second son-in-law, is always the 'top man in cardiology in Galway University Hospital'. Leonard is a school principal, but it's a posh school, so he's 'very well respected in the field of private education'.

I dread to think what my add-on is. 'Very low down in the guards', I imagine.

We had a big falling out a few years ago when I got sick of her snide remarks. In Nora's estimation, my house is too messy – well, it is, but four people live there, not just me – I don't cook enough home-made meals and Kieran always looks scruffy. I mean, come on – her grown adult son doesn't dress in top hat and tails and it's my fault? We've patched it up now, in that Irish way of never discussing it again and carrying on as if nothing had happened, but I suspect Nora Munroe is never going to be my biggest fan.

Kieran always tells me to ignore her. He's good to her, but he's always backed me when she sniffs about me not being classy enough, and he says she drives him daft too with her notions.

Like last year she horrified the whole family. She went a bit quare in the head and got obsessed with an American politician, some distant relative of 'Fergus, who is very high up in the Bank of Ireland'. To be fair to him, Fergus explained at every chance he got that he didn't know the man nor the sky above him, but it made no difference. Nora was going to be the reason Ballycarrick had its American moment. Ballyporeen had Reagan, Wexford had Kennedy, County Down had the Bush family, Mayo had Biden, Moneygall in County Offaly even dug up a few relatives for Barack Obama. And Nora was going to have her day, hell or high water. She decorated the house with American flags and everything. She was a laughingstock in the town because of it, until it all came crashing down because your man, whatever his name was, dropped out of public life due to some scandal or another – don't ask me what – and 'needed to spend more time with his family'. So that, to the intense relief of the Munroes and the rest of Ballycarrick, was that.

Nora has been subdued for months since then, and I've seen even less of her than normal. In fact, now that I think about it, I've not seen either her or Kevin in ages.

We're a bit early, and our table isn't ready yet, so we order a couple of drinks at the bar. Kieran has a pint of Guinness, and I get a red wine. I'd been going to stick to fizzy water, as we have both my car and Kieran's van with us, but thinking about Nora makes me want to drink, and I decide we can get a taxi home then back in the morning; we're only a couple of miles outside the town, so it won't break the bank.

'Thanks, Tatiana,' I say as she puts down our drinks.

'You're welcome,' she says sternly. She isn't a smiler, or a woman to use more words than strictly necessary, but she has a kind heart, and she runs this place so well that I don't think I've ever had to come in here with my garda hat on to deal with anyone. I asked her once how she did it, and she gave me her typically blunt but accurate answer.

'Other bars give drink to people when they are already drunk. That is greedy and stupid. Me? No. I stop giving drink before that, and it is better for everyone. Nice people now come here, your mother, Joe, you and Kieran, Sharon and Trevor, because you know there will not be some fool talking rubbish, or a fight, or something stupid like this.'

She's dead right. When Benny was in charge, we wouldn't have dreamed of coming in, unless I had to as the local sergeant. But now the place is lovely and peaceful.

Sharon and Trevor arrive at the same time as the drinks, and me and Sharon embrace each other while Trevor and Kieran shake hands and do a bit of shoulder slapping. Sharon and I have been best friends coming up on forty-six years. We've rarely had a fight, just one or two squabbles over the years but nothing big really. Trevor and Kieran get on great, thank goodness. Kieran calls a Guinness for Trevor and a vodka and tonic for Shar, and the two men sidle up the bar together, towards the telly, where a team in blue and white is playing a team in red and yellow in whatever bit of the World Cup is on at the moment.

Sharon takes Kieran's stool at the bar. She looks gorgeous in a glittery shirt and tight jeans, as stylish as ever. 'How's everything, Mags?'

'Pretty much the same as when I spoke to you yesterday. How'd it go this afternoon?'

She's applied for the position of manager in a graphics place in Galway, and I'm dying to find out how the interview went. Graphics wouldn't be her first choice of career; she always worked in fashion retail when we were young. But then she married Danny Boylan, who was loaded, and became a stay-at-home mother, and then when they broke up, she kind of disintegrated and did nothing for ages, so now she's desperate to get a proper job and earn some money.

Trevor's a musician with his own band, Tequila Mockingbird, and used to be in big demand at pubs and nightclubs and things like that. But since Covid, people have changed their habits a lot. People go to the pub less now; it's cheaper and easier to have people round and eat and drink with them in your own house and not worry about getting a taxi home. So as a result, he's not flush with money. Plus Sharon's still refusing to look for a single penny from her slimy ex, Danny Boylan, a noble but self-destructive move. Trevor spends his now plentiful spare time fixing up his late mother's house. If they can rent it out, it will take some of the strain off their finances, but it's going to take a while because he's having to do all the work himself.

'Disaster,' Sharon says glumly. 'The money is rubbish and the hours worse, so it won't work even if I did get it, which I won't. The one who interviewed me thought she was uber-cool and all angles, you know? She had a black dress for all the world like a kite and a white lace thing under it, jet-black hair in a mullet – I swear, an actual mullet – with a fringe that looked like it had been chewed off by an Alsatian, and she looked me up and down like I was something the cat dragged in. So no. Definitely not.'

There's a loud cheer from the men around the TV. Blue and white are beating red and yellow, it would seem. And that's a good thing. As you can see, sport bores me senseless. It's all 'they did some sport, then we did some, then they did more and now they're the winner, but next week we'll come back and do more of this and hopefully better than them'... Honestly, why do people care?

'Maybe it went better than you thought?'

'Not a bit of it. The one interviewing me was about twelve, and she kept saying things like "backloading inventory" and "growth hacking" and "bio breaks", and when I said I didn't know what she was on about, she says, "I suspect a disconnect. Can you just restate your definition of this concept?"' Sharon imitates your one's stupid accent and I laugh, but she shakes her head glumly. 'Maybe I'm just too old, Mags, seriously like.'

Even though I've been feeling exactly the same way since yesterday, I don't want to listen to it from my best friend. 'You're not too old. Don't be daft. And you didn't really want to work in graphics anyway. What would you love?'

'What are we on, *Highway to Heaven*? "What would I love?"' She scoffs.

'Seriously, just answer the question. If you could have any job you want, what would it be?'

'To be Hugh Jackman's private dresser? Taste tester for Veuve Clicquot? Willy Wonka?' She rolls her eyes humorously. 'I don't know, do I? If I had a dream job, I'd have trained for something, I suppose, wouldn't I?'

'OK, try it a different way. What do you want from a job?'

'Well, that's easier. I want enough money to make it worth my while – not loads, like, but enough. I want to not have a huge commute and spend ages in traffic. I want flexible hours that if I've to take Sean to the dentist or to see him in the school play, then I can do that.'

'OK, and what are your skills?'

She laughs. 'Are you interviewing me for a job in the station, Mags? 'Cause I'd be a terrible guard.'

'You would. They don't let us wear heels for starters, so that's you out.'

'I know, reason six million and fifty why I never joined the guards. The uniform is so... – I'm just going to say it, Mags – unsexy.'

I chuckle. 'Do you know, Shar, I'm fairly sure, back at the foundation of the state when they were designing the uniform, they didn't think, "How can we make the national police force sexy?"'

'Well, just as well that wasn't their goal, because they failed miserably. That dress is lovely on you, by the way. Definitely sexy. Kieran will have it off you tonight in no time.'

'But then the poor man will encounter my new shapewear and have to go for his hammer and chisel.'

As we're laughing, Tatiana reappears to tell us our table is ready, and the men return from the end of the bar and tell us with great delight the outcome of the game. Blue and white are Argentina, and some man called Lionel Messi is 'the goat'. I look at them like they're speaking in tongues. Sharon tells me I know nothing about modern culture because GOAT means 'greatest of all time' and that even the dogs on the street know that.

I watch fondly as Trevor helps Sharon down from the stool and puts his arm around her as we all make our way to the restaurant.

I'm so glad my best friend has found love again. She is well and truly over Danny Boylan, but it took some time. She married him when we were in our twenties, and I knew then, what was confirmed later, that he was an absolute snake, and sure enough he cheated on her all the time. The amazing thing is Sharon is gorgeous and he's only very average. But he broke her heart, and it's really only now she's back to her old self.

There was a time I'd thought she'd be like Julie from the chemist's and never get over it, but she's truly copped on about Danny now. He is a man-baby, and even when he takes Sean out, the boy comes home with stories of missed films, closed shops and sitting in the car while his father talks on the phone. Like last week, Danny collected Sean from school for an overnight visit. Sharon was in Galway visiting her aunt in a nursing home but had texted Danny to say Sean's jersey was drying on the line in the garden and for him to take it because Sean had a match the following morning. Of course when she got home, the jersey was still on the line and Sean was texting frantically about needing it for the match. Sharon drove it over to Danny's house, and he came out to meet her, saying he'd had to take a very important call when he got her text and forgot about the jersey. 'Oh, for God's sake,' Sharon said in exasperation. 'Did I marry you or have you? What was I thinking? You're a waste of space.' She shoved the jersey at his chest and walked away.

So you can see, she's not afraid any more of Danny trying to take Sean away from her, like he tried to do one time, egged on by his new woman, 'Chloe from the chipper'. Now Danny just tries to buy Sean's affections with expensive presents, but it doesn't work. Sean is a smart cookie and knows what his father is like.

Poor Chloe from the chipper thought she was really after landing on her feet when she had an affair and then two children with Sharon's husband. But leopards don't change their spots, and Danny Boylan was soon up to his old tricks again, messing around with married women and young ones, and Chloe is at home, minding his children. She's an eejit and deserves it, and Sharon is well out of it, but you'd have to wonder how the likes of Danny get away with it. I shudder. He's an absolute creep, but there's no accounting for taste, I suppose.

Meeting Trevor Lynch has been the best thing for Sharon. Trevor is decent and kind and funny and loyal. OK, he makes some very dodgy clothing choices, a big fan of snow-washed denim, leather things around his wrists, and for a long time, he had a bleached mullet, but she's tamed the worst of his '80s rock-god look. And anyway, he is a dote, so all is forgiven. On top of everything else, he gets on fantastically well with Sean and does loads with him.

Tatiana sets us at a table overlooking the stream that flows behind the pub, and the food on the Samovar menu looks as good as we've been told it is. Kieran and Trevor order the steak served with hand-made chips, medium rare (which in Ballycarrick means well done, but I assume Tatiana knows that), and Sharon asks for the sea bass with celeriac mash. But I ask Tatiana what her favourite is, and for once she smiles and says they have a new sous chef, a Polish woman, who makes a wonderful Polish hunter's stew. 'She serves it with Polish *pampuch*, but I don't put it on the menu because this is Ballycarrick. We just eat it in the kitchen by ourselves. You want try it, Mags?'

I take the risk – you only live once. The stew turns out to be a spicy mix of sauerkraut, white cabbage, beef and sausage, along with a handful of spices, and the pampuch is a kind of plain steamed dough-nut. And it might sound strange, but I can tell you, it is incredibly delicious.

After desserts the men disappear to the bar to catch the end of another match, which to their delight has gone to extra time, and Sharon and I order Tatiana's famous coffee to wash down our choco-late tart. The waitress, Rachel Mahony's older sister Hazel, an abso-lute pet who takes after her mother, brings it in a lovely cafetiere complete with little china cups and a tiny home-made piece of short-bread from Teresa's Bakery in the saucer.

'Tatiana still won't say where she gets this coffee,' Sharon murmurs as she inhales its blissful aroma.

'I know. Ronan Brady was telling me that the number of patrol cars from Galway that need to drive by Ballycarrick is huge since she started doing takeaway. Everyone knows it's the best for fifty miles.'

'You know Teresa in the bakery is dying to find out – she told me she's after asking in every way she can think of. But our Russian is tight-lipped, swears it's just the stuff from the cash and carry, but it isn't of course. Teresa even sent her nephew – you know, the fella with the ears? – she sent him to go rooting in Tatiana's wheelie bins to see if he could find a wrapper or something, but of course she had a giant padlock on her bins. I mean, who does that?'

I grin. 'People who don't want nosy neighbours going through their rubbish, I suppose?'

'People with something to hide, more like.' Sharon taps the side of her nose with her finger, nodding knowingly. 'I'm guessing there's a lot of funny business goes on in this town that even you don't know about, Mags Munroe.'

'And a lot more I wouldn't even want to know about,' I agree sincerely, also wisely tapping my nose.

# CHAPTER 3

*I*'m up to my eyes with paperwork before the Circuit Court tomorrow, and I'm hoping no one will turn up for the week's neighbourhood watch meeting, but no such luck. Garda Delia McGovern pulls an apologetic grimace as she sticks her head around my door.

'So sorry to interrupt, Sarge, but Lavinia Moran and Joanna are here already.'

My heart sinks. I've found it very hard to like those two since they came up with a scheme last year to kick the Travellers off their perfectly respectable and long-established halting site. Only a very emotional town hall meeting, where most of Ballycarrick rallied behind the Travellers, put a halt to their gallop.

'And Mrs Flanagan and Oscar...'

It gets worse.

'And Derry and Annette...'

I cheer up. Derry is the lovely former primary school principal, and Annette is a sensible woman of around sixty who runs the local organic vegetable farm with her wife, Martha, and they're good at supporting me.

'...have sent their apologies...'

My heart sinks again.

'But Annette emailed in the minutes, so that's good. Oh, and Ronnie Atkinson is here.'

My heart has now settled for good in my deeply unsexy garda shoes. Ronnie is the local councillor, and he's been coming to the odd meeting for the last few months. I should be pleased to have a member of Galway County Council taking an interest in Ballycarrick. But he's also the local Green Party secretary. Now don't get me wrong – I'm very interested in saving the planet and I recycle as much as I can and won't buy fruit from New Zealand because of the air miles, but honest to God, this fella would give you a pain in your head just listening to him. He's so sanctimonious, going around on his bike, with his hand-knit jumpers and his vegan ways. He's got sandy hair and a straggly beard that seems to only grow in patches, and there's a weird smell of damp dog off him. And to cap it all, he has a very annoying mid-Atlantic accent even though he comes from Leitrim. Actually, that doesn't cap it all – what caps it all is that when he talks, he punctuates his speech with air quotes made with two fingers on each hand and then counts off the points he's making on his fingers.

Delia reads my expression accurately. 'You want me to settle everyone with a coffee and tell them you'll be another five minutes? I did suggest I could take the meeting, but I'm not 'high up enough to do anything useful'. That's a direct quote from Lavinia, by the way.'

I roll my eyes. You wouldn't want a sensitive bone in your body in this job. I thank my stars I'm so lucky with the officers in my station. All four of them, Delia, Nicola, Michael and Darren, are hard-working, decent young people who do their jobs well, and we pull together as a team.

They've even been taking turns to clean the station while we try to replace Mrs Harris, who has just retired. There is a budget allocation for a cleaner, but nobody seems to be looking for that type of work these days. I'm not too worried. The lads are doing a good job, and to be honest, it's not as hard to keep the place tidy as it used to be, because it got an upgrade after I was shot in the line of duty a couple of years back. The top brass probably thought it was the least they could do for me at the time, after ignoring all my warnings about a dangerous sex trafficker operating locally. In the revamp, all the old fittings and furniture that had been there since the '50s – whoever decorated it back in the day had a great dedication for dung brown and cat-sick green – were taken out and the walls painted cream, and we got new blue hard-wearing carpets and a proper ladies' dressing room with showers instead of a toilet in a broom cupboard. The room where we hold the neighbourhood watch meetings even has a coffee machine.

I get up and put on my jacket. The full uniform lends an air of authority, which is handy around the likes of Ronnie Atkinson, who thinks he's the boss of everyone. 'Fine, I'll hold the meeting myself, but you come and sit in anyway. Maybe we can get them to see you're quite as capable of listening to them as I am.' I walk out into the public office and then turn left into the meeting room.

I find them all sitting around looking expectant.

Lavinia Moran, a tiny bird of a woman, has taken the seat at the top of the table, as if she, not me, is going to be in charge of the meeting. She has a Prada handbag and is making sure everyone knows it by placing it in front of her on the tabletop instead of at her feet like a normal person. Joanna Burke, the gossipy doctor's receptionist, is on Lavinia's right, and next to her is Elsie Flanagan, a small wasp of a woman they've recently adopted as a new member of their clique.

Elsie wrecks my head. She has yellow – honestly, it is yellow, not blond – hair cut in a severe style that ends at her earlobes, and she is dressed as she always is, in golfing gear. I know the brand because we buy it for Kieran's dad every Christmas. TravisMathew. To the best of my knowledge, Elsie has never swung a golf club in her life and isn't a member of the local club, but she just always wears golf clothes. I can't explain it. Any more than I can explain how she has made a rather successful career out of selling paintings to tourists. I mean, that's not weird in itself, obviously, but the thing is, she only paints one scene, which is the castle on the shore of Carrick Lough three miles from town. She paints it repeatedly, like hundreds and hundreds of times, the same chocolate boxy castle, green fields, blue lake and two swans. And as for when she gets onto the subject of her daughter, Noreen…

Still, there's no crime against being odd, which is just as well, because if there was, I'd have to arrest the whole village.

I greet Lavinia and her gang warmly and smile at Oscar O'Leary, another pothole to be avoided usually, but only because he has developed an obsession with religion in recent years, in particular his favourite saint, St Gertrude, who is the patron saint of cats. Otherwise he's harmless.

I find it harder pretending to be pleased to see Ronnie Atkinson. I can tell from the look of him that he has something 'important' to say, but I do my best.

Two months ago, Ronnie's important thing was newts. There are some newts – I've never seen a newt in my life, by the way – apparently living in a pond in Gerry the hairdresser's garden. According to Ronnie, Gerry's ride-on mower was disturbing the habitat, and Ronnie wanted me to – wait for this – impound Gerry's lawnmower to save the newts. I did mention the issue to Gerry, asked him to maybe let the grass grow around the pond while the breeding season was on, but he acted like he thought I was joking, and fearing for my roots, I decided to retreat from the discussion. Maybe that's where the blond streaks came from, I suddenly realise.

I have barely taken my seat at the other end of the table from Lavinia, with Delia on my left, when Ronnie starts. 'Sergeant Munroe, I've several important matters I need to raise with you –'

'Perhaps we should have the minutes of the last meeting first, Ronnie?' I suggest, looking at Delia, who has a copy of them in front of her, sent in by Annette. But Ronnie waves my words aside with an impatient flap of his hand.

'I haven't really got the time to wait for the minutes – I have a very important council meeting to attend. But this won't take long, just three or four pressing things.'

'Perhaps if you're in a hurry, you can call me later?' I try to stop him, but he's on a roll.

First, using his finger to mark off point one, he complains that people are using turf in their fires, which is perfectly legal, by the way. I try to explain that I am not the guardian of the planet but of the peace, and if someone is not breaking the law, no matter how reprehensible he deems their behaviour, there is nothing I can do about it. He snorts. I hate that.

The next point is that I should prevent (here come the air quotes) 'Karens' – I hate that word; it's just an excuse to be misogynistic – from parking their 'gas-guzzler mom buses' within five hundred yards of the primary school because of the emissions giving the children brain damage. This gets him a filthy glare from Lavinia, who owns exactly the kind of vehicle he's talking about and has a son at the school. For once, I win her approval by pointing out to him that parking is legal except on yellow lines, and that all cars are checked annually for emissions and have to be below acceptable standards to be considered roadworthy. He snorts again. See what I'm dealing with? He gives the green agenda a bad name.

Finally, he gets to his main point, and his third finger. 'The thing is, it is vital, absolutely vital, Sergeant, that the habitats at Horsehead are maintained.'

'That's private property, Ronnie, so I'm not sure what you want me to do.' Horsehead is a gorgeous if very run-down old estate house on the edge of the town, the home of Noelle and Doreen Hurley, twin sisters, both of whom recently died within days of each other. I don't even know who owns the place now.

'It's not going to be private property for much longer. I'm currently asking the council to CPO the house and grounds and turn it into a wildlife park,' says Ronnie, preening a bit.

I'm surprised. I've never known the Galway council to use their powers to put a compulsory purchase order on anything, even the building next to Gerry the hairdresser's, which looks like it's been hit by an earthquake and is pulling his roof down with it.

'So in the meantime, I expect you to police the place properly, Sergeant. There are ancient native trees there, yews and oaks, not to mention newt habitats and...'

I start to point out that I'm a garda, not a park warden, and then

Oscar comes to my rescue, simply by being Oscar. 'Of course it's all of our duty to protect the animals. I'm reminded of St Francis of Assisi, who said, "Not to hurt our humble brethren is our first duty, but to stop there is not enough. We must be of service to them whenever they require it."'

'Yes, yes indeed. Well, as I was saying…' Ronnie, who is a proud atheist, turns back to me, but Oscar is pursuing his own agenda.

'We are indeed blessed to be surrounded by God's magnificent creatures, and we should look out for them, shouldn't we, so wouldn't a little prayer session be a nice idea? Maybe we could have the children in school draw pictures of all the animals in Horsehead, and we could have a special Mass, or even a series of Masses, one for each species? Or maybe one for squirrels and another for birds and newts and things? I wonder, would Father Doyle like to do that, do you think?'

I smile and nod. 'That's a lovely idea, Oscar.' I know Father Doyle would swing for me if he heard me supporting the idea of extra Masses; he is already worn out from Oscar's very enthusiastic brand of Catholicism. Like most parishes in Ireland now, the whole show is being run by a single elderly man, vocations being very thin on the ground, and poor old Father Doyle is barely coping as it is; he should have retired long ago. But I have strong self-preservation instincts, and hopefully this will head Ronnie off.

Ronnie is frustrated, I can tell, to be stopped mid-rant, but then Elsie jumps in. I suspect she's been primed for this by Ronnie, because he beams at her.

'Mags, listen here to me now. It's not just about trees and newts and stuff…'

Ronnie stops beaming and looks indignant.

'Horsehead needs policing. My Noreen above in Dublin deals every day with government ministers and the like, is absolutely astonished and dismayed that community policing is failing so dramatically.'

Delia glances at me without moving her head, only her eyes, but I can't look at her. Only last week she was telling me how Mrs

Flanagan told her that Noreen had won an award at the library for a readathon. Delia, who has never met Noreen, thought she was a child, so asked Mrs Flanagan what class Noreen was in. Poor Delia hadn't meant any offence, but Elsie Flanagan was outraged, it would seem.

I know that if Elsie gets on a roll about 'her Noreen', we're all done for, even more than when Ronnie was fixated on Gerry's newts. The younger Miss Flanagan is a timid little mouse of a girl who has an unremarkable post in the department of fisheries, but according to Elsie, her daughter is in the ear of the Taoiseach himself. There isn't a person with a pulse for fifty miles who isn't an expert on the many and varied achievements of Noreen Flanagan. Poor Noreen is a nice girl and totally horrified that her mother is always painting her as such a high-flier.

'If you'd like to make a formal complaint about me, Mrs Flanagan, then please do so. Garda McGovern here will be happy to take your statement.' This might seem a strong reaction on my part, I know, but it's always best to go full formal with this kind of thing.

Elsie reddens. 'Ara, Mags, will you have a hair of sense? Write a statement? I will in my eye. Only for you to put it through the shredder?'

'Mrs Flanagan, that is a serious accusation –'

'Well, here's another accusation for you, Mags. The unsavoury things that do be goin' on in there are nothing less than...' – she pauses for dramatic effect – 'satanic.' She finishes with a hiss, while Ronnie nods furiously.

I'm startled. Is something genuinely going on at Horsehead? Is this one of the things that Sharon jokingly accused me of not knowing about? 'Satanic? What are you talking about?'

'Ha! You didn't know, did ya? Obviously, you guards don't give a tinker's curse what goes on in this town.'

It's my turn to glance at Delia, who is a Traveller, and it's her turn to sit staring impassively ahead. Tinker is a racist term for Traveller. I decide from Delia's expression that she doesn't want me to make a thing of it.

'I'd urge you to be cautious with your words, Mrs Flanagan,' I say quietly.

'Cautious? Surely to God you know that unsavoury elements are using the place as a drug den and God knows what else, Mags?'

'And chopping down native trees for their fires.' Ronnie Atkinson jumps in. 'And disturbing a colony of pine martens who are very important for keeping down the spread of grey squirrels so the red squirrels can return to the area.'

I've never been sure why red squirrels are considered more worthy of preservation than grey squirrels in the environmentalist handbook; maybe it's a case of what's common being worthless, like the children of the poor. But I do want to know about the drugs.

'Mrs Flanagan, what is it you want to tell me?'

'It's the young ones from the social housing, of course. They've been going up there at the weekends. Ronnie was waiting in the bushes last Saturday and saw them at it, so he did. You're so brave, Ronnie, unlike some people I could mention…'

Ronnie inclines his sandy head, acknowledging his superiority to the local guards.

'Did you recognise any of the kids in particular, Ronnie?' I ask calmly.

'Well, no, but it was definitely kids being badly behaved…'

'So you don't know who the young people were exactly?' I hate all this jumping to conclusions about whole groups of people. Ballycarrick recently got a new social housing development, three-bedroom units built on the empty land behind the posh estate where Elsie lives, and there's been a lot of muttering about property prices. Though judging by the figures shown in Foxy Clancy's window – he's the local estate agent – the price of houses is still going up and up, which is why social housing is needed in the first place. And now the estate has become the new halting site when it comes to crime, getting all the blame for anything that happens in the town.

Elsie's chest swells indignantly. 'Ara, come on, Mags, who else would it be with the drink and the drugs and the rituals they do be doing? And you do know who's selling them the drugs, I suppose?'

I decide to say nothing. I just sit, waiting for her to get it all off her chest.

'Travellers from Galway!' she finishes triumphantly. 'No offence, Delia.'

Delia McGovern might be a fully qualified guard, but in the eyes of this town, she is a Traveller first and foremost. I half wish now I hadn't asked the poor young woman to sit in on this meeting, as this always happens – someone always manages to blame the Travellers for something. Still, I guess she knew what she was getting into when she joined the guards in the first place, and like I said, you need a thick skin to survive in this business.

'Elsie, I will investigate, of course, but in the meantime, you need to refrain from making unsubstantiated allegations,' I say firmly.

Elsie goes red, which sits uneasily with the yellow hair. 'Did I name names? No, I did not!'

It's true; she merely collectively smeared two whole social and ethnic groups.

'Sergeant Munroe, the important thing here is, they're lighting *fires*,' says Ronnie Atkinson, dragging things back onto the environmental track. 'Which apart from the immediate damage to native trees, releases carbon into the atmosphere.'

Well, well, this is a new one. It seems the Travellers and the poor aren't just to blame for every crime committed in the town – they're also responsible for global warming.

* * *

AFTER THE MEETING, I go back to my office and pick up the phone.

A pleasant young woman answers. 'Clancy and Golden. How may I help?'

'Hello, it's Sergeant Munroe from Ballycarrick. Could I speak to Mr Clancy please?'

'Certainly, Sergeant, one moment.'

I waited as Neil Diamond explains powerfully how sweet Caroline really is.

The climax of the song is interrupted by Foxy's nasal greeting. 'Mags, how're ya doing?'

I can just visualise him, his dyed hair, his suit shiny with age and wear. He has a very red nose, the sign of a whiskey drinker according to my mother, and he goes to every funeral for fifty miles. Where there is death, there is property, and nobody can ever accuse Foxy Clancy of being slow off the mark. For all that, though, he is all right. He had flame-red hair as a kid, and instead of allowing nature to take its course and let it go grey, he's decided to dye it to an alarming orange colour. His wife is a surprisingly well-spoken woman from Germany, a physiotherapist in Galway; what she sees in Foxy is anyone's guess.

'Fine, Foxy, and yourself?' I reply. I pretend not to know that he's up on a tax fraud charge soon. The thing about community policing is that you have to be friendly enough not to have anyone think you've gotten ideas above your station but aloof enough to do the job. It's a thin line, and I regularly mess it up. It's further complicated or helped, depending on the day, by the fact that I grew up here. Foxy Clancy is like a lot of locals here, down the Samovar on a Friday night taking the mick out of me and my colleagues, but then he has bald tyres or no tax and we're suddenly bosom buddies. You get used to it; it comes with the job.

'Ara, grand, you know yourself, Mags. Draggin' the divil by the tail the whole time.'

'I do, Foxy, I do indeed. Come here to me – I was ringing about Horsehead. Apparently, it's been sold? I'd like a contact for the person who is responsible for securing the property.'

'Well, it's not me, that's for sure, Mags.' He sounds alarmed, like I might go accusing him of something.

'I know that, Foxy, but whoever owns the place now needs to secure the property or they might be liable for any accidents that take place on the grounds.'

'What sort of accidents might they be, Mags?' He's still being cautious.

'I've been told that people, probably young ones, are using it for drinking and parties.'

Foxy chuckles and relaxes. 'Ah sure, Mags, kids will be kids. Didn't we have plenty of nights ourselves back the in the castle grounds? I remember when I was a *garsún* acting the maggot back there plenty of times, and I'm sure you were there too.'

Foxy was a year ahead of me in school and an eejit even then.

'Indeed, and I was not,' I say. 'Marie Kelleher wasn't going to have her precious girls up there, so she wasn't.' I laugh to make light of it, but also it's true. Mam had the good sense not to allow me or my sisters to hang around drinking with the likes of Foxy Clancy.

Foxy takes no offence. 'I suppose you're right, Mags. You and Jenny were never ones for the craic, though your sister Delores now, well, she was another matter. God, she was a right messer. She's in America living up a tree now or something, isn't she?'

'She's fine, thanks, Foxy. I'll tell her you were asking for her.'

I'm not going to be drawn into discussing Delores, who as it happens is now called Lori, and who is living sustainably in a hippy commune in Montana with some lad who has dreadlocks down to his bum and a beard that could well have several small mammals living in it. My other sister, Jenny, is completely different. She lives in Dubai with her husband, Ahmed, and their three boys. Jenny is fine. She is a bit uptight, and everything must be just so. She buys designer hand-bags, and her hair is like something from an ad. Lori, on the other hand, is just daft. I love them both, but I don't have that much in common with either of them, to be honest.

'Do that, Mags, do that, and Jenny too. She's another one I haven't seen in ages. Sure, where do the years go, eh?'

This is another thing about Irish social interaction – you have to allow a certain amount of this drivel to get to the point.

'Sure, I know, Foxy. Time does fly,' I say, joining in the dance of pointlessness.

'Did you hear about your man that hit Brian Magee a clatter on Friday? I suppose you were called?'

Foxy is fishing for gossip, no doubt, but even if I did know anything about it, which I don't, I'd never discuss it with him. It doesn't stop him trying, though.

'I didn't, Foxy. Anyway, I need a contact number for whoever has the responsibility to secure the property –'

'Poor Brian was only just back from a long cycle. Sure you know he goes miles on that bike. When he opened the door and found Eamonn Gerrity on the doorstep, and he with a big bull head up on him, savage he was. I'm surprised you didn't hear about it. My poor Anya had to go and meet his missus for a gin and tonic in the Samovar after it – she was no more good.'

I'd forgotten Foxy's wife and Brian's were good friends. I am resigned now to hearing the whole thing, so I make a noise I've perfected after years in the job. It's a cross between an *ah* and an *eh*. It indicates mild surprise but also a vague question. It says everything and nothing and gets me out of a load of things.

Anyway, Foxy is now in full flight; best keep up.

'You know Otter Magee died recently? Brian's father. God be good to him.'

He'd worked for the county council and was nicknamed Otter for some reason lost to the mists of time.

'I heard that,' I say.

'Well, apparently, Eamonn Gerrity lent him a fiddle in 1973 and Otter never gave it back. Brian knew nothing, of course, but the fiddle is in his place, and Gerrity decided to ask for it back. He must have worked himself up into a right lather on the way there, because to the best of everyone's knowledge, Gerrity never asked Otter for the fiddle back. But he decided the O.K. Corral would be Friday, so when poor Brian opened the door, didn't your man roar at him that he could keep the bloody fiddle and stick it where the sun don't shine, then hit him one hell of a clatter into the face and off he went in high dudgeon.'

Now this is the kind of tale one gets to hear regularly in Ballycarrick. Delivered as if it makes perfect sense, but of course it doesn't. Best not to ask but take it on face value.

I make the noise again. And it seems to do the trick, because he says, 'So that's the story now,' while sounding satisfied.

'Now, Foxy.' I try again. 'I need to contact the new owner of Horsehead –'

'Well, good luck with that, Mags,' says Foxy, and finally, he gets to the point. 'Look it, the Hurley sisters left Horsehead to a nephew of theirs, a man called James Whitsun, but he lives in South Africa and he doesn't want it – he's never set foot in Ireland and has no interest in doing so. So he's asked me to put it on the market for him, and I have. But the only offer is from the council for half of what it's worth, so I told him to turn them down and sit on it. But now the council's after getting a flippin' compulsory purchase order on it, so they are, on the grounds the house is going derelict.' He sounds disgusted, presumably because this will hurt his commission.

'For a wildlife park?' I ask, amazed that Ronnie might have actually achieved something on the council.

'No – who told you that? For Ukrainians,' he says, still annoyed. 'Women with children.'

'Ah...' That sounds more plausible. I know the government has pledged to look after several thousand Ukrainian women and children while their husbands stay to fight the war. And if it's true, it will be interesting to see Ronnie's reaction to the news. I wonder if he will be as eager about saving innocent human beings as he is about saving trees. But right now, I have Elsie's concerns to address.

'So securing the place is the council's responsibility?'

'All I know is the council are in the process of buying it for half of what it's worth, and so you'll have to take it up with them eventually, I suppose.' Foxy sounds slightly miffed that I am still questioning him. 'And maybe I shouldn't even be talking to you about this, Mags, when there's no contracts signed or anything, but I wanted to do you a turn.'

Which will no doubt be called in at a later time, I note. 'And I appreciate you telling me, Foxy. We'll just have to wait and see, I suppose,' I say, backing off.

'Indeed we will, Mags, indeed we will.'

I end the call. I should get back to the paperwork. But it's time for elevenses, and Teresa's Bakery beckons.

# CHAPTER 4

*I* decide to call into Mam and persuade her to come with me to Teresa's, and I head up Main Street in the direction of her shop, past the Samovar and the flower shop, Julie the chemist's and Gerry the hairdresser's.

Most people smile and nod when they see me, and some stop for a quick chat.

'Howya, Mags,' mutters Bobby Buckley, an old boy with long hair and a Grateful Dead t-shirt. He's known around here as Sniper's Nightmare, or Snipe for short, on account of his very pronounced limp. Apparently, he was born in America and his parents came back to Galway when he was a child, but he went over as a young fella and kind of bummed around. He was at Woodstock, and then he got drafted to Vietnam, where he had some kind of a leg injury. He's been invalided out, and now he hobbles happily around the place.

'Hi, Snipe.' I smile. He looks for all the world like Willie Nelson with a limp. Bandana around his head, denim jacket covered in badges – you get the picture.

Eighteen-year-old Finbarr Turner, Annette and Martha's son (well, Martha's son and Annette's stepson), strolls by on the other side of the road with his best friend, fifteen-year-old Olivia McGovern, one of

30

Delia's many cousins from the halting site. Finbarr has Down's syndrome, and he's an absolute darling. He and Olivia are both mad into animals, and Finbarr spends loads of time at the Drumlish site with Delia's father, Jerome McGovern, helping with the dogs and horses and chickens and rabbits. Both of them wave to me, and I wave back.

I pass Bertie Mahony, local butcher and a backbone of the Church, standing in the doorway of his shop, but he scurries back inside without saying anything. He's avoided me since the night I caught him up to no good in the woods with a load of other like-minded people living out their sexual fantasies. One of the worst nights of my career, that. There's a reason the adult film industry is populated by young beautiful people and not middle-aged, pasty, paunchy Irish ones. That's all I'll say – I'll spare you the picture. Unfortunately, I can't ever unsee it.

Anyway, you see what I mean? People think it's the kids from the council estate who are the issue, and I'm not saying they never are, but I can assure you, there are plenty coming from the fancier developments – and 'respectable' adults as well. I hope none of those present in this morning's neighbourhood watch meeting are in for a nasty shock about their loved ones if I do decide to investigate the alleged goings-on at Horsehead.

On the corner of the street, I stick my head into Dillon's Menswear because it seems wrong to walk by without saying hi. 'Hello, Joe?'

'Hi, Mags,' he calls from the back, where he's opening a box of variations on a theme of blue V-necked sweaters, the chosen jumper of most Irishmen over sixty.

'How're you, Joe?' I've always liked Joe Dillon, and since he and Mam married, he's blended seamlessly into our family.

'Ah, grand altogether, Mags, but I'd be better if I could get your mother out from behind that bloody counter and get her to live a bit.'

'Exactly what I think,' I agree cheerfully. 'I'm just on my way to drag her out to Teresa's, if you want to join us.'

'I'd love to, but I'm expecting a second delivery of these jumpers.'

31

How many blue V-necked sweaters does one town need?

'You're as bad as Mam, Joe, never leaving the shop.'

'I'm not, though. I've been suggesting we go on a cruise at Easter, the Mediterranean maybe. I mean, we're not exactly spring chickens, the pair of us, we're well past retirement age.' He shakes his head. 'But Marie won't hear of closing up for any length of time. She's a stubborn woman, Mags, a wonderful woman, but as obstinate as Delaney's donkey.' He grins at me. Though they are only married a short time, Joe and Mam have been friends for years and have easily slipped into the kind of good-natured banter that is the hallmark of marriages much longer than theirs.

I grin back at him. I remember the song. My dad used to sing it at parties when I was small, before he got sick, the Val Doonican hit.

For a second I am back, sitting on the floor looking up at Daddy, who is standing up and having everyone sing along.

'And there was Reilly, pushin' it, shovin' it, shushin' it. Hogan, Logan and everyone in town - lined up, attackin' it and shovin' it and smackin' it. But they might as well have tried to push the town hall down. The donkey was eyein' them, openly defyin' them, winkin', blinkin' and twistin' out of place, Reilly reversin' it, everybody cursin' it, the day Delaney's donkey won the half-mile race.'

I feel my eyes prick with tears. I haven't cried over my dad in years and years. He was sick for so long, and I was only a kid when he died. But here now, standing in Joe's shop, him mentioning Delaney's donkey transports me back in time. It's so strange, isn't it? Losing someone, I mean. Something weird will trigger a memory and lead to such a sharp stab of loss.

'Ah, Mags...' Joe looks stricken. 'I didn't mean... I mean, your mam is marvellous. I'm crazy about her. Sure I was only joking...'

I shake my head and wipe the tear away with the sleeve of my jacket. 'It's not that. My dad used to always sing "Delaney's Donkey",' I manage.

'Ah, he did too. I remember him belting it out. He was a great man for a song was Milo Kelleher.' Joe smiles, relieved he's not offended me. 'He had a head for lyrics. No matter what it was, he'd remember it. Great craic altogether, and what a dancer – he was the Fred Astaire of the parish. Himself and your mother put the rest of us clodhoppers to shame.'

He pulls me into a hug and gently kisses the top of my head, and I'm overwhelmed with affection for this kind man. I kind of forget that he knew Daddy all his life, from when they were at school together.

'Thanks, Joe. And you're right about Mam being stubborn as that donkey, and I do think she needs to shut up shop and have some fun. Maybe I should say something to her about it?'

He looks panicked. 'Do not tell her you've been talking to me, Mags. I'll be murdered.'

'I won't mention your name, trust me. And I'll have a good think what to say and how to say it – I won't go jumping in there with two flat feet.' Mam isn't getting any younger, but I know if I even hint she needs to slow down or take it easier, she'll not thank me for it.

And it's not that I think the shop is too much for her; it's just that she's worked so hard all her life, caring for Daddy and then for his fearsome mother, my Nana Peg, who'd terrify a vampire. Mam loves Joe, and I want to see her enjoying married life. She's done it all alone for so long, and I think she should let Joe fuss over her like he wants to do.

* * *

I FIND her writing up sale signs for the window.

'Having a clear-out, Mam?' I ask as she looks up from the fluorescent star she's writing on in a thick black marker. I hope her business isn't hurting with the post-Covid recession that seems to be hitting a lot of small shops. There's nothing fancy about my mam's boutique, but this little shop reared me and my sisters, and I'm not surprised Mam is reluctant to let it go.

Anyway, what would the women and girls of Ballycarrick do without her? She dresses them for communions, confirmations, weddings, anniversaries. If you have an occasion, Marie's Boutique is where to go. She instinctively knows what looks good on people, and even people who have no interest in fashion know that if Marie dresses them for an occasion, they'll be there looking their best. And they trust her even more because she always looks well put together herself. Today is no exception; she has cream tailored trousers, a royal-blue tunic and patent-leather ankle boots. Her hair was long and red when she was young, and it is short but stylish now, threaded with silver and gold but always blow-dried properly, and she wears a little make-up. No wonder Joe and that Argentinian doctor, Teo, both fell for her; she looks great for her age.

'I am, love,' she says. 'And don't worry. It's not that I'm having a problem shifting stuff. It's just I need to make way for the spring stock.'

'So plenty of customers still?'

'Era, I tip away. This place is paid for, so I've no overheads as such except stock, and I have my regulars. I was a bit worried about Covid. The trade magazines were all about the pandemic getting people buying online and it being hard to get them back to the shops, but I can't say I've noticed.'

I run my hand along a rail of stylish women's jackets, admiring them. 'I'd say that might be true for the big shops maybe, but what people like about coming here is the personal touch, the way you can tell them nicely that the frilly dress in cerise pink and blood-clot red is maybe not the best thing for their mother's funeral. And the way you make sure the clothes will fit them and not be two sizes too small.'

She chuckles. 'That reminds me – I got that cardigan in Nora was after, the longline blue one. She saw it in the window a few weeks ago. She swore she would fit a ten, but it wouldn't button across her stomach, so I said it must have been labelled the wrong size and I'd contact the manufacturers for a replacement and to come back to me in a few days. That was three weeks ago, but she still hasn't come in for the bigger size.'

My face must have registered something, because my eagle-eyed mother gives me a funny look.

'What?' she asks.

'Nothing really. Kieran mentioned to me that Nora and Kevin are having a bit of a spat at the moment is all.'

Mam shakes her head. 'I can't imagine Kevin Munroe ever sticking up for himself enough to have a spat, but if he has done, fair play to him.' Mam is normally diplomatic to her bones, but she really doesn't like Nora, just because of how Nora's treated me all these years.

'I'm sure they'll work it out, but yeah, it's new territory for sure. Maybe that's why she's not out and about so much.'

'Well, tell Kieran if he sees her to mention the cardigan.' She deftly puts the discount signs around the small shop as she speaks.

'Anyway,' I say, getting to the point of this visit, 'I'm in need of a trip to Teresa's, my treat, so maybe you can shut up the shop for half an hour at least?'

She hesitates, but then the lure of Teresa's overcomes her work ethic. 'Well, maybe just for twenty minutes...'

* * *

TERESA'S BAKERY is known locally as the Pit of Despair. Her cakes are so irresistible, there isn't a healthy eater on the planet who could resist. Teresa herself is like a whippet, but the rest of us are wearing her cream horns and custard slices on our hips and bums.

Elaine, who runs the slimming club in the dank meeting room of the local hotel, declared war on Teresa years ago, but Teresa doesn't rise to the bait. She knows the worth of her own product and simply goes on doing what she does.

I used to go there, to Elaine's, I mean – I have always and will always go to Teresa's – but it was such a depressing experience, I gave it up and promised never to return.

Imagine trying to explain the concept of a slimming club to aliens. 'So, little green fella, here's how it works. We all go here, to this woman, every week, and we give her a tenner. Then we get up on a scale and she tells us not to eat so much, so we leave, despondent that we've failed again, go home, eat too much to cheer ourselves up and go back the next week, another tenner, more scales jumping and more sad disappointment on the face of Elaine or similar. Repeat for a lifetime.'

And when the little green man asks why we do it, what answer would we have? 'Because we're trying not to eat so much and be smaller than we are.'

'And does giving this woman a ten euro help? Does she know things you don't know? Has she some kind of magic potion that makes this happen?'

'Absolutely not,' we say with confidence.

'I'm confused,' says the little green man. And well he might be.

Once, when we were younger, Sharon and I went together. She's greyhound breed anyway, but we were both going heavy on the beer-and-pizza diet and it was showing a lot on me and a little on her.

Elaine, or whatever she was called then, told us we could only have eighteen strikes in a day. They call the food we eat strikes – can you believe it?

So we're going in the door and I say to Shar, 'Did you stick to eighteen strikes?' I knew I'd eaten way more than that. Like a plain old ham sandwich was about ten.

'I did of course,' she says incredulously. 'Didn't you?'

'Closer to thirty,' I say miserably, fully prepared for the ritual humiliation of communal weighing.

'What did you have?' she asks, her brow furrowed.

'Just my normal breakfast, lunch and dinner, but it adds up to too much. Why? What did you have?'

'Well, a pint is two strikes, so I had nine pints of lager and a salad with no dressing.'

Before I have time to digest this, no pun intended, she hops up on the scale and the one almost squeaks with delight. 'Down two pounds! Well done!'

I follow next and get the equal and opposite reaction, a shaking of the head and a pitying smile. She looks like she is sympathising with me at a funeral of my nearest and dearest.

'Up a half, Mags...'

Sharon gets a sticker and I get a sigh.

Moral of the story: Drink nine pints of beer and eat nothing. No thank you.

We order and take our coffees and cake down to a table. As usual the place is almost full. Teresa is probably a multimillionaire, impossible that she isn't.

'So anything strange this week?' I ask, cutting into a slice of jammy, creamy, buttery, sugary cake. Heaven.

'Joe wants to go on a cruise,' Mam says, rolling her eyes as she digs into her own slice.

'Oh, wow, that's amazing. It sounds fabulous. I'd love to go on a cruise.' I know it's not what she wants to hear, but I did promise Joe I'd try.

'Sure, how in God's name can I go away for a week on a cruise? He's off his head, but he keeps going on about it.'

'Well, when does he want to go?' I ask. It's a bit sinful of me to imply I haven't just been talking to him about this very thing, but then I did promise not to implicate him in anything I might say.

'Easter, if you don't mind!' Her tone of voice makes it clear she thinks Joe has gone stark-staring mad and that I'd better not start backing him up or else. 'As if I could go away at Easter, and the mothers of the brides and grooms all up in a heap over the summer weddings?'

'What sort of a cruise?' I ask noncommittally.

'A Mediterranean one, going to the Greek islands. Ara, Mags, what's the point of us even discussing what sort of a cruise? It's ridiculous, him expecting me to down tools at the drop of a hat, and just as the girls will be coming in for their communion dresses.'

'Well, maybe it would be nice for you to take some time away from the shop?' I venture, and know she'll get the hump.

She bristles. 'Time out for what? Time to sit around waiting for my dotage, is it?'

'No,' I say calmly, not rising to it. 'Time to spend some money on yourself, to see the world, to feel the sun on your face. Time to spend with Joe. Isn't that what he's looking for, more of your company?'

She leans closer to me, her sleeve dangerously close to a big blob of cream. 'Would you believe, he's even been talking about...' – she lowers her voice with the horror of it – *'retiring.'*

'Is he now?'

'Yes! He's off his head, so he is. He'll be gone senile in a week. That's what happens when you stop.'

'Well, I'm sure he's not meaning to stop altogether, just do something else,' I say. 'I mean, he has had that shop since God was a child. Maybe he thinks there might be more to life than thermal vests and V-necked jumpers? Come on, Mam, I don't think he's off his head to want a change of scene and enjoy his life with you.'

She sighs and relents a little. 'I suppose he is older than me. Maybe that's part of him wanting to slow down a bit.'

He's six months older than her.

'Well, what if he did shut up shop and you went part time, not to retire, just to go on a few holidays together?'

For some reason, she laughs, and her blue eyes sparkle. 'Do you know what happened with Deirdre Hickey?'

I'm a bit thrown by this non sequitur. Deirdre is the Ballycarrick Irish dancing teacher who has not got off the chair for the last forty-odd years, only bellowing at the children from where she sits, beating time with her walking stick. She is absolutely ancient.

'No, is she all right?'

'All right? She's grand. But Eithne and Alice, her two daughters, have been on and on at her to retire from the dancing since she turned eighty, and they even got worried about her using her own kitchen after she nearly burnt the house down. Sure that was an accident that could happen to anyone, Mags, but they tried to set her up with that day-care place – you know, the new one up by the garage? So she'd get her lunches there and wouldn't have to cook during the day, and they'd bring her dinner in the evening.'

'Not the worst idea ever.'

'Oh, do you think so? She'd already refused point-blank to go even on the over-sixties day out to Knock because it's for old people. And anyway' – Mam pauses for a last mouthful of cream cake – 'they went behind her back, knowing she'd never agree. They were terrified to tell her they'd booked her in there, to the old folks' day-care place, so they let the woman that runs it, Eileen something, a cousin of Hetty O'Hara, do the honours.'

'And what happened?' I ask, fascinated.

My mother peals with laughter. 'Well, poor Eileen rings up Deirdre, asking will she come into the care home on lunchtimes, and Deirdre thinks for a minute and says to her, "I will, I suppose. I can do Thursdays and Fridays all right." Eileen was delighted because she'd heard Deirdre might resist, but then Deirdre pipes up, "Like I usually only teach the young ones, but I'm sure I'll be grand. What time do you want me to give the dancing classes?"'

I crack up laughing as well. You have to hand it to Deirdre – she's going down fighting. And then I have an idea. 'There's a favour I've been meaning to ask you, Mam. Ellie's been asking me can she do a couple of hours for you on Saturdays, and I said I'd ask for her.'

It's not true, but it will be after I've talked to Ellie this evening. Old-lady cardigans and dresses don't float her boat, but I'll point out that if she gets some experience in Mam's, she can apply for one of the cool fashion shops in Galway when she's sixteen and will have an edge of having worked in a clothes shop over all the other young ones who'll want it.

Mam instantly falls for my cunning plan. She loves her granddaughters and would do anything for them. 'Oh, of course, if she wants it. She'll be great. Sure hasn't she been in here helping me since she was a tot, herself and Kate and it would be nice for her to have a bit of pocket money of her own.'

'Now don't be paying her, Mam, unless she's going to actually do it properly and let you go off for a few hours and not just be sitting around watching you do everything.' I'm not really offering Ellie up to work for free, but I have to force Mam to take a break.

'Sure, I don't mind giving her a few bob for keeping me company...'

'Mam, she's fifteen. She's going to be hurt if you don't think she's able to look after your shop for an hour or two without burning it down. Sure I leave her babysitting Kate sometimes, don't I? And I'm very fond of Kate.'

She relents. 'Well, maybe. And Joe will be pleased. He wanted to take me to the pictures last Saturday, to see *The Banshees of Inisherin*, but I was too busy as usual. So maybe if I can get away for an hour or two some Saturdays, that will stop him mithering on about the Greek islands.'

'Well, if she works out doing the few hours on Saturday, she might be able to give you a few days off during the school holidays, and yourself and Joe could go abroad then maybe?'

'Mags…' There's a warning tone in her voice, and I back off.

'Anyway, whatever you decide, Mam. But either way she's her head screwed on, so I'm sure she'd be fine, and myself and Kieran would be around to help if anything happened.'

Mam laughs. 'If Geraldine Doherty needs a bigger size in the Cross Your Heart bra? I can just see Kieran being brilliant at that.'

'Well, he still has trouble defining the difference between a skirt and a dress, and the only thing he knows about cups is what you put your tea in, but in the event of a hold-up or something.'

'Ah sure, that's a weekly occurrence.' She winks. 'I blame the guards myself.'

'You might as well, Mam. Everyone else does,' I say as I pay, and we take our leave of Teresa and head in two different directions along the street, her to her beloved shop and me to the station.

# CHAPTER 5

*I* don't finish until six thirty. When I get in the car, I intend to go straight home, but the neighbourhood watch meeting has been playing on my mind, and halfway there I find myself taking a detour down a side road with grass growing up the middle and parking outside the high gates of Horsehead.

I get out, button my uniform jacket against the chill evening air and stand looking through the rusty iron bars. The old house and its grounds must have been a lovely place once upon a time, but the sisters were very elderly when they died and everything is neglected and overgrown. You couldn't drive a car up that avenue; the brambles would scratch it to bits, and you'd probably get a flat as well.

Anyway, when I try the gates, they are rusted shut.

There is a gap, though, where one of them is half off its hinges, and on a whim, I squeeze through. I have a nasty moment when I get stuck halfway – I'm even fatter than I thought I was, and I'll have to call Kieran to rescue me, and Ellie will never let me live it down – but I make a fierce effort and pop out the other side like a cork, shedding two buttons off my uniform in the process. On the ground just inside the wall are a couple of fizzy drink cans and a scrunched-up takeaway food wrapper, so I'm not the first person to come this way. I think for a moment about leaving it and returning with Darren or Michael for backup, but I'm here now, and sure what else would I be doing? Only relaxing at home with Kieran and the girls, maybe a TV dinner and a nice glass of red.

I struggle along through the undergrowth, pausing now and again to disentangle myself from thorns and broken branches. Sticks snap like gunshots, and crows fly up squawking. I see one of the pine martens Ronnie was on about and mentally apologise for 'disturbing' the creature. And finally, I come out into a clearer space and can see the house, with the sunset behind it.

It's big. Not a stately home, but it's what you'd call a strong farmer's house. Double-fronted, two-storied, a front door one-and-a-half times the size of a normal front door, two small limestone steps up to it. The windows are original, sliding sash. The woodwork was once painted white, but the paint is all chipping off. There are a few tiles off the roof, there's grass on the chimneys, and one of the upstairs panes is cracked, but it's liveable, not falling down. Still, the sisters must have been rattling around in there like two dried peas in a jar. You'd wonder why they didn't move somewhere more convenient, but I suppose they were attached; the family were there for generations.

I'm doubtful about the satanic ritual thing, and I don't see any signs of human sacrifice, but I can see Ronnie and Elsie were right about people, probably kids, using it for parties. There are loads more crumpled cans, lager and cider as well as fizzy soft drinks, and empty bottles of those hideous alcopop things. A fire had been lit near the foot of the steps. I crouch down over it. The remains are black and cold, and there are a couple of empty cigarette packets half burnt in it. Just as I go to stand up again, I notice a small clear plastic bag tucked under the lowest step, where a bit of stone has cracked off and left a cavity. The broken bit of limestone is lying there on the ground. Someone must have pushed it back in, but it's tumbled out again, leaving the stash behind it visible. I coax the bag out. Inside is another cigarette packet, Benson and Hedges, and inside that a very small lump of cannabis resin, barely enough for one joint. I replace it in the box and the box in the bag, put the whole thing in my pocket and stand up.

I need to think about what to do next.

* * *

THE ROAD HOME IS QUIET, and when I get in, Kate is baking buns in the kitchen while Ellie pores over her books. A picture of domestic bliss. I am immediately suspicious.

'What's going on here?' I ask as I walk in with an eyebrow raised. The whole kitchen is tidy-ish – well, tidy by our standards anyway.

Ellie lifts her head and glares at me. 'Exactly what it looks like. Kate is baking, and I'm studying for my English test tomorrow. Why? What did you think was going on behind your back?'

'Hmm. I'm not sure, but normally you two are thrown in front of the TV, ware all over the floor and the kitchen like a bomb's hit it?'

'"Suspicion always haunts the guilty mind. The thief doth fear each bush an officer,"' Ellie quotes pointedly.

Kate and I share a glance. She loves her sister and they're thick as thieves, but she's worn out from all the quotations too.

'Well, I'm glad to say I've nothing to feel guilty about,' I say lightly.

'Don't you?' She sounds really accusing, and I wonder what I've done now. Then decide I don't want to know.

'How are you, Kit Kat?' I kiss my younger daughter on the head; her hands are all full of cake mixture.

'Good. Dad is working late again, so the reason the place is tidy and we're all organised is Granny Marie came round to give us our tea. She made roast chicken, and Joe bought us cream puffs from Teresa's for dessert. She made up a plate each for you and Dad – they're in the fridge. But we ate all the cream puffs, I'm afraid. That's why I'm making you and Dad these buns.' Kate gives me a cute grin. I feel a pang of love for her, my youngest child. She is a ray of sunshine.

'That's wonderful, pet. I'll have one with a cuppa when Dad gets home.' I wink at her as I take a plate of roast chicken, carrots, parsnips, potatoes and stuffing from the fridge and pop it in the microwave. My mother is a marvel. I'd be lost only for her. I can't imagine why I'm trying to encourage her to go away on long cruises. Which reminds me…

Damn. Now I *am* feeling guilty. I hadn't expected Mam to be here this evening. I wish I'd warned her not to say anything about the Saturday job in the shop before I'd spoken to Ellie… But then, how could I? I'd gone and told her it was Ellie's idea in the first place. What a tangled web we weave, as Ellie might quote at me.

I sit down at the table to eat my dinner while surreptitiously checking my daughter's face for signs of outrage. She ignores me; her deep-blue eyes are focussed on the textbook. She is keeping whatever thoughts she has to herself. So maybe Mam didn't say anything? Maybe Ellie's just in a mood because she's stressing about tomorrow's test – she's a high achiever – rather than annoyed at me for arranging a Saturday job for her without even asking. Though I'm sure she will be delighted to earn a few bob working for her adoring granny.

Or will she?

I love my oldest daughter so much, but she's hard to understand sometimes. I worry that we're not as close as we used to be. She used to tell me everything, but she seems so cagey these days. Mam says it's just teenage hormones, that it will come back, the closeness. I really hope so, because I miss her. She is more complicated than Kate, lightning quick, brightest in her class and full of ambition. Kieran and I are so proud of her. She took the lead in the Galway Youth Theatre's production of *Dancing at Lughnasa*, and I know I'm her mam, but she was honestly mesmerising. At fifteen she had them eating out of her hand as Kate Mundy, a hard role to do, and she fully intends to make it as an actor. Any other kid, I'd say it was a pipe dream, like wanting to be a professional footballer or a rock star, but I can't see anything stopping Ellie if she sets her mind to it.

I look at her, and my heart aches for the child she once was. The mop of dark curls is pulled into a ponytail, and she's grown into a beautifully curvaceous girl. It makes me anxious to see how men look at her now. I spend too much time in my job in the minds and lives of predatory, unscrupulous people, and honestly, if you let it get to you,

you'd never let your kids outside the front door. It frightens me how already she can't wait to get out of Ballycarrick; the day-to-day life here is a source of total boredom to her, it seems. She's decided she wants to study drama in New York when she finishes school. That's not for another three years, so as Kieran says, 'Let's pick our battles.' But that's not happening, I can assure you.

'So what's the test about, Els?' I ask. This roast chicken really is delicious.

'English,' she replies, without looking up.

'What aspect of it?' I try again.

She slams the book and looks at me straight in the face. 'Why did you lie?'

I am caught completely off-guard, and my face must show it. 'Ellie, I… What?'

Kate stares at us, clearly surprised. She has paused in the act of licking cake mix off the spoon.

Ellie's blue eyes blaze with contempt. 'You're always telling us we're not to lie, that lying is the worst thing you can do. It destroys people's trust in you, and trust takes such a long time to build back again. And then you went and told Granny a massive lie about me wanting to work in the shop.'

Oh, dear Lord, Mam must have spoken to Ellie after all, and she must have felt so let down and disappointed when Ellie told her she knew nothing about it and had never asked for the job in the first place.

'And so I had to lie to her as well, and I hate lying! I had to pretend I knew all about the job and was only dying to do it. It's as well I'm a good actor, especially when Joe was even thanking me for letting them go off on a two-week cruise in the summer. Obviously it never crossed your mind I might have my own life with my own plans.'

'Ellie, let me explain…' I'm so relieved she covered for me, but I need to get a word in. 'I'm sorry, I really am, for putting you in that position, and thank you so much for not saying anything to Granny about me not having asked you first, but –'

'I didn't do that for you. It was for her sake. I love Granny and didn't want her to know you'd told her a big, fat lie,' she says coldly.

'That's still really sweet of you, Els...' I do love how she loves her granny.

'Stop patronising me.'

I take a deep breath and try again. 'Look, I'm sorry, Els. I know I shouldn't have said anything before agreeing it with you first, but I honestly thought you'd like to do it, especially as your granny's going to pay you.'

'Mam, that is *so* not the point.' Her cheeks are pink with fury. 'The point is not whether I *will* do it or not, because I will now that I *have* to. The point is, you didn't ask me.'

'It was just that I was trying to think of a way to get your granny to slow down a bit and enjoy life –'

She rants straight through my attempt to defend myself. 'And the reason you didn't ask me is because in your mind, I'm still a child, and you think it's OK to go arranging my life for me. And by the way, I *know* you think you can stop me going to New York to study drama. I *know* you want me stuck in bloody Ballycarrick forever, just like you are. You probably want me to take over the shop from Granny when she retires and live here my whole life.' Suddenly unable to even stand the sight of me, she grabs her books and storms out of the kitchen and up the stairs.

I sit, staring miserably at my cooling plate, not hungry.

Kate pops the tray of buns into the oven and comes to put her arm around me. 'Don't worry about Ellie, Mam. She's delighted for the job – she said it to me even after Granny and Joe left just now – so it's not like she won't get over being cross about it.'

Bless her; she's so kind. I smile at her. 'Love you, pet.'

My appetite returns enough for me to finish my dinner, although I'd better go easy if I plan on squeezing back into the grounds of Horsehead any time soon.

Kieran is still not home by the time I've put my plate in the dishwasher. I go up to Ellie's room and tap on her door. I know I should

46

probably leave her alone to simmer down, but I hate a tense atmosphere in the house.

'What?' she says sharply from inside.

'It's Mam. Ellie, I just want to say I really am' – her door opens abruptly – 'sorry, pet. The thing is, Joe wants them to spend more time together, and I thought if I sort of made out to Mam like she was doing you a favour – she loves you so much – rather than trying to make her take time off for her own sake –'

'Fine. Can I go to Cat and Trish's house on Saturday night, after I've slogged away in the shop all afternoon?'

I'm taken aback but very relieved she's talking to me again, and in a normal-ish voice. 'Oh...right. But weren't you coming with us to Luigi's?'

Kieran and I have a 'family date' planned for Saturday, all four of us. Luigi is really called Lenny and is from Offaly, not Milan, but he makes nice pizza and the best knickerbocker glories, and the girls love going there.

'Nope. I'd rather hang out with my own friends, thanks.'

'Um...OK.' Now that I think about it, of course we've planned the outing without consulting her, so it's not like she's agreed to something and then changed her mind. 'Well then, we'll drop you on the way to Luigi's and collect you on the way back, around ten. Is that all right?'

'I might stay over. We're watching all the Hunger Games films back to back, so it might be late.'

Ah. Now she's testing how much she can get away with while I'm on the back foot over the shop thing. I choose to sidestep instead of risking another blow-up by pushing back. 'I'll see what Dad says. I'll let you know.'

'Mam, he'll be fine about it. "It is a wise father that knows his own child."'

'Let me guess, *Hamlet*?' I'm trying to be a good sport about the quotations.

'*Merchant of Venice*.' She rolls her eyes at how thick I am.

'Oh, right. Well, let's ask your wise old dad when he gets back and we'll see, will we?'

I know it's a parenting cop-out to let it all hinge on my husband, but I'm through with being a parent for one day. It's definitely a lot harder work than being a guard.

# CHAPTER 6

*I* need to know what I'm dealing with regarding the drugs, but I don't want to get into it with the drugs squad. Of course, I have to nip the Horsehead situation in the bud before it gets any worse and more people start congregating there and maybe cause damage to the house. But I'm pretty sure I'm dealing with a few bored kids, not major drug dealers, so I don't want to call in the heavy brigade unless I have to.

In the morning, after doing an hour in the office answering emails, I take my own car and drive through town, up a long lane between fields, and park outside a little cottage with a beautifully kept garden, which at this time of year is bright with daffodils. Annette Deasy and Martha Turner keep their house and garden beautifully, in between tending their organic vegetable garden in the polytunnels behind the house.

They're a couple now. They got married last autumn in a registry office wedding with a handful of guests, including me, Kieran, Jerome and Dora McGovern, and of course Finbarr, Martha's son who had Down syndrome, along with his best friend, Olivia McGovern. Jerome and I were the witnesses, and it was a lovely celebration, which we all needed after the terror of Finbarr disappearing overnight that summer. He'd been at the McGovern halting site when it got trashed by a very unpleasant and dangerous man acting on behalf of some developers who wanted the land. The McGoverns were all away at a wedding, and Finbarr tried to stop the attack single-handedly, but the man hit him and chased him, and poor Finbarr ran in terror until he found a ditch to hide in. And he was too scared to come out again in case the man was there waiting for him. If Jerome hadn't found him the next day after all of us searching high and low, who knows what might have happened.

Both women are in the kitchen when I knock on the door.

'Ah, Mags, hi! Come in? Cuppa?' asks Annette. 'Kettle's just boiled.'

'Lovely, thanks.' I smile.

She jumps up to make me tea, while I stand with my back to their solid-fuel range and enjoy the warmth and the smell of incense and turf smoke, baking and soil. Their house always has as earthy and as wholesome an aroma as you can imagine.

On the wall near the back door is a framed picture of Finbarr and Olivia. I walk over to look at it. It's a cutting from our local paper, the *Western People*, from when Finbarr and Olivia entered Jerome's bantams into the poultry competition at the Summer Show last year and won first prize. 'The Happiest Hens in Ireland' reads the headline.

'It took us months to get around to framing it properly, but we got there,' says Annette cheerfully.

'Looks great. Where's the man himself?'

'Oh, he was up and about very early this morning. He's cutting lawns for people these days and earning a few bob for himself. He's very happy now the grass is growing again after the winter, all the more work for him.' Annette's voice is filled with pride for her stepson.

I smile at her. 'Good for him. He's a great lad. I wish Ellie was as keen to put her hand to the plough. I've just bounced her into doing a couple of hours for Mam in the shop on Saturdays, and you'd think I'd sold her into slavery. Martha, is that me you're cutting the fruit cake for? I really shouldn't – I'm trying to cut down on the sweet stuff.' I pat my ever-expanding waistline ruefully.

'Nonsense, Mags, it's only a small bit' – it isn't – 'and anyway, we need your opinion,' she says as she slips the slice onto a blue and white side plate and places it next to where Annette has just set down my tea. 'Come on, you have to try it. We made it from our own currants that we dried last year, and we need your verdict.'

'Well, you've come to the right person then. I'm the world expert on cakes.' I sigh, pull up one of their súgán chairs to the table and take a mouthful of tea and then a bite of the fruit cake. It creaks when I sit, you know those old style chairs that are made of wood with rope work seats and backrests? Not flattering. But the cake, oh Lord. It's the best I've ever eaten, rich and moist, and the currants are wonderful. I say so, and the women are delighted.

'So, Mags, is this just a friendly visit or are we in trouble?' Annette winks as she and Martha pull up their chairs to the table.

I grin. 'No, you're not in trouble. Even if you were, I'd let you off after eating this cake. But it's not just friendly either – I've an off-the-record question for you, Martha.'

'Shoot, if I can help, I will,' she says openly, and I think how different she is from the guarded cagey woman I first knew. Martha came to Ballycarrick initially as Annette's lodger but got into all kinds of bother for growing cannabis. She ended up with only a suspended sentence due to extenuating circumstances. Annette has terrible arthritis, and Martha was growing it for medicinal purposes, but that's not legal in Ireland, and now they just grow organic vegetables. Or so they tell me.

Annette's arthritis came back badly while Martha was standing trial, but she's hopping around like a spring chicken now, and to be honest, I don't want to know. I'm just glad she and Annette are a match made in heaven. They are so happy now, and I'm delighted for them.

After another mouthful of the cake, I produce the plastic bag I found under the step, take out the cigarette packet and shake its contents onto the table.

Martha looks startled, and a hint of the old caginess creeps back in. 'Mags, I know nothing about this...'

51

'Ah, I know that. I found this little stash in some woods at the weekend, and what I wanted to ask you is, what am I looking at exactly?'

Martha relaxes and examines the lump of resin, sniffing it. 'Poor-quality stuff...'

'So not strong then?'

'I'd say not, but...' She smiles slightly. 'There is one way to find out.' She raises her eyebrows in question, and I nod slightly, sipping my tea.

She reaches behind her for a tin that's on the dresser and sets it in front of her, taking out a packet of outsize Rizla papers and a pouch of tobacco. She crumbles the small bit of resin over the tobacco, deftly rolls a joint, lights up and takes a drag. As she inhales, I instantly know something is wrong. She stubs it out and winces, which gives way to a fit of coughing. Clearly this is not what she's used to.

'Martha, what is it?' Annette is concerned, and a very strong smell is coming from the stub of the joint in the ashtray.

I open the back door to let in some fresh air, and Annette brings her a glass of water. Annette picks up the still smouldering joint off the table and gets rid of it in the range with a grimace, like she's disposing of a dead cockroach.

Martha recovers enough to drink some of the water, though she's pale. 'Where the hell did you find that stuff, Mags?' she asks. 'That's not just resin. That's contaminated with something. Heroin, I'd say.'

'Heroin? What? Why?' I'm shocked.

She finishes her water. Her colour has returned. 'Yeah, I know, totally immoral, but dealers often cut poor-quality resin with heroin and things like that to make people think they're getting the good stuff.'

'Is it easy to overdose on it?' I am extremely worried now.

'On pure Heroin, yes, of course, but this resin won't kill anyone – it's way too diluted. But still, it's not a good idea, and there's always a risk another batch will have too much in it. I hope this isn't going around the kids in the town?'

'I don't know, Martha, but I'm intending to find out.' The whole business with Horsehead has just got a lot more serious.

'We should legalise it, Mags, then none of this would be your problem,' Annette says quietly.

I know a lot of people think it would be better if drugs were decriminalised in Ireland, so we could get rid of the gangs and unscrupulous dealers and stop people selling rat poison to the unwary. 'Maybe we should, Annette, but it's not up to us, is it?' I say, and I finish my tea and leave to return to the station.

\* \* \*

I PONDER this new turn of events as I drive back through the town. I have to do something. As Martha says, it could be much worse the next time, and it's very worrying. But I'm still fairly sure it's just kids involved, even if one of them has been sold some contaminated resin in Galway or somewhere. So what I'm thinking is, a short, sharp raid by us local guards might be enough to do the trick, taking them all by surprise and frightening the hell out of them, followed by cautions all round and some compulsory education about the dangers of drugs. There's a crowd in Galway who are happy to give talks and workshops about it; some of them are recovering addicts themselves.

The problem is, it's hard to see how we can catch whoever it is by surprise. Ideally we would whizz up the avenue with a few vehicles, but you couldn't get a garda car up there even at a snail's pace, and if we go on foot, they'll hear the twigs snapping and the crows and bloody pine martens getting alarmed, and whoever they are will have plenty of time to melt away long before we get there, taking their drugs along with them.

Back at the station, I go straight into my office, pick up the phone, ring Garda HQ in Galway and request to be put through to fleet management. A few clicks, then a voice answers.

'Fleet management.'

'This is Sergeant Munroe from Ballycarrick –'

'Howya, Mags!'

I smile. It's Colette Donnelan, one of the officers in charge. She's a great person to deal with. 'Hi there, Colette.'

'What can I do for you, Mags?'

'Well, Colette, it's an odd one. I need some kind of a vehicle that can be driven up an overgrown lane. We can't get a patrol car up there – it would be destroyed with briars and brambles, and I can just imagine the drama if it has to be resprayed. So would you have anything I could use?'

'Hmm…let me think. We've a van, but that's not going to work. Oh, hold on, I've just the thing. Does it need to be fast?'

'Not at all. This isn't a chase – this is a shock-and-awe mission.' I chuckle. 'A bunch of kids are drinking on private property, but we wouldn't be able to catch them because the old house is up an over-grown avenue. We'd have to approach on foot, and it's surrounded by woods, so they can get away easy enough. I need to give them a bit of a fright. Flashing lights, sirens, you know yourself.'

My general approach to policing is gentle and relies on good rela-tionships with the community, young and old. I've never wanted to be the kind of police officer people only see when there's a problem, and so I make sure I and my team are very visible and that we get involved with non-law-enforcement events in the community. I've done it this way since passing out of Templemore twenty-seven years ago, and it's how I'll do it to the day I retire. Mostly I use the carrot, but some-times, thankfully rarely, a stick is needed, and I've decided that this is one of those times. I could get the drug task force involved, but that's using a hammer to break a nut, so I'll try a good fright first.

'I do know, Mags. You'll need to look a bit scary. Well, I'll tell you what we have now, and it might suit you. It's an old armoured Land Rover with bull bars. It's ancient and about to be decommissioned actually, but it's driving fine. But no pickup – you'd be quicker on a bike on a clear road. So you can wreck it and nobody will care. It's going for scrap.'

'Ideal. Thanks, Colette. I'll send my lads down for it this afternoon if that's all right?'

'Not a bother, Mags. I'll have it ready.'

Time for a meeting with my team to discuss the next step.

I put down my phone and check the rota, and I see Nicola and Michael are on duty next Saturday night anyway. I'll sign off on over-time for Delia and Darren, and then we'll all be available. On the internal phone, I call Nicola, who is on the front desk, and ask her to arrange Delia, Darren and Michael to come in for a meeting after lunch so everyone can hear my plan.

# CHAPTER 7

*I*'m confused as to why I'm here. As I was finishing work, Kieran rang me and asked me to come up to his parents' house. But he wouldn't say why except no one has died or had an accident or got cancer all of a sudden. Everything's fine. It's just he doesn't want to tell me the reason on the phone and he can't leave his mother by herself.

So I'm still in uniform as I ring the bell of their bungalow, and through the frosted glass of the front door, I see Kieran come to answer it.

'Hi, love, what's up?' I ask.

Instead of bringing me in, he steps outside and leads me around the corner of the house. Kieran Munroe is the least dramatic man on earth, so this is very out of character.

'Kieran, what is it? I'm getting nervous now.'

He runs his hand through his silvering hair. 'Mags, my father has left her, says he won't stay here any more apparently, has had enough and is gone.'

'What?' I take a step backwards; I'm literally reeling. Kevin Munroe, the monosyllabic man who wears grey trousers and a blue V-necked jumper from Dillon's Menswear every day of his life, who

56

never speaks, who keeps his grass cut with precision, has left his wife? No way.

'I know.' He looks haggard and tired. 'She's locked herself in the bedroom. I tried to talk to her, but she won't speak to me about it, and she says she won't talk to Gearoid or the girls either.'

'But what happened?'

'God only knows, and she's refusing to tell me. She won't even say where he's gone, though she must have a fair idea – she knows every place he would think of. And surely it's not far, as he can barely drive with the bad hip.'

'You've called him, of course?'

'Of course. Loads of times. His mobile is ringing out, and I'm so worried. I hate the idea of him out and about and hardly able to drive safely, let alone walk. She's so upset as well, but she won't tell me anything.' He looks at me pleadingly. 'I know this is mad, but I was wondering if you could have a word with her, Mags, see if you can get her to tell you something, anything...'

'Me?' I say, aghast. 'Sure she can't stand me! She barely speaks to me at the best of times.'

'Mags, please, I'm scared he'll do something stupid. Like, he's never done anything remotely spontaneous in his whole life, and Mam said he and she had a desperate row altogether. Will you go and talk to her, Mags, sort of put your garda hat on and get her to understand she has to tell me where he's gone as a matter of safety?'

I exhale. Nora and I are not best friends, and she'll bite my head off for sure, but Kieran looks on the verge of tears. I love him so much; I have to do this for him. 'OK, ring Marie and ask her to pop in on the girls, and tell her we'll get Luigi to deliver a pizza to them for their tea so she doesn't have to be cooking at this short notice. Then ring the girls and tell them Nora is feeling a bit under the weather and we're here taking care of her because your father's hip is very bad.'

'Right. Marie, pizza, girls.' He nods, and I give him a hug.

'It will be grand, love, probably just a spat. Maybe he finally stood up to her and she couldn't take it,' I add with an encouraging smile, though even while I'm saying it, it sounds daft. His father is such a doormat, never, ever challenging Nora, even when she is being utterly snobbish.

'He stood up to her when she was horrible when Gearoid came out as gay,' Kieran reminds me quickly. He is very fond of his dad and hates how his mother bosses him around; he wants to feel proud of him for something.

'True,' I say kindly. 'He did.' Although to be honest, the big 'standing up' moment consisted of no more than Kevin escorting a weeping Nora out of the room while whispering to Gearoid, 'Knew it all along, son. You were always very neat.'

Nora is now delighted with Gearoid, by the way, and refers to him as 'my son who is very high up in the arts'. He runs two theatres and the Galway drama festival and is seen at all the right places, not just in Galway but also Dublin, London and New York. He seems to be single again – it's hard to keep up – but apparently, none the worse for it. He is handsome and has a glint in his eye. Ever since he was a lad, he has always been stuck in some devilment. He is unashamedly himself and cares not a jot what some people think of him or his life.

'Right, let's do this,' I say, trying to sound confident. I button up my garda jacket, wishing I was wearing my police-issue stab-proof vest, and walk in through the front door.

The house is spotless as always and smells of that sickly lavender room spray. It's decorated in a very 1980s style. I pass the sitting room that contains a floor-to-ceiling mahogany unit that houses the TV and a forty-year-old hi-fi and goes the full length of the room. On the top shelves is a set of those old encyclopaedias that only posh people had back in the day, the Encyclopaedia Britannica. Nora explains frequently how she insisted on having them; they were very expensive but worth it to 'enhance the children's education'. Kieran tells me he only ever looked at the pictures and never saw any of his siblings reading them either, but today I notice one of the volumes has been taken down and then shoved back upside down, which in my house would be standard practice but in this house looks very odd and out of place.

The other shelves and every square inch of the walls are a shrine to the many and varied achievements of Kieran, Aoife, Orla, Catriona and Gearoid Munroe. Certificates, photographs – there is even one of those glass-fronted corner cabinets for the medals and cups they have won over the years. Nobody could accuse Nora of not being proud of all her kids, that's for sure.

My Kate won a cup last year for something – don't ask me – and recently announced that it was a perpetual trophy and needed to be given back. Could I find it? Course not. No clue where it went. I had to ring the school and ask them if I could buy a new one, to be primly told I couldn't because the recipients of previous years had their names engraved around the base of it. Then I remembered, thanks be to the Lord and St Anthony, employed to great effect by my mam, that following the school's firm instructions, I'd left it into the jeweller's to have Kate's name put on it eleven-and-a-half months ago and totally forgot about it. So you see? Mine and Nora's parenting styles are a bit different.

I carry on down the corridor that runs through the middle of the bungalow to what Nora insists on calling the master bedroom. There are only four bedrooms, and they are all the same size, but she would remind you of that one off the telly, Mrs Bucket, the one who insisted on calling herself Mrs Bouquet, remember her? Such notions of grandeur.

I pause before the closed door. How does Kieran imagine she'll agree to speak to me? But I've said I'll do it, so I gently tap on the wood.

Silence.

'Nora? It's me. Can I come in?'

Nothing.

I try again. 'Nora, it's Mags. Can you open the door?'

I hear shuffling, and then to my amazement, the key turns in the lock. The door opens a crack and there she is.

I'm shocked. I've never seen my mother-in-law in any condition other than perfectly groomed. Hair done, make-up on, pressed and perfect clothes. She never wears trousers. She wears skirts and cardigans and blouses, and if she is really slobbing out, a skirt and a jumper, but always tights and patent shoes with a heel. Pearls at her throat and in her ears. It is like a uniform.

Now her long grey hair is hanging in messy strands down her back. I never knew her hair was so long – she wears it in a chignon every day. She's got no make-up on and is dressed in a navy dressing gown, her feet in slippers.

My heart goes out to her, very slightly. 'Can I come in?' I ask gently.

She opens the door fully to admit me, and I walk past her into the bedroom, a room I've never been in though I'm married to her son for almost two decades. The room is a study in Laura Ashley flowers that makes my eyes hurt. Pink and purple flowery bedspread, flowery pillowcases with pink lace trim, matching curtains and pelmet. The carpet is pink too. And there are two chairs upholstered in the same material, with a small table between them on which is a lamp with – yes, you guessed it – the same fabric on the shade. No wonder poor Kevin had enough; this room looks like the inside of a bordello.

I sit on one of the awful chairs, and Nora perches on the end of the bed. She's been crying; her eyes are red rimmed and her face is puffy. The wastepaper basket – yup, pink and purple flowers – is full of used tissues. All very *Gone with the Wind*, I think to myself.

'Right,' I say, as she sits in stony silence. 'What's this all about?'

Long seconds pass and she remains silent.

'Nora, if you tell us, we can help, but we've no idea, and it's so hard for Kieran not knowing where his father is. Anything you can say to help us find out if Kevin is safe is very important. The first twenty-four hours after someone goes missing are crucial.'

I'm laying it on a bit thick. Kevin is a grown man, not an abducted child; completely different rules apply to him. But his son is sick with worry, and I want to get that look of terror out of his eyes.

She looks startled, but it works, because after a while spent dabbing at her eyes and twisting another tissue in her hands, she asks in a feeble voice, 'Do guards have to keep a secret if they're told it? Like priests and doctors?'

I'm taken aback but say instantly, 'Yes, if it's told to me in the line of my duty and is not relevant to an ongoing crime.'

She eyes my uniform. 'And you're on duty?'

I mentally put on my garda hat, as Kieran asked me to do. 'I am.'

'So if I tell you where I know he is, you can't tell Kieran, or anyone?'

'Well, no...' Ugh, this is going to be bad. 'But I think you should tell Kieran yourself, Nora. He's outside and –'

'No!' she gasps. 'I can't tell him, and you can't tell him either.'

I sigh. 'Nora, whatever it is, we'll figure it out, but you'll have to tell me where he is at least. It's a matter of safety with him driving while he's recovering– he might not even be insured – so let's focus on that first, will we?'

'You promise you won't tell Kieran?'

She's putting me in a terrible situation. 'Nora, the important thing at the moment is to make sure Kevin is safe and stays safe. We can deal with the family angle later.' I think this is what my husband would want me to say. He did ask me to put my garda hat on, and now I have.

She sits in silence for another long while, shaking her head. Then she finally comes out with it. 'I looked at our bank account on my phone,' she mutters, shredding another tissue, 'and he's paid for three nights in the Mallon's Inn in Galway.'

It's not easy to run away these days, when your every move is plastered all over the internet. But I exhale. No harm can come to him in a three-star family hotel surely.

'That's good. And what did you and Kevin fight about, Nora?' I ask directly.

Her voice trembles; more tears leak out. 'He's gone, Mags. He won't come back. I've lost him...'

'I'm sure that's not true. It was probably just a silly fight, and when everyone cools down and gets some time, we'll sort it out.'

Nora sighs and droops, and suddenly I see an old woman who is carrying the weight of the world. She's in her late seventies but until today she never looked it. Now she does, and a few more years with it.

'Kevin left me because I told him the truth,' she whispers. 'I thought it would stop him going on at me, but it didn't. It just made everything worse.'

I wait. Being a guard has some advantages. You learn early on in the job that the awkward silence is your friend. I go into investigator mode, and we sit in the quiet.

'I should never have told him, never. I would have taken it to my grave but for those stupid encyclopaedias.'

OK, now I'm bewildered. But she is talking at least. 'Start at the start,' I say gently.

She looks at me, and for a second, she's young, scared and vulnerable. She closes her eyes and exhales slowly, inhales and exhales again. She licks her thin lips, and her fingers twirl the engagement ring on her left hand, round and round. She says no more.

# CHAPTER 8

*T*he next half hour is a blur of arguments. Nora stays locked in her room and won't let Kieran in no matter how much he begs. Kieran is furious I'm keeping his mother's secret about where his dad is. And I'm really fed up at being caught in the middle.

'I can't believe you're not telling me, Mags,' he says for the hundredth time.

We're standing toe-to-toe in his parents' living room, among all the trophies and awards and the Encyclopaedia Britannica, which is apparently mysteriously connected to this case.

'I know. I hate it too,' I say, trying to keep my voice steady and calm, 'but it's the only way she'd tell me where he was, if she could do it with me acting as a garda and not your wife.'

'Isn't it possible to be both?' He is really hurt.

'Kieran, it was you who asked me to put my garda hat on, so I did. I can't just whip it on and off to please you – it doesn't work like that. So frankly, no, sometimes it isn't possible to be both.'

Unfortunately, this reminds him of the time I knew his younger brother was gay long before Gearoid told Kieran himself. The reason was, Gearoid's then boyfriend had got beaten up in Galway one night and Gearoid was in court because the victim of the assault was his partner. So I'd been on garda business when I found out, and I couldn't tell Kieran, and he was seriously upset when he found out I'd known all along.

After briefly reiterating what I'd hoped was old history, Kieran storms off to remonstrate with his mother once again through the locked door. I take the chance to leaf through the encyclopaedia, the A–E one, all the way from aardvarks to Ezekiel, The Book of.

Nothing jumps out at me.

Kieran returns and announces angrily, like this is all my doing, that Nora now wants me to go and find his father by myself and make sure he's all right and that he's not going to miss his appointment for the hip operation.

'I will if you really want me to,' I say stiffly.

'Since when did you ever need my permission to do anything?' he snaps.

'I'm not talking about you giving me permission. I'm asking if you want me to do this, because if you do, I will.'

He sighs heavily. 'I do, you know I do.'

'And what hat would you like me to wear while I'm doing it?'

'Whichever one you want to wear, Mags. Please yourself.' And he slumps on the sofa, pale and defeated. I pause on my way out of the room to touch his silvery hair, but he moves his head away, not sharply, just slightly, and my heart aches.

\* \* \*

I FIND Kevin Munroe in his room in Mallon's Inn off Shop Street in Galway. He limps to the door when I knock, registers my presence with a curt nod of his head and goes back to lying on his bed, looking as old and ill as his wife and clearly in a lot of physical pain as well. There's a box of Solpadeine beside him, and an empty glass, which I take and refill from the water jug beside the kettle.

He says nothing and I say nothing. Like I did with Nora, I just sit down in the armchair by the window, watching the Corrib go tumbling by beneath. It's the fastest-running river in Europe, beautiful and dangerous, and glittering with reflected city lights.

Eventually Kevin cracks. 'She sent you, did she, Mags? Well, you can tell her I'm not going home.' It's a long speech for Kevin Munroe. His voice is creaky, like old leather, with lack of use.

I look at him now. 'She's not asking you to come home, Kevin.'

'Then what does she want?' His voice holds no compassion; it's chilling.

'She wants me to make sure you're all right and that you'll be having the operation on the fourteenth as planned.'

'Ah.' He puts his hands behind his balding head and stares at the ceiling. 'Right.' Still no hint of emotion, just coldness. It's bizarre, like there's been an invasion of the body snatchers.

I have to ask. 'Kevin, what's happened between you and Nora?'

Silence. Between the two of them, this is serious blood-out-of-stone territory.

'Is it really that bad, Kevin?'

He makes an odd noise, a sort of angry sob. 'She hasn't told you?'

'She said it was something about an encyclopaedia, that's all.'

'Oh yes, the encyclopaedia.' His voice is sneery. 'Which we bought at great expense because she "cares about her children so much", though it turns out she doesn't care a bit. It's all appearances, that's all that woman cares about.'

'Kevin, please...' Even I am beginning to think he's being a bit unfair now. I'm no fan of Nora Munroe, quite the opposite, but there's no doubt she loves her family – well, all of them apart from me. 'Of course she cares. She loves every one of you.'

More odd noises, and then, like if he keeps it in any longer, he will burst like a frozen pipe, he chokes out, 'Then why did she lie to me about our son?' And he lies with his eyes squeezed tight shut, his face going red, suppressing tears.

I sit there, stunned, and try to process what he's just said to me. I can't. It's too strange. Which son has she lied about, Kieran or

Gearoid? And what could she know about either of them that she wouldn't want her husband to find out? Everyone already knows Gearoid is gay, so it's not that... And anyway, it was Nora who found that hard to come to terms with, not Kevin. 'I literally don't understand what you're saying, Kevin.'

'She has her faults, God knows, but I love her...*loved* her, I did, and I thought I knew her. I thought at the bottom of it all, she had a good heart. But now I find our whole life together has been one big lie, from beginning to end.'

Oh God. Their whole life together? What...? How...?

My brain is scrambling. And then the only possible explanation leaps out at me. One of their two sons, either Kieran or Gearoid, is the product of an affair. Sweat breaks out on my forehead as I think back to that cringing, beaten-down old woman I left sobbing on her bed, no longer respectable, unable to look me in the eye...

'Which son?' I ask through numb lips, terrified of the answer.

'Do you really want to know?' asks Kevin bitterly.

* * *

I RING down to room service for tea and sandwiches, and at Kevin's request, a stiff whiskey. Kieran's dad rarely drinks, and he shouldn't be doing it at all while taking pain meds, but sometimes the devil drives.

The whiskey on top of the codeine loosens his tongue, and for the first time in living memory, Kevin finds his voice. And when he starts, I just need to listen.

Apparently, Kevin Munroe's family was very respectable and well-to-do. They lived in Castleknock in Dublin. His father worked for the bishop's office, and his mother was a matron in Holles Street Hospital. Then he fell for a girl called Nora whose parents owned a fish-and-chip shop in Cabra, and his mother and father were disgusted.

I fight to keep my face neutral. For my whole marriage, Nora has made me feel like I'm not good enough for her precious son, and all this time she was once in the same boat? How could she have been such a cow to me over the years when she knew what it was like to be on the receiving end? But I push these angry thoughts away – this isn't about me and Kieran – and go back to listening.

Kevin went to university in Galway; the course he wanted in biochemistry was there. Nora wanted to do a secretarial course in Galway to follow him, but her mother said it was too expensive and she was needed in the chip shop, so he left her behind, working in Dublin.

This new Nora, the one from humble beginnings, is a stranger to me. I remember something. 'I thought she said you were both from Galway?'

He shakes his head. 'No. Dublin. But when we settled here and... Well, she said it was easier to say that, and she dropped the Cabra accent as quick as lightning. I suppose I should have realised then that she was a natural-born liar.'

'Ah, Kevin, I don't think that's fair...'

His mouth sets in a stubborn line. 'Why should I be fair, Mags, after what she's done to me?'

I say nothing, because I don't know what she's done to him, and he takes another slug of the whiskey before saying gloomily, 'I suppose she'd say I was a liar myself, because she knows I told my father I'd finished with her.'

I look at him, still neutral. He stares into his glass. He's clammed up again, and I make my special noise, the one that's a cross between an *ah* and an *eh*.

'But that's only because my father was a very strict man and told me if I wanted to go to university and have him pay for it, I had to finish it with Nora. And I needed my degree, you see, and it was very expensive in those days, so I did tell him I'd left her. Only my plan was to get him to pay for the degree and then once I was qualified, we'd get married.'

Well, yes, that was a big lie, all right. It's hard to imagine Kevin Munroe as such a maverick, but then Nora isn't who she seems either, so who knew?

'Anyway, whatever about what I said to my father, and whatever about her staying behind in the chip shop. The night before I moved to Galway, I proposed to her on bended knee and gave her a ring and everything. We were engaged, and we...' He stops and blushes slightly for some reason.

I make the noise again but realise what he's saying. Seeing Kevin and Nora as young people in love, not willing to wait until they married to make love, is such a peculiar realisation, but it humanises them for me in a way that has never happened before.

'So I went to Galway, and then when I came home for the Christmas holidays, her mother told me she was gone away to her aunt's in England for a holiday. I didn't understand why she hadn't waited in Dublin for me, or even written to say she was going. I was broken-hearted. I wrote so many letters, but I never got a reply. I assumed she'd found someone else, but I still wanted an explanation.' His eyes pleaded with mine for understanding, he wasn't the kind of man who left a girl high and dry. He went on,

'That next summer I went round again. She was still gone, and this time her parents wouldn't say where. I knew then she'd given up on me, but all the same, I didn't give up on her. I was mad about her, you see. The next Christmas I tried the chipper again. I hardly dared hope...but there she was, my precious little Nora, working behind the counter, as lovely as ever. And I waited until no one else was in the shop to approach her and begged her to come and meet me after her shift.

'She did, and she told me that after I'd gone, my own parents had come around to her house and warned her off me and her own parents had sent her away. I was so angry with them all, Mags. I asked her if she'd still have me after the way my parents had treated her, to leave with me that very day. I'd get a job and pay the rest of the tuition myself, and so that's what happened. She came to Galway, we got married, I wrote to my family, and they replied I was dead to them and that they never wanted to hear from me again.' I could hear the bitterness there, even after all these years.

'Your parents cut you off, just for marrying someone you loved?' I'm so shocked.

'They did. She wasn't good enough for them, and that was that. But the dean of the university was very understanding. I worked in the labs, cleaning them in the evenings and things like that, and worked in a factory at weekends, and Nora worked in a shop, and between us we made just enough money for a small flat in Salthill. And then I qualified and got a good job, and we moved here to Ballycarrick, and we had Kieran, and the girls, and Gearoid...'

I breathe again. So Kieran is his son.

'I thought everything was wonderful. I loved her for the way she'd stuck by me through thick and thin. It wasn't until I took down that encyclopaedia, to look up what it had to say about bones, because of the hip replacement coming up. I was looking under "B" and there under "baby", stuck right back between the pages, I found the picture of her and a newborn baby, the image of Kieran...' He stops, gulps more whiskey.

I'm so confused. 'But what was the problem with that?'

He looks at me like I'm stupid. 'The date on the photo. The baby in her arms was almost two years older than Kieran! And then I looked at her hair, and it was cut really short, and when Kieran was born, it was lovely and long.'

Again I fight to keep my face expressionless. I can't believe this. Super-respectable Nora Munroe had a baby with someone else when she was young? Poor Nora. Poor Kevin.

'It took weeks for her to admit it, Mags, but she finally did. She... fell...you know...on the night before I left, when we...'

'Hang on, Kevin, back up there a wee bit. Are you saying this baby is –'

'And she had a baby boy and gave him away. And when I came back for her, she never mentioned it, ever, so there's a son of mine out there in the world I have never known. And now she's pretending not even to know the date he was born, or where. She doesn't want him found. She's always pretended to be this wonderful mother, but oh, oh, Mags...'

Whiskey, codeine, misery, incomprehension, anger...they all combine, and he sobs and sobs and sobs, and I sit on the bed and put my arms around him. This man, who if you look up stoic in the dictionary, it says 'see Kevin Munroe', is sobbing against my shoulder as if his heart would break.

# CHAPTER 9

*T*he secret is out. Kevin rang Kieran from the hotel room while I was still there and told him, so now I'm off the hook and can go back to being the supportive wife I need to be in this situation instead of having to wear my garda hat.

The girls are in bed by the time I get home. Kieran hugs me for a long time, and I hug him back. We both apologise for being snappy with each other earlier, and then he spends an hour on the phone to his brother and three sisters, letting them know the whole story, or what we know of it, and asking them all to go and talk to Nora.

It's nearly midnight by the time he comes back into the living room, where I've been sitting for the last hour, staring at the television without really knowing what I'm watching. He pours himself a glass of red wine from the bottle on the sideboard.

'How did Gearoid and the girls take the news?' I ask as he sits down beside me.

I like Kieran's sisters well enough, but we're not really close. They'd never confide in me, nor me in them. Orla is the one I get along best with; she lives here in Ballycarrick, and her Evie and my Kate are best friends. Tom is her other child, a nice kid but a bit geeky, into computers, and she is married to 'Fergus who is very high up in the bank'. Fergus is the misfortunate soul who happened to mention to Nora about his distant cousin running for the US Congress, leading to Nora going a bit doolally over it all, but he's sound. I knew his sisters going to school. I like Orla, and she's really helpful if we are stuck for a spin for Kate, but again, we wouldn't confide in each other.

I get on really well with his youngest brother, Gearoid, though, and my girls think he is the coolest person on the planet. Last month he took them to a film premier of a huge budget thing made on one of the islands. All of Hollywood turned out for the party in the Westbury in Dublin, and my two were rubbing shoulders with them, even getting selfies with the stars. It was, according to Ellie, the best night of her life, and it's where she got her idea from about studying drama in New York.

Kieran sighs. 'Not great. But not the worst. Catriona is a bit horrified – you know what she's like, takes after Mam – and the Dublin chipper thing came as a shock. But Orla and Aoife and Gearoid, well, they're more confused than shocked, and also curious about this man as well. They want to know more.'

'And you? How are you about it?' I ask gently.

He gives a deep sigh that seems to come from his toes. 'I honestly don't know. Like, I'm bewildered as to why she never said a word in one way, and in another I'm not. You know how she is, and if she heard that bit of gossip about someone else, she'd dine out on it for a month. I suppose she thinks everyone in the world is as small-minded and as gossipy as she is.'

'But apart from your mother not saying, how does it feel to know you have an older brother?'

'It depends on what he's like, I suppose. The first thing is to find him.'

* * *

EASIER SAID THAN DONE. In the last three days, all of Nora's children have spoken to her, but she won't tell anyone anything, not the date this boy was born – at least we think it's a boy – nor the name on his birth cert, not even what mother-and-baby home she was in when she had him, if that's where she was. It's like she wants to wipe the memory of him from the face of the universe.

Although if that's true, why did she keep this picture hidden away where she thought no one would ever find it?

Kevin Munroe's not wrong. It must be a picture of the mystery child even though the little boy is the spit of Kieran as a baby, because in all the pictures of Nora with Kieran, her hair is shoulder-length and shining, while in this one, her hair is cropped very short, almost like a boy's. And the unknown baby has a mark in the centre of his forehead, which Kieran's baby pictures don't have. It's the kind of mark they call an angel's kiss. Funnily enough, Ellie had one of those when she was born; it must be genetic. And to top it all off, there is a date written on the back of the picture, presumably the date the photo was taken, and it is nearly two years before Kieran was born.

Kieran and his siblings are all gathered in the living room of Nora and Kevin's bungalow for a family meeting. I'm here as well – Kevin wanted me to come – but I feel conspicuous in that I'm the only in-law present.

Nora's hiding in her room, but Kevin is here in the living room with us. Kieran managed to persuade him to come home, at least until he's had his operation, so we can look after him while he's disabled, but he and Nora are still not talking to each other. They are existing like ghosts, moving around each other without speaking. He's living in Kieran's old room, while she stays locked in the 'master' bedroom. Occasionally she drifts out to make herself food, but she has taken a kettle and all she needs for tea to her room, and there she stays.

'So what do you want to do, Dad?' Gearoid asks his father, who is looking a hundred years old and has his jumper on back to front, something that would never have happened if Nora was looking out for him. Gearoid feels very deeply about this awful situation, I know that, but he still manages to be dressed in an exquisite suit that's like it was made for him, and I realise that it probably was. He is very charming and very good-looking, helped by a few shots of Botox and filler here and there and a wardrobe of designer clothes, but despite him being an absolute peacock, I love him to bits.

'I want to find my son,' says Kevin simply.

'I know, but if Mam won't tell us...'

'We have the date on the photograph. It must be near enough to his birthday, the newborn in it.'

'Yes, but if Mam won't agree to look for him...' Gearoid tries to be reasonable.

'I'll find him myself. I don't care what she thinks.'

'Dad,' says Catriona firmly, in her mother's 'stop talking now, Kevin' voice, and he responds to it like a well-trained dog, going quiet and slumping in his armchair.

The truth is, however much Kevin wants to do this, Gearoid is right. Only the birth mother can register for information with the adoption services, and Nora is still refusing to have anything to do with this. Everyone in the family has tried to get a bit more out of her, but she is like a clam. Nothing. And if whoever this missing child is – I mean, whoever this *man* is, because he must be fifty-eight by now – hasn't also registered with the service, even she won't be able to find him.

'Surely birth records are public information?' asks Aoife. She is just bursting to get on board with this. She and her husband, Leonard, are both principals of private schools in Limerick, and they are so right on, it is a bit painful. Organic tofu, vegan sandals, gifts of goats for Africa – you know yourself. All very laudable, of course, but a bit wearisome too.

'Can't we just search all the records for around that time and see if there's a Munroe? Or a Connolly?' Connolly is Nora's maiden name.

Technically, Aoife's right, but as I point out, the birth records kept by most of the mother-and-baby homes are in the hands of the religious orders and it's not easy for anyone to get access to records held by the nuns.

'Maybe we can go to all the different convents near where she was living and ask direct?' suggests Orla.

Again, technically, Orla's right. We could try that. But the nuns from that time are ancient or dead, and anyway, everyone knows they shut up like clams when asked questions about the baby homes.

'So is that it? We just accept he's lost and that's all there is to it and move on from this?' Catriona puts a sad face on, but I wonder if 'moving on from this' isn't her preferred option. She hasn't said she's against finding her surprise new brother, but she is the least enthusiastic for sure.

Catriona is the most aloof of all of the Munroes, and the most like Nora. Her husband, Seamus, is the head of cardiology at University Hospital Galway, and she is the perfect wife. Slim, well groomed and at his side as and when she is needed. She does a lot of charity work, Nora explains regularly; that's track seven of Nora's greatest hits played on repeat. It drives Kieran mad that Catriona is so uninterested in this new twist in the Munroe tale, but I suspect this is not the kind of story that she and Seamus would like to get out. She's only here, I'd say, because Orla and Aoife made her come.

'No, we don't accept it.' Kieran bristles. I shoot him a warning look not to snap at her, and he takes a breath and calms down a bit. 'We just have to work out a way.'

Catriona sniffs but picks up the baby picture, which is between us on the coffee table, and tries to look concerned.

Kieran continues. 'Me and Dad have been looking on Facebook groups, and we found a few, but to be honest, they were less than helpful to us. They are very women-orientated understandably, and since we weren't children trying to find our mothers and without Mam's input, they didn't really want to get into it.'

'So we're at an impasse unless we can get Mam to tell us more,' Orla says gloomily.

'Well, yes. Unless we go public,' says Kevin.

'Dad!' says Catriona again in her Nora voice, and he shrinks into himself.

'Going public how?' I ask, smiling at him.

He sits up straight again and clears his throat. 'Well, just that. Going on radio, those TV shows that find people, putting an ad in the paper, asking online, that sort of thing.'

Catriona looks shocked. 'But then everyone would know,' she protests. 'Mam would never allow that, not in a million years. Sure, she won't even talk to us about it, let alone having the whole place know her business. You can't do that to her, Dad.'

Ah, yes, I see it now. Catriona isn't entirely against finding this man but only if it can be kept quiet. Herself and Seamus don't want to be the poster family of a long-lost, born-out-of-wedlock baby, thank you very much.

'She'll never agree, Dad,' she finishes, in Nora's 'end of the argument' tone of voice, and it looks like she's won, because Kevin's gone all quiet again.

But then he rallies and slams his fist on the arm of his chair. 'I don't care if she does or she doesn't, Catriona! He's my son and your brother, and we are going to bloody well find him no matter what we have to do!'

'Dad!' She is genuinely shocked, and it's not just her – we all are. We've never heard him raise his voice before.

'I don't know, Dad,' Orla begins doubtfully.

But Aoife pipes up. 'Well, I think it's a good idea. I'm sure Mam deep down wants to find him. She was obviously traumatised by the whole adoption thing, and she can't start the healing process until we bring this out into the light.'

Kieran winces at Aoife's choice of language, but says, 'I agree with Aoife. This is Dad's son too, and he needs to be able to look for him if he wants to.'

And Gearoid says, 'I'm with Kieran and Aoife.'

Catriona's cheeks flush under her perfectly applied foundation, the expensive type that never sinks into the cracks, just plasters over them, and she jumps to her feet. 'No, wait,' she protests. 'This isn't fair on Mam. You're bullying her.' And before anyone can say anything more, she bolts out of the living room. We can hear her in the hallway, knocking loudly on the door of the bedroom, calling, 'Mam, it's Catriona here. You've got to let me in.'

Almost immediately, the door opens. There's a murmur of voices, then the door closes and there's silence.

We all sit looking at the carpet. After a while, I glance at Kieran. He is drawn and ashen. Kevin looks mulish. Orla is upset. Gearoid is inspecting a speck on his jacket. Aoife is shifting uncomfortably in her seat, probably worried about what tales Catriona is telling her mother.

I'm just thinking this might take a while and will I put the kettle on, when the distant door opens again and feet stride down the hall. We look up as Catriona comes in, and then everyone sits up straight as, a moment later, Nora shuffles after her into the room.

Like Kevin, Nora appears to have aged decades in a matter of days. It's the second time I've seen her in the last week without her 'face' on her, as she calls it, no lippy or mascara or blusher. Her trailing salt-and-pepper hair is even greasier than three days ago, and she is dressed in what looks dangerously like a mauve velour leisure suit, made popular by the walking women of Ireland circa 1985 and thankfully not seen for years.

She comes to a halt just inside the room and stands with her wrinkled old hands clasped together. 'Catriona's told me...' She falters and stops. Catriona puts her arm around her.

'Do you want me to say it for you, Mam?' she asks softly, and Nora nods.

Gearoid has always been Nora's favourite, but Catriona is more like her mother than the rest of them. I'd say she understands Nora's deep desire for respectability and has been quietly supporting her all along, rather than banging on about 'circles of healing' or whatever Aoife's been pushing on her, or Gearoid's 'let it all hang out, who cares what anybody thinks', or Kieran begging Nora to be kinder and put her husband first for once, or Orla doing her best to please both parents.

Now Catriona looks coolly at each one of us. 'What Mam wants to say is, you're only causing her pain. This man you want to find, he's been living his life, and no doubt it's a good one, and she's asking us now, as her family, to just let it go at that. Isn't that what you wanted to say to us, Mam?'

'It is, Catriona. That's what I'm asking.'

Her voice lacks its usual certainty, though. Nora is a self-proclaimed authority on everything. One night Ellie told a story over a family dinner with all the grandparents of how a kid in her class was now nonbinary and how everyone was dealing with it, including the kid, and when Ellie tried to explain it to my mam, who looked bewildered, Granny Nora exclaimed that when she was a girl, she knew lots of nonbinary people. I mean, fine, maybe as a concept it existed, but the idea that there were loads of people wandering around Ireland in the '40s and '50s openly identifying as trans or nonbinary – come on, Nora. But she was adamant. There isn't a subject on earth about which she doesn't know more than someone else. It is bizarre. She only last Christmas tried to explain to me how the law was being misinterpreted by gardaí on the subject of drinking and driving. So yeah, we've all had to listen to a lot of that.

This trembling unhappy voice, though, it just doesn't sound like Nora.

Nobody speaks. The tick of the Laura Ashley china clock on the mantelpiece is the only sound.

'No.' It comes from Kevin. 'We won't let it go, and we won't forget about him the way you seem to be able to do.'

Nora flinches and puts one hand to her heart, and I think the gesture is involuntary, not dramatic. Kieran and I exchange a silent conversation. What to do now? He leans forward, looking at his mother with his dark-blue eyes.

'Mam,' he says gently, 'it's not really up to you, do you understand? You gave birth to this boy, but Dad is his father, and it wasn't his choice to give him away.'

She flinches again; it's like we're all stabbing at her. 'A choice, was it? That's what I had?' she says under her breath. 'Were you there, Kieran?'

'Well…' Kieran looks puzzled. He's thinking, as we all are, that she had a man who wanted to marry her; she could have told him for a start.

'You could have told me!' snaps Kevin, voicing our thoughts. 'But you chose not to!'

'It wasn't like that.' She looks scared now, and oddly young under her aged face.

'Then what *was* it like, Nora?' he asks furiously.

'Dad,' says Catriona, in Nora's voice.

He ignores her completely. 'What was it like, Nora, giving away our son? Why won't you tell me that, Nora? Why won't you tell me anything about him, not even his name?' He's leaning forward in his chair now, jabbing his knuckly finger at her. 'You think he's nothing to do with me. You think because I'm only a man, I don't count, I shouldn't even care. But I do care. Very much. He's my flesh and blood, Nora, and I want to know why you let them take him away without telling me. Maybe he's fine – I hope to God he is – but what if he's not? What if he needs help? Needs a family? I need to know.'

'Do you now?' A flash of the former Nora rears its head, and she steps away from Catriona's protective arm. 'Do you, Kevin? You want to make me live it all over again? Do you? You want me to tear out my heart like I did back then and let the whole lot of you stamp all over it for good measure?'

'Mam...' Gearoid gets up and goes to her. He's her baby and always her favourite, but for once she won't let him comfort her. She pulls away, won't let him touch her, and her eyes are fixed on Kevin, burning with rage and pain.

'You want to know what I went through? Fine, I'll tell you then, and then maybe you'll know why I never told you.'

'Mam, maybe sit down,' murmurs Catriona, taking her arm, but Nora pushes – actually pushes – her away and turns on Kevin again.

'The night you asked me to marry you, I was so happy. I thought it was OK to act like we were married. You said it was. You said it never happens the first time. But then you went away and left me, and I was three months gone before I realised I had fallen. I was only a girl. I knew nothing. I was terrified. I didn't know what to do. I was afraid for my life. My parents were God-fearing – I knew they would be horrified. I couldn't go to our doctor – he'd surely tell them – so I went to the maternity hospital in town. I put on the ring you gave me and gave them Mrs Kevin Munroe as my married name, and the doctor there congratulated me for "being with child".

'I remember that day back at home, Kevin, hiding up in my bedroom, telling Mam I was too sick to work in the chipper. I was scared to death. I knew I had to go to Galway and find you and tell you and hope you still wanted me even though I was pregnant. I was going to get the bus first thing in the morning, but around nine that evening, someone came to the door downstairs. I heard voices and crept out to the landing. My older brothers were gone from home then, both working in England, so it was just me and my mother in the house. My father was working in the chipper because I was supposed to be sick.'

She swallows; the very memory is traumatising her.

'It was your parents at the door, Kevin. The doctor at the hospital was a friend of theirs and asked them were you really married to me – that's how they found out I was pregnant. And the way they spoke to my mother, like I was some kind of a streetwalker and not good enough to clean their shoes. I heard Mam screaming for my dad to come in from the shop, and then I was summoned downstairs in my nightie. My mother was hysterical, and my father was stony-faced...'

She wipes away tears with the back of her hand, and my heart goes out to her, despite all that we've been through over the years.

'Your parents called me terrible names, asked how dare I pretend their precious son was the father of my baby. They said it couldn't be yours, that you'd broken up with me ages ago. I showed them the ring and I said how we were engaged, but your mother laughed and turned her nose up at it and said, well, that proved it, that if her Kevin had proposed to me, he'd have used his grandmother's emerald ring that was promised to his future fiancée, not some cheap bit of tin. And your father said you'd promised him on your grandmother's grave to leave me, because that's the only way he would pay for your college education. Imagine what it was like for me to hear that, Kevin, that you'd sold me for money!'

Kevin stirs in his chair and mutters, 'I didn't...'

But her eyes flash. 'You never told me about that lie, did you, Mr High-and-Mighty Kevin? No, you didn't, so what was I to think?'

'Nora...'

'You asked me to tell you what it was like, Kevin. Now do you want to hear me out or not?'

He subsides, his head down, his shoulders up around his ears.

'Right then,' she says grimly, 'I'll go on. So I was banished upstairs while they discussed me and my life. Next thing I knew, about an hour later, a car pulled up and my mother came into the room. She silently packed a bag of my things and told me to go downstairs. I was still in my nightie, so I got dressed and did as she said. Of course I did. I was only seventeen, and I was scared to death.'

Her voice has been getting lower and lower in the telling, and it is barely more than a whisper now.

'There was a priest there – I never saw him before. And without a word from any of them, I was put into a car and driven to a place in Cork. All through the night, we drove. The driver said nothing, and neither did the priest. I'd never been to Cork before. The house was a big one, up a long driveway. It had a red door – I remember that. The priest let me in, had a few words with a nun there, and I was brought into a room.'

The air is heavy in the house. Kevin is still shrunken. Nobody speaks.

'She said I was a sinner, and that I would now have to atone for my sins.'

'Did you not ask her to write to me?' croaks Kevin suddenly, without lifting his head.

Nora's eyes flash with contempt for his stupidity. 'I did, and she said I was a foolish girl, that if she had a shilling for every girl that let a boy do as he pleased to her because he put a bit of gold on her finger, she'd be a wealthy woman.'

'I didn't lie to you,' he chokes out.

'How was I to know that?' A touch of the erased Dublin accent creeps into her voice.

'You either lied to me or to your father, Kevin, and how was I to

81

know which? And the ring wasn't even gold. It wasn't your granny's ring, was it? It was tin. Cheap and worthless, like me.'

'Oh, Nora...'

She looks away from him, stares out the window into the neat spring garden, and her voice drops again, becomes flat. 'They changed my name to Esther, and she brought me upstairs to a dormitory. There was a faded blue dress and underwear, and a pair of second-hand shoes on the bed. She told me to put them on and to give her my bag and my clothes, and so I did.'

I glance at Kieran, and he looks sick. He knows well the stories of women and girls being incarcerated in those places, their babies dying or being sold on by the nuns; it is in the news every day now. Catherine Corless, a very brave woman in Tuam, just a few miles from us in Ballycarrick, recently managed to uncover a grave of babies in a septic tank on the grounds of a convent, a place that was once a mother-and-baby home. There seems to be no end to the horror.

But to hear the story from his own mother... It's a shock.

Yet why is it a shock?

And that's when I realise, we've all had our heads in the sand. The Nora Munroe we know is so respectable that it's hard to believe... No, that's not fair. This isn't about Nora. It's about us. We just can't conceive of such a thing happening in our own family; we're too respectable ourselves. Deep down, without even going there, I suspect we've all been imagining a *nice* sort of mother-and-baby home. The sort to which wealthy men – judges and businessmen and politicians – used to send their mistresses. Nice discreet B&Bs located right next to private hospitals.

But Nora is from a chipper in Cabra. She's 'Nora from the chipper', like Chloe is 'Chloe from the chipper'. Bottom of the pile.

Catriona has just realised this, and she wants it to stop. She tries to put an arm around Nora again. 'Mam, do you want to sit down now, and I'll make you a nice cup of tea?'

Nora shrugs her away angrily. 'Sit down yourself, Catriona. You need to hear this too.'

She turns back to her husband. 'I worked so hard, Kevin,' she says passionately, 'scrubbing floors, cutting grass, weeding paths. No tools and in all weather, and everyone there was expecting too. We weren't allowed to speak to each other really, only an odd whisper at bedtime, and you were punished severely if you revealed anything about yourself, where you were from, anything like that. And I was so scared of what was coming. I hadn't a clue, not an iota, about babies and childbirth and all the rest. My mother would have rather died than talk about such things.'

She stops and wipes her eyes on her sleeve, and my heart breaks for her. My mam told me the same about her own mother. There'd been such shame about bodies and that kind of thing back in the day.

'You're so much better now, you young mothers,' Mam said to me recently. 'Much more open and no silliness. I remember only a few weeks ago, Kieran picked me up to bring me over to your house and Ellie texted him, asking him to buy her tampons. He didn't turn a hair, just went into the service station shop and got them for her. It's like a different world, honest to God it is.'

I dismiss the memory and concentrate on what Nora is saying.

'So I stayed there, until it was my time. I'd seen girls in labour by then and knew it wasn't nice and it hurt a lot and sometimes you died, and the nuns wouldn't do anything to help you. I was so terrified. I can only remember that feeling. I was just so scared.'

She takes a breath, steeling herself. 'One day, my waters broke, on the floor of the refectory where we ate. The nun in charge got very cross with me and made me get a bucket and a mop, and I had to clean it up in front of everyone and my dress was soaked. I'll never forget the pain. I cried and begged for help, for them to do something, but I was just brought to a room with a single bed covered in a blue rubber sheet and left there alone. The pain was incredible, and I was so afraid I'd die there alone.'

Tears flow down her face, and I blink back my own. The barbarity of it.

'Then a nun came in, and the baby came out of me, and she gave him to me to hold while she cut the cord with a big scissors. He was tiny and screeching and covered in some kind of white stuff, and I remember thinking he looked like a little monster. I didn't want to be near him or see him again. I just wanted the nightmare to be over and to be allowed to go home.'

'Oh, Nora,' says Kevin, and he puts his head in his hands.

She moves a step closer to him, standing over him, forcing him to hear this. 'They took him then, and let me sleep. I had no pillow or blanket or anything – I was just left there, like an animal. Then a girl I recognised, one who'd had her baby a few weeks before me, came in and helped me to the bathroom and washed me and gave me clean clothes. The next day I was back to work. And I was in such pain, and the milk came in, and in between scrubbing, I had to feed him. But you weren't allowed to cuddle them or anything, just feed them and leave. I hated feeding him – everything hurt.'

'But the photo, Nora,' groans Kevin into his hands. 'In the photo, you were smiling. You looked happy.'

'Oh yes. One day when he was two weeks old, they said they needed to take pictures of the babies in the nursery. They didn't tell us why, but I know now it was so they could get a passport. The day he came, all of the mothers were lined up and sent to the nursery. They let us hold our babies before the photo so they'd be content and not crying, I suppose, and they told us to smile for the photographer or we wouldn't get our dinner. And that day, when I picked him up, he was all dressed up for the photo in a white suit and a white knitted cardigan. And Oliver opened his eyes and gazed at me –'

'Oliver...' gasps Kevin, raising his head.

'Yes, Oliver.' She smiles at him, but it's an ugly smile. 'I called him Oliver, but there's no point looking for him under that name – he'll have been given a different one by whoever adopted him. They didn't let us name them, oh no. We'd probably have given them common unrespectable names, but I didn't do that, did I? I called him Oliver. That's a respectable name.'

He gazes hungrily at her. 'Oliver Munroe?'

'Murphy. They all got the surname Murphy. Just until it got changed.'

He flinches, then rallies. 'What colour were his eyes, Nora?'

She smiles again, but more softly. 'He had dark-blue eyes, if you must know, like Kieran's, and that day he locked his little eyes with mine while I was holding him and…' – her voice cracks briefly – 'and his hair was black and his cheeks were rosy.'

'Ah…'

She half closes her eyes. 'When it was my turn, we went in, and the man asked if I'd like a photo of my own. He'd take it and develop it and give them out to us the next day he came, unbeknownst to the nuns. Salving his conscience at what he was doing, I suppose.'

Probably she was right about that. So many people had to be complicit in order for the machine of cruelty to work. Not just nuns, but priests, parents, boyfriends, bosses and – yes, I'm ashamed to say it – the guards. We brought girls who ran away from these terrible places back, though they'd committed no crime. It is a dark stain on the history of the organisation I work for and love.

'Well, he took it, and I smiled as he asked. And then I went back to work and he went back to the nursery. Three weeks later I went up to feed Oliver as usual, but he wasn't there. He was gone. Just like all the babies before and after. Nothing to be done.'

'Oh…' Kevin begins to weep, big fat tears squeezing through his fingers.

'Yes, Kevin,' she says fiercely, 'Oliver was gone. Gone. I begged, I cried, I tried everything, but he was gone. I'm sorry to make you feel so unhappy, but you insisted on knowing, didn't you? And it's hard to bear now, all these years later, isn't it? Can you imagine what it was like for me?'

She bends over him. She's forcing him to hear this, forcing him to feel in some way what she went through herself, and I realise with a shudder of revulsion and pity that she is relishing his tears.

'About a week after that, they called me in from the kitchen garden one day. I was given my old clothes and my suitcase, told to get dressed, and when I went to the Reverend Mother's office, my father was there. He had come to bring me back to work in the chipper like nothing had ever happened. And the only thing he ever said to me about it ever again was on the way home, on the train. He said in this flat voice that I was soiled now, for giving birth outside of marriage, and that if I really wanted a chance with someone as decent and nice as you, Kevin, I was never to tell you about it, even if you came back for me, because then you would never want me and my chance of a respectable life would be gone forever.'

'But you didn't get yourself pregnant.' I am so outraged, I can't help interrupting.

Nora shoots me an odd look, something between bitterness and amusement. 'But that was the way of it then, Mags. The girl was the one with the loose morals, not the boy, and you never got pregnant the first time, so what was Kevin to think, only that it was at least my second time?'

'So what did you do?' I ask, because she's stopped again and everyone else is speechless.

She shrugs. 'I went back to work in the shop, and then Kevin came for me.' She turns back to her husband. 'And I was so afraid of losing you, Kevin, and never, ever being respectable, I didn't dare tell you. And then weeks turned into months, and two years later, we had Kieran, and it was like looking at Oliver all over again. My heart was broken, but I'd pretend to myself he was Oliver come back to me. And the years became decades, and I...I just tried to forget.'

There's a softness in her voice now – it crept in when she was talking about Kieran – and Kevin looks up at her and tries to take her hand.

She whips it away, and her voice is hard as flint. 'And I did forget him. I was fine and happy until I was stupid enough to move that photo from where it was because we were going to replace the carpet, and I only put it in the encyclopaedia for a while because no one ever looks at them even though they cost the earth. And then *you* of all people found it, and you've never read a book in your life.'

'I'm sorry, Nora...'

'Sorry, are you? So is this good enough for you now, Kevin?' She's gone back to being a ball of fury and grief. 'Am I humiliated enough now, telling the lot of you this story, or are you still planning to drag my name through the mud of Ballycarrick and break my heart all over again for no good reason?'

'I don't want to drag you through the mud, Nora. I just want to know my son –'

'You say that's what you want,' she rages at him, 'but you just want to hurt me all over again, like you did before.'

'I didn't mean to hurt you, Nora! I never knew –'

'Oh yes, I can hear them now. "That Nora Munroe who thinks she's better than anyone." Don't think I don't know what they say!' she bursts out fiercely, before Kevin can try to contradict her. '"Look at her, that Nora Munroe, who had a child outside marriage and lied to her husband about it, and all this time looking down that nose of hers at us." That's what you want to put me through, after all I've gone through, after all I've suffered to get a respectable name?'

'Maybe people will be kinder than you think,' he says weakly.

She pauses, considers his words, then smiles slightly. 'Kinder than I would be if it was someone else, you mean?'

This moment of self-awareness is unprecedented but intriguing.

Kevin, fair play to him, smiles back at her. 'Maybe so, Nora. Maybe we can all learn.'

Again he reaches for her hand, but again she whips it away, and her rage is back, full-on rage, rage against the world, rage at him, at us, at everyone who wants to drag her down.

'Oh, I learnt my lesson long ago, Kevin Munroe. I learnt the hard way what women like me could and couldn't get away with in this world. I didn't have it soft like all of you here in this room' – she glares around at us, spitting out her words – 'brought up with money and love and softness. I did what I needed to survive, and I won't be looked down on again, not ever, not by the people of Ballycarrick, and certainly not by my own family.'

She storms to the door, pausing to glare at us before leaving.

'Do you hear me, you bunch of bullies? All of you, go away and leave me alone.'

Moments later, her bedroom door slams.

Orla and Aoife both stand up, but Kevin heaves himself to his feet despite his bad hip and waves at them to sit down again. 'Leave her to me, leave her...' He hobbles off down the hall, and we can hear him tapping on her door and saying her name, over and over, but she doesn't answer. After a while the door to Kieran's room closes as well, and the two old people are back where they were, trapped in the angry silence of their own rooms.

# CHAPTER 10

*I*t's Saturday, and tonight is the night we'll be springing the surprise raid on the revellers at Horsehead.

The plan is, we'll join forces to lift open the rusty gates, and then myself and Michael will charge up the avenue in the old armoured Land Rover with the bull bars, clearing the way for Nicola and Darren and Delia to follow us in the two patrol cars and the prison van, and there'll be megaphones, handcuffs, the whole lot. I'm determined to teach these kids a lesson they won't forget in a hurry.

The day goes by quickly, and at the handover, all the staff remain on. The station is closed and lights turned off. We all depart in our own cars. The police vehicles, including the old 4x4, two patrol cars and a prison van to be driven by Darren have been parked up behind the secondary school all day, so in case any of the juvenile lawbreakers are concerned about our whereabouts, it just looks like the cops are all gone home for the night and won't be back.

We're going to reconvene behind the secondary school at ten thirty, so there's plenty of time for our family date night at Luigi's pizza restaurant, and I'm looking forward to it.

I'm a bit disappointed when Ellie reminds us she's not coming. I'd forgotten we'd agreed to drop her off at Cat and Trish's on the way, to watch films and sleep over. Still, she's done a good day's work in the shop according to her granny, so fair enough. She's old enough to make her own decisions about where she spends her time. When we leave her at the entrance to their estate, Kate looks a bit crestfallen, but at least Ellie remains on the pavement waving sweetly to her as we drive away. And it works out rather well. We're able to give our full attention to our baby girl, and it's nice not to have to deal with the usual snide remarks from Ellie about Ballycarrick being the back end of nowhere and how she can't wait to get out of here to New York where the Italian restaurants are run by real Italians and not by a man called Leonard from Offaly.

'So when we get home, can we all watch a Harry Potter film together, like Ellie is watching the Hunger Games with Cat and Trish?' asks Kate hopefully as she smears knickerbocker glory all over her face.

I smile at Kieran, who is on his second glass of red wine. I'm not drinking, so he has the half carafe to himself. 'It's up to your dad, Kit Kat. I have to go out for a while.'

'Oh…' She digs in her spoon. 'Where?'

'Just something to do with work.' I smile at Kieran again. I haven't told him about the raid. It's not that I don't trust him to keep it a secret, but it can't be one rule for me and another for my officers. Something like this has to come as a total surprise to everyone. Nicola knows not to tell her boyfriend and Michael not to tell his fiancée. Darren and Delia are going out together, but they won't say anything to their brothers or sisters or their cousins-thirteen-times-removed, even if they suspect one of them might be better off staying home tonight. So you see, if any of my officers find out at a later date that Kieran knew about the raid in advance, then I will lose their trust. And trust, as Ellie reminded me earlier this week, after catching me barefaced lying to her beloved granny, is easily lost and a lot harder to get back.

So I've told Kieran I'm going out for an hour or two, but I've said it's a joint patrol with Delia around the primary school, which had a window broken last night and we want to catch the culprit if they show up again. It's true about the window, but I checked the CCTV footage this afternoon and I already know it's Gary Desmond, the infamous Chloe from the chipper's eleven-year-old brother. God knows what manner of grudge is driving him to this ridiculous behaviour; maybe the teachers tried to teach him something. I'll be dropping in on him next week, just when he's started to think he's got away with it.

I don't think Kieran totally believes me about the school, because he gives me an anxious look when I get up from the sofa at 10:15 that evening and follows me to the front door.

'Are you all right, love?' I ask, pausing in the act of putting on my garda hat.

Kieran has had some mental health issues in the past. He got very anxious after I was shot a couple of years ago, and he began to resent my job and tried to keep me safe by living in my ear – driving me mental in the process – before eventually he broke down saying how he was having nightmares about something terrible happening to me. He went for therapy, specialist counselling provided by the force for PTSD, and he is so much better now, but I still worry about him sometimes. He knows that he needs to protect his well-being mentally as much as physically.

'I'm fine, love. I know you worry, but I'm grand.' The worried look vanishes as if he forced it to, and he smiles.

My heart melts. I love this man more with every passing year. The fireworks of the early years, in every department, have given way to a more gentle, calmer, arguably more harmonious relationship. I notice how we rarely if ever fight now. It's like over the years, we've rubbed each other's rough edges smooth, and we just get along together. OK, so the mad passion of our youth might have gone, but we replaced it with a deeper connection and true friendship. He's totally on my team, and I'm totally on his.

Like I'm trying to organise nursing care and a family rota for when his father comes home from the hospital after his hip operation. It's happening next week now because there's been a cancellation. The Munroe business is still in a terrible tangle, with Nora and Kevin not speaking, hence the need for paid care, and Kieran is so upset about it all. It's such a lot for him to take in.

On the doorstep of our house, we hug each other, and then I leave and try to put the Munroes out of my mind. I've a job to do. The village won't police itself, so the story of the missing baby and his unhappy parents needs to go to the back of my mind.

My officers are all waiting when I arrive at 10:25. We get into the police vehicles, then drive slowly in a convoy out of town, through the country lanes to the gates of Horsehead. There are a couple of old cars and a quad bike parked there already, up on the grass verge, so a few of the kids must be old enough to drive, though I'd say the quad is 'borrowed' from some unsuspecting farming parent.

As I climb out of the Land Rover, I can just about hear the music from the road, the bass throbbing in the still night, so good news – the party is in full swing. Darren has brought bolt cutters, and he slices the rusty chain off the gates, and then between the five of us, we very carefully lift the gates off their hinges and lean them down among the brambles. They're heavy – it's a massive effort – and to my annoyance, I burst off one of the two buttons that Mam patiently sewed back onto my jacket after my last encounter with Horsehead.

Then we all get back into our vehicles. I stick my arm out of the window with a beckoning gesture, and we strike. Michael is driving the Land Rover, and he crashes headlong through the undergrowth, the briars and stumps of trees tearing at the armoured body, but I don't care. Behind me are Delia and then Nicola driving the patrol cars, and Darren is driving the prison van. All of our sirens are on and blue lights flashing. As we approach the front of the house where the music is blaring out from speakers and a big fire is lit, there are kids scattering in every direction.

Our vehicles squeal to a halt in a semicircle. We turn on their spot-lights, and I grab the megaphone.

'Remain exactly where you are!' I yell through it as I leap out of the Land Rover. 'Stand still and place both hands on your head where we can see them. Failure to comply with our instructions will result in criminal charges being brought against you and a night in the cells.'

Everywhere, the fleeing kids stop dead, slowly raising their arms, placing their hands on their heads.

As I repeat the instruction, I see Nicola already handcuffing young Rachel Mahony, who looks out of it. That figures. Bertie the butcher's daughter is going out with a fella from Galway. He is too old for her and known to us as a minor dealer, so it stands to reason he is using her to get to the young people of Ballycarrick. I can't see him here, but I'd bet money on him being the source of the resin. Rachel is only fifteen, the same age as Ellie, and she's no Pablo Escobar, but she's out of control and needs to find out there are consequences. Bertie is such a Holy Joe and his wife is not on this planet at all when it comes to teenagers, so Rachel can run rings around the pair of them.

Not that there will be over-the-top consequences. My plan is still just to bring her and the rest of them all into the station, call their parents to come and fetch them, then haul the miscreants back in over the next week for a caution – which is basically just a tough talking to by me, no charges or court appearances or anything – plus a commitment to attend a workshop on the dangers of drugs, which will be held in the local community centre.

Exactly as they've been trained to do, my officers continue making arrests, and one by one, the young people are put into the cars and the van to be brought to the station. I see a lot of familiar faces, and they're certainly not all from the social housing estate. There are a number of offspring from 'respectable' houses, the sort of homes where the parents would be furious if we disgraced them by bringing their darling child home in a garda vehicle.

Lavinia Moran's sixteen-year-old nephew, for one, and Joanna Burke's granddaughter of the same age, and I'm pretty sure the kid staggering past me with Darren holding him up is Elsie Flanagan's son. This is going to teach the neighbourhood watch to blame everything on Travellers and kids from the social housing, I think grimly, and I wonder where the parents think their children are. Probably they've covered themselves by pretending to be at each other's houses, while in fact they're out littering private property with broken glass and takeaway food wrappers, drinking underage, smoking weed and lighting fires.

I see one of the downstairs windows of the house is broken now, which it wasn't the last time I was here, and remember what Foxy said about the Ukrainian refugees who will be moving in here. I hope the kids haven't the interior ruined, breaking and smashing things and thinking it's great craic.

I climb the limestone steps and test the front door, and sure enough it swings open, so someone must have climbed through the broken window and unbolted the door from the inside. I cast my flashlight around the dark hallway.

It's a mess. Graffiti on the walls, one of the banister uprights kicked out, a large porcelain sheepdog smashed on the floor, a moustache drawn on the oil painting of a shepherdess, mud on the Turkish carpet, a trail of which leads to the stairs.

Mindless destruction it seems, is such great craic.

Seething, I stand in the hall, listening out. There are voices upstairs. I stick my head back out of the front door and beckon to Nicola, who has just rounded up a few more of the eejits and got them into the van, which is nearly full. I want her with me when I go upstairs. It's not that I'm afraid to go up by myself, but caution is important in police work. Because you never know what you're going to run into, there are rules about doing things in pairs. Not that it always works. I had Delia with me when we intercepted the sex trafficker, but there was a gun involved that time, which changed things a bit. Tonight we're not expecting anything like that, though we are of course kitted out for low-level trouble.

Like you'll probably think this is overkill, but we're all wearing stab-proof vests and have extendable batons and pepper spray on us, and as the only officer in the station with a firearms licence, I also carry a taser. No guns, mind you. It's a subject of deliberation in Ireland, the fact that as gardaí we are unarmed, but we have such a low gun-crime rate compared with other countries that I think we'll stay unarmed as long as we can. Kieran thinks it's ridiculous; he said he'd prefer if I carried a weapon all the time. But like I said, he's just a bit nervous since that time I was shot.

Nicola joins me. I put my finger to my lips, then point up the stairs, and we start to creep up together, testing each tread as we go in case of wood rot and also to avoid anything that might squeak.

Off the upstairs landing, we can see into a big bedroom that has a four-poster bed in it, no curtains on it, and there is a tangle of five or six teenagers lying on the bare mattress, passing around a joint and swigging from cans of beer. Girls and lads who should be at home doing their schoolwork.

We stand in the doorway. One of them looks up and sees us watching them, and instead of being alarmed, he winks at us. Of course he does. It's Ger 'Winky' Costello. His dad is 'high up in the Gaelic Athletic Assocation,', as Nora would say. All those Costellos are cocky, and this youngest one has a right gob on him. Always the one with the smart remark. He says something to his gang. There's a big stoned guffaw, and everyone looks around at us.

'Right, everybody, on your feet now,' says Nicola calmly. 'We're bringing you all in to the station.'

Still giggling and woozy, they start to get off the bed, swaying and colliding into each other. One of the less-stoned girls – I think she might be in the class above Ellie – is a bit tearful at getting caught, but Winky gives her a poke. 'Don't look so worried, Debs,' he drawls. 'Sure the guards can't do anything to us – we're all juveniles. It's nothing.'

'But...' She can't help glancing towards the joint, which someone has hastily thrown into the corner, where it lies very obviously against the skirting board.

'Debs, a bit of possession for personal use, nobody cares, not even PC Plod there. Isn't that right, Mrs Plod?' He actually winks at me as he speaks. He's clearly seriously stoned; whatever they've been smoking is very strong...or laced with heroin.

I walk over to pick up the joint, to catcalls and giggles. 'Do ya like a puff yourself, Mrs?'

One of the other stoned boys chortles as I pull out an evidence bag. Nicola is standing like a statue in the doorway, with one hand on her baton in case any of these eejits decide to make a break for it, and I can sense her bristling. I'm sure she would love to do something to wipe the silly grins off these lads.

Some gardaí say the respect is gone, that people don't have the same regard for us or what we represent any more, but I don't think that's true. I think there were always gougers and there always will be. The vast majority of people I meet in the course of my working day are nice and reasonable and have no occasion to feel resentful or treat us with anything but common courtesy, as we do them, but as I say, there are always the few. And these kids are the few. And I've had enough.

It's time to put a stop to this dangerous nonsense. It's not just about respect for authority; it's about personal safety. No one is dying of an overdose on my watch if I can help it, and if the respectable mammies and daddies of Ballycarrick have an issue with their darlings being up in court on a variety of public order offences, then maybe they should parent their offspring a bit more effectively. I know this is going to cause waves, but they are breaking the law, and much worse, they are endangering themselves and others by smoking contaminated drugs. And also I'm sick of them getting away with it while everyone else blames the Travellers and the less-well-off people from the social housing.

'OK, Nicola,' I say calmly as I put the now cold spliff in an evidence bag. 'Read them their rights. We're arresting and charging these people with trespassing, breaking and entry, wilful damage to property, setting fires, endangering wildlife and possession of illegal drugs.'

'What...? Ah, would you go 'way with yourself now. You can't charge us with anything...' Even Winky looks shaken, and Debs bursts into noisy tears.

'I can and I have, and you're going to have your day in court. Nicola, go ahead.'

Nicola begins intoning their rights. The two other girls are sobbing as well now and clinging to each other, and the three lads are in a flat panic – they want to run, but there's nowhere for them to run to. Once their rights have been read, Nicola and I cuff them, bring them downstairs and put them in the van, and then I inform Darren and Michael that we are now charging and arresting every single one of these kids. They nod and get out their notebooks, professional as you like, no argument. I suspect they are delighted we are taking more decisive action.

Then Delia approaches me through the dark from behind the house, and I know by her face something is wrong. She is gripping a very drunk boy by the arm, who keeps shouting, 'Do you know who I am? My father is a detective sergeant!'

With a guilty twinge of *schadenfreude*, I recognise Duckie's appalling son, Tom Cassidy, the one who goes to the private school in Ballycarrick.

Duckie Cassidy, the bane of my life, was promoted a couple of years ago to detective sergeant and is now even more insufferable, if such a thing is possible. Everyone knows it was nepotism, because Duckie comes from a long line of guards. I didn't want the job anyway; I love where I work, and I love my work-life balance. There's not even any difference in rank or salary, but Duckie loves rubbing my nose in it all the same because there is a difference in public perception. Detective sergeant is a plain-clothes job, therefore 'glamorous'. I'm still in uniform, and therefore I'm still a 'PC Plod', as Winky made the mistake of calling me.

'Everything OK, Delia?' I ask her, and then add loudly for Tom's benefit, 'I've just given orders to arrest and charge everyone with trespass, breaking and entry, wilful damage to property, setting fires, endangering wildlife and possession of illegal drugs.'

Tom's head lolls around wildly. 'I want to speak to my father! Do you know who I am? My father is your boss. You're nothing but a, but a...' he rants drunkenly. 'When he finds out, you'll be sacked.'

'I'll talk to you in a minute, Sarge.' Delia bundles the very drunk young boy into the Land Rover, a good choice of vehicle for him as it's going for scrap, so it doesn't matter if he pukes up all over the upholstery. When she comes back, I'm busy kicking soil over the embers of the campfire; I don't want to leave anything burning. She's still looking worried.

'What is it, Delia? Give us a hand here? Or a foot, rather.'

'Sarge...'

'What? You're not worried about arresting Duckie's son, are you?' Duckie Cassidy hates Travellers and thinks they're all criminals. And he really hates the fact that Delia is a qualified guard and a very good one too, so she should be quietly over the moon to have his son, Tom, under arrest, even if it would be unprofessional for her to say so out loud.

'Course not, Sarge. But I found him sitting with a bunch of girls. They're younger than him or the others, and several of them are very drunk. I've already popped them into my own patrol car, and I was thinking, if you didn't mind, I'd bring them straight home instead of to the station.'

I shake my head as I stamp out a glowing ember. Michael is securing the front door of the house with a padlock, and Darren and Nicola are checking that all the kids have their seat belts on; we're wrapping up here and nearly ready to go. 'No, Delia. When I said arrest everyone, I meant everyone.'

'No, but, Mags, these girls...'

'Delia, *everyone*.' I'm firm. I'm beginning to wonder if one of these girls is a cousin of hers, but I can't have her playing favourites; it would be an abuse of her power, and surely she knows that. 'It's not like anyone is going to prison,' I reassure her. 'Trespass and possession for personal use and drunk and disorderly without causing fear or attempting to intimidate another person will get a fine and a bit of community service most likely, a rap on the knuckles, that's all. Nobody, including me, wants it to be anything more than that, and it won't be, but these kids have to face a judge if for no other reason than to scare them a little.'

She draws closer to me. 'Sarge, one of them is Ellie, and she's very, very drunk.'

Blood pumps in my ears, and I feel like I'm going to be sick. My Ellie, my daughter.

Swallowing my emotions, I say as calmly as I can, 'Everyone, Delia.'

* * *

IT'S COMING up on midnight, and the garda station is in chaos. Parents are collecting their errant offspring, some mortified, others furious at their kids, more of them furious at us. We don't react, just cite the laws broken, advise them their children have been charged and are now being released into their custody to await a court date.

Duckie's wife, a miserable downtrodden woman, has come to collect Tom. She keeps her head down and avoids my eyes. I wonder how long it will be before Duckie comes into my station again. He normally calls in whenever the humour takes him, for a reason nobody knows apart from flirting with Nicola and throwing dirty looks at Delia, but hopefully after this, he'll be mortified into staying away for a while. So that's one good thing at least. I can't bear him, with his halitosis and misogyny.

Bertie the butcher is just as cowardly; he's sent his own wife for Rachel. Maura is a sweet woman who keeps murmuring her apologies as she coaxes her pale and sweaty daughter off the premises. Elsie Flanagan has sent her sister, Flo. I'm not a bit surprised she doesn't want to face me tonight, not after her insistence on it being the kids from the social housing and Travellers from Galway.

Willy Costello is fuming when he arrives. You'd think having family in the GAA top brass, and a brother who plays for the senior Galway hurling team should exonerate Winky from murder, let alone a little thing like trespass and drugs and breaking and entering. It crosses my mind to breathalyse Costello Snr on the spot. He is crimson around the gills, and I'm sure I can catch a whiff...but I decide against it. Don't judge me. He only lives a couple of hundred yards away; for all I know, he could have walked.

I've not spoken to Ellie yet, and she's huddled miserably with Jess, the girl who was bullying her last year but who for some reason Ellie seems to still be impressed by.

Ellie. I can't even look at her, let alone speak to her. My own daughter. How could she have been so stupid? How could she lie so easily like that about sleeping over with the twins? I knew we'd been having the usual mother-and-teenage-daughter arguments, but underneath it all, I'd genuinely thought we had a strong relationship. But honestly, I just don't know any more.

I will have to deal with her as a mother, of course I will, but for now I've asked Delia to call Kieran. When everyone else is gone home, I'll go home myself and we'll talk then.

I see Holly and Don, Jess's parents, arrive looking like thunder. They are very well-to-do. He has a big management job somewhere in the Shannon Enterprise Zone, and Holly, the mother, is a gorgeous tanned, toned yoga teacher.

'Mags...' Don begins.

'If you'll just join the line there, Garda McGovern or Garda Carney will process Jess,' I say calmly.

'Ah look, Mags, there's no need for this surely.' Don tries again. 'They're just kids. And I know Jess shouldn't have gone to that party, but...'

'Like *everyone* else' – I fix him with a steely glare – 'Jess has been charged and will be processed through the courts in due course. Once she has signed her statement, you are free to take her home. Now if you'll excuse me.'

'I bet your Ellie won't be charged with anything,' mutters Holly furiously, but loud enough that a number of other parents look around to listen.

'Excuse me?' I face her down as I've wanted to do since her little brat forced Ellie to do her homework for her. But I'll maintain my composure and professionalism. If it kills me.

She's braver now. 'Our Jess wouldn't even be here if it wasn't for her. Your daughter is the ringleader, and now *our* daughter is the one in trouble?'

'Like everyone else, Ellie has been charged and will be processed through the courts in due course,' I say, in the same flat voice.

'I'll believe that when I see it,' sneers Willy Costello as he hauls

Winky out of there, and there are murmurs of agreement among the other parents waiting.

'You will see it,' I say quietly.

I retreat to my office, meeting Michael in the corridor on the way.

'If Willy Costello gets into a car, bag him please,' I say. It's not vindictive; it's enforcing the law. Well, maybe it is a bit vindictive, but if he's driving drunk, then he deserves it.

'Will do, Sarge.' Michael thankfully doesn't give me a look of pity or empathy but just goes about his business.

I get to my office, close the door and lean against it, my eyes closed and my heart pounding. I need a break. I'll make myself a coffee. Kieran and the girls bought me my own coffee machine for the office as a birthday present, and I love it. I fetch down a cup from the shelf, and as I do, there is a knock. I wait – usually my officers open the door after knocking – but nobody comes. I go to open it.

Kieran pushes past me into the room, his face as angry as Holly's and Don's, closing the door behind him without asking.

'Kieran, I'm busy working –'

'Really, Mags? You look like you were just about to make a cup of coffee.' He points to the empty cup in my hand with a look of contempt. 'Now please tell me what Darren Carney just said is a bluff, that you haven't had Ellie charged with a list of public order offences as long as my arm?'

I can't believe him. Instead of being furious at our daughter, I'm to blame? For doing my job? I manage to maintain my composure, but I'm fit to scream or cry or both.

'She's been charged with the same offences as the others, Kieran, and I can't talk to you now.'

'Our daughter?' His voice goes up several notches, but he quickly lowers it, hissing now. 'You're giving our own daughter a criminal record? Am I having a nightmare?'

'Kieran, as you well know, I have to prosecute Ellie the same as anyone else – not to do so would be wrong. But as we are explaining to all the parents, she's under eighteen, so her case will be heard in the Children's Court. If Ellie ends up with a conviction because of this, it will be her own doing, not mine – she's the one breaking the law. Now can you please take her away and leave me alone? I'm at work.' A weariness washes over me, and I wish more than anything I could just get into my car, drive away from him, from the kids, from this whole village, check into a hotel far away and sleep.

'Ah, for God's sake, Mags.' Kieran runs his fingers through his hair, and I see the tension in his shoulders. 'What are you doing? They're *kids*, local kids, the sons and daughters of our friends, our neighbours. I don't understand it. What the hell did you think you were doing?'

I will not have this out with him here. 'Take Ellie home, Kieran. I'll be there when I finish doing my job. I'm not going to discuss this with you at work, and I need to get on, so please, just take her home.'

'I can't believe you, Mags. You knew you were going to raid a bunch of kids, but you never said anything about it to me or the girls. Did you not think for one moment it was possible that Ellie –'

'No, Kieran, I didn't. Did you? Did you think our fifteen-year-old was drinking and taking drugs with boys older and more experienced? Because if you did, then perhaps you might have mentioned it? Or were you going to leave that to me along with everything else?' I'm furious now – how dare he? 'So no, I believed our lying child when she said she was watching a film with her friends, but even if I didn't, even if I thought for one second that she might be there, I would still not have mentioned it. It can't be one rule for her and another for everyone else.'

He stares at me with his mouth open. Like he can't believe his ears. Finally, he looks me up and down, a horrible, scathing look, and marches out, leaving the door open.

So much for us being a team.

After giving him ten minutes to take Ellie and go, I walk back out into the public office, my head held high. I would love to stay hiding away at the back, away from all the angry respectable faces and muttered insults, but I have to show my face and keep showing it. Parents keep coming up to me, pleading their own little darling's case and repeating versions of Holly's inference that I'll be letting my own daughter off, but I just keep saying the same things over and over again: The law has been broken, these are the consequences, and their children are better off learning them before they turn eighteen and it becomes a serious matter.

Anyway, the wheels have been set in motion, and I can't do anything to stop whatever's coming next. Not that I would if I could. There's going to be no overdoses in this town on my watch. Which reminds me, I have that joint in my evidence bag. I'll get Nicola to send it off to Galway, for forensics to check it over.

# CHAPTER 11

*T*he next morning is Sunday, and the station is closed. I sleep on later than I usually do and wake to find Kieran gone. The girls were asleep and my husband was on the sofa with the TV on by the time I got back, so I didn't go into the sitting room but just went straight to bed. Now the house is silent, and I check my phone; it's nine thirty. I lie there for a few minutes, wonder if the girls are here or not – more specifically Ellie.

Everything is very quiet.

I get up, take a shower and stand there in the stream of hot water, trying to figure out how to best handle this family crisis. I need my husband to support me; I don't know how I will ever get through this without him.

I've always been on his side. I stood by him through all of our marriage, even when things were less than ideal. When he started his roofing business, it was hard financially. We needed to buy a lot of expensive equipment and the insurance was astronomical, but my secure, permanent government job meant he could do it. And now of late, this business with his parents and the brother, I'm doing my best with that too.

It isn't like he doesn't support me either. He does, even though I know secretly he wishes I wasn't a guard, but that's only because he fears for my safety.

Or is it? I just don't know. Maybe he's more like Nora than I realised. Maybe he does think of me as Mrs PC Plod, a woman with a tin-pot job of no particular importance. It doesn't seem to bother him that Ellie has humiliated me in front of the whole town and that I will henceforth be known as the sergeant who can't police the behaviour of her own child. Our daughter has made it immeasurably harder for me to do my job in the future. I'm going to be under scrutiny the whole time, and if I put a foot wrong, I'll never regain the respect I once had.

But none of that seems to have entered my husband's head.

I need him to step up. I need him to be on my side and blame her for what she has done to me – yes, I want him to take my side against our daughter. Does that make me a terrible mother? I don't think so... But then I don't know any more.

I get out of the shower and dress in jeans and a hoodie – I've no intention of going out today – and wander downstairs to find the kitchen tidy and the place empty. I make a cup of tea and then realise I have to call Foxy about the state the kids left Horsehead in. After all, he's the one in charge of selling it to the council for your man in South Africa. I should be able to get him at home on a Sunday morning; he's not one for Mass.

'Hi, Foxy, it's Mags Munroe...'

'Mags!' And straight away he is off with the chat and the stories and, like I've said before, the dance of pointlessness, but I'm just not in the mood today and I cut through it all.

'Foxy, we raided an illicit party at Horsehead last night, picked up a bunch of kids from the town including' – I might as well get it over with; it's going to be all over the town within hours if it isn't already – 'my own daughter Ellie.'

'Ellie?' Foxy guffaws, delighted. He thinks I'm no craic at all, and he's thrilled. 'Your Ellie?'

'Yes, I'm afraid so.' I hate this. 'I'm calling to apologise on her behalf for the damage caused by her and her friends –'

He is still chuckling. 'Ah, Mags, don't be apologising. Sure they were just messing, being kids. Weren't we all that way once – well, maybe not you or Jenny, but your sister Delores. Ellie must take after her. She'll be living up the same tree next...'

If this is Foxy trying to cheer me up, it isn't working.

'I'm afraid this was more than messing, Foxy. That's why I'm calling you. They broke windows, damaged the fixtures and furniture and scrawled graffiti on the walls. I'm sure the judge will order them to clean it up as part of their community service – that's what I'll be asking for anyway – but if you have anyone looking around it within the next month, you might need to organise a clean-up job and ask the judge to have them reimburse you.'

'Not at all, don't be worrying. Horsehead is off my hands now. I closed the deal with the council last Thursday. Not a great price, but it will do.'

'Have you a number then for the right person to talk to on the council, warn them about the state of the place?' Another conversation I'm not going to relish.

'Ah sure, the council won't mind. 'Tis only for the Ukrainians,' says Foxy comfortingly. 'They're coming from a war zone, so they're well used to it.'

I hardly know how to answer this blatant racism and appalling attitude, but thankfully there's a knock on the back door. 'It's Mam,' I say with relief. 'Foxy, I have to go now.' And I cut him off in the middle of whatever ridiculous thing he's saying.

'Hi, love, how are you?' asks Mam, coming in and taking off her coat.

I plaster on a smile. 'Good, you? Tea?' I don't feel ready to tell her yet about last night or Ellie's role in it. I will in a while, but right now I don't want her to face this reality of her precious granddaughter. My sister has three boys, but Mam has only met them four or five times. They speak English, but their culture in the Middle East is so different, it can be hard to really connect, so my girls are her world.

'Please,' she says, sitting down and looking around her. 'Where are Kieran and the girls?'

'I've no idea, Mam. I'm not long up. Kieran was gone when I woke, and I looked in to the girls' rooms and they're not there, so they must have gone somewhere together, maybe up to Nora and Kevin's to make sure they're eating at least.'

'Poor Nora,' says Mam. Then adds, 'And Kevin, I suppose.'

She knows the story about Nora and the baby – I got Kieran's permission to tell her – and despite her intense dislike of the woman, she is much more sympathetic towards Nora than towards Kevin. 'It certainly explains the poor woman's frantic determination to be seen to be respectable,' she'd said when I told her. 'She had it beaten into her, didn't she, what happens if you step out of line in this society.'

'But it's different now, Mam, so she doesn't need to keep –'

'Doesn't she though, Mags?' She'd cut across me. 'You think this town is past tearing down a woman who slips off her perch?' She got out the cardigan she'd been keeping for Nora, on which she'd deftly replaced the size twelve label with one saying size ten, and wrapped it in tissue paper for me to bring up to her. 'I'd say give this to her as a present from me, but then she'll know that I know and she'll think I'm pitying her, so tell her she can drop the money in when she's passing.'

'So, Mags,' she says now, as I put a mug of tea in front of her. 'I'm afraid I'm here to warn you that that gossip, Joanna Burke, came up to me and Joe after Mass and tried to tell me Ellie was at some sort of wild party last night. Of course I told her not to be spreading rumours, that my granddaughter spent Saturday afternoon working in my shop and then went off to a sleepover with Cat and Trish, but I thought you needed to know, because God knows who else she was telling before I put her in her place.'

Poor Mam. This is going to mortify her.

'It's true, Mam.' The words drop like stones.

She smiles, puzzled. 'What's true? True about what?'

'Ellie, our Ellie, my daughter Ellie, was at the party, a rave on the Horsehead property, drunk off her head.'

'What?' She is totally shocked. 'Our Ellie? Sure she's only –'

'Fifteen,' I finish for her. I hear the defeat in my own voice. 'I was up there with all my officers. We sprung a raid to teach the young ones a lesson, and we had to charge them all, and then there she was, getting drunk with that Jess one – you know, the kid that used to make Ellie go over to their flashy house and do her homework for her? Well, my eejit has fallen under her spell again, it seems.'

'But Ellie told me she was going to –'

'Exactly. And that's what she told us too. She said she was with the twins, but she was with Jess.'

'Oh dear, oh dear, oh dear.' Mam shakes her head and sighs deeply, but by and large, she seems to be coping with the news. It's a relief. I thought she'd be more upset, to be honest, but I forget she's had a lot more experience than me with this kind of thing. She's raised three girls of her own, and one of them was Delores.

'I'm so sorry about the position Ellie put you in with Joanna, Mam.'

She flaps her hand. 'Oh, don't worry about that. I never go near the woman anyway. She never comes into the shop – she doesn't wear anything that's not out of Brown Thomas, for all the good it does her. The state of her. Everything she has clashes with her complexion. She wears maroon, and it makes her look yellow.'

With a faint smile, I sit down opposite her with my own tea. I'm finding this conversation comforting, me and Mam in our little bubble against the world. 'I wish I could avoid the whole town, to be honest. There's a lot of parents raging I'm sending their kids to court. Don and Holly were spitting nails at me when they came to pick Jess up from the station.'

'Outraged at *you?*' She is indignant now, back in her comfort zone, rushing to my defence, bless her. 'More in their line to know where their kids are, don't mind blaming you.'

'Except I didn't know where my kid was either, Mam,' I say glumly. 'And now everyone thinks I'm the worst in the world, and Kieran thinks I'm the worst mother.'

Her brow furrows. 'I'm sure he doesn't. He knows he's her parent too. It was both of you she had fooled. In fact, that's probably where they are right now. He's dropped Kate to a friend's and taken Ellie off somewhere to give her a good talking to for being an eejit for being led astray by that Jess.'

'I don't mean he's upset with me for not knowing where she was, Mam. He's upset with me for arresting and charging her along with the others. When he came to the station, he was raging at me. He slept on the sofa last night, and now he's left the house without saying anything to me or even leaving a note or sending me a text.' My shoulders slump; I put my face in my hands. God, I feel weary, and I'm so hurt.

'But you didn't know she was going to be there, and you can hardly let your own child off and charge the rest of them now, can you? It would ruin your reputation altogether. Kieran will see sense, and if he doesn't, I'll make sure he does.'

I raise my head, surprised at her tone. I think this is the first time in twenty years my mother has said anything negative against my husband. I know she's always in my corner, but usually if I give out about him, she defends him gently and tries to soothe troubled waters. And sure enough, the next moment, she's doing exactly that. 'Look, why don't you text him, Mags. He'll have calmed down by now, I'm sure. He was probably just shocked last night. He knew you'd be exhausted this morning and was letting you rest on.'

I sigh. Doubtful, but she's right that I need to make contact sooner rather than later. I know that most conflicts benefit from a bit of time being put between the incident and the reaction. This is certainly the case for me and Kieran. But this issue isn't going to be resolved without communicating, and besides, we're not teenagers.

I text: *Woke but no sign of anyone. Assume girls with you? x*

I put the kiss on as a white flag, indicating I'm ready to talk. I need to do this face to face. What I feel is too much to put in a text message. I need to see him, to talk to him about Ellie and, more than that, his reaction in the station last night. I was hurt and upset and furious, and he was… Well, I'm honestly not sure what he was.

The phone rings, Kieran's number flashing on the screen.

'Hello?' I say cautiously.

'Hi, Mam, it's Kate. I'm in Nana's living room. Daddy gave me his phone to play Fortnite because he's in the kitchen with Granda. Nana is still in bed, and Ellie is doing something out in the garden and didn't want me to watch her. I can see her kneeling over by the flowerbeds – I think she's weeding as a surprise for Nana Nora.'

My poor little Kit Kat, clueless as usual. She's the baby of the family, and maybe we all mollycoddle her a bit. She's not a street-smart tween, put it that way. Though I don't know any more. I wouldn't have said Ellie was a teenage drinker who lies to her parents, so maybe I'm not a good judge. What I would say right now is that Kate's sister is most certainly not weeding and is probably vomiting. Good enough for her. I've no sympathy.

'Can you get Dad for me, love?' I ask.

'OK, Mam. Is everything OK with Nana? Dad is being really weird. He wouldn't let me sit in the kitchen with him and Granda, and now they're in the kitchen with the door closed and Nana is in bed.' I hear a crack in her voice. 'Is Nana dying, Mam?' she whispers.

'No, darling, she's not. They're just planning a birthday surprise for her. Look, I'm here with Granny Marie...'

I cover the phone as Mam mouths something to me.

'Granny Marie says she needs a hand in the shop for an hour – there's a tenner in it for you if you want to?'

'I'd love to!' She is delighted. She was a bit fed up when Ellie got the Saturday job in Mam's shop, and I don't blame her really; she's put a lot more hours into that place than her sister, and I've never let Mam pay her for any of it, though I'm sure Mam slips her the odd bit of pocket money. A tenner is a fortune to Kate.

'Great, we'll be there in fifteen minutes.'

'That's great!' I hear her brighten at the thought of escape. Then she says, 'Will I call Ellie too?' Though her voice falters a bit at the idea of sharing the tenner with her sister.

I also hesitate. I'd rather not see Ellie today, to be honest, but then I realise this is ridiculous. She's my daughter and we need to talk.

'Yes, call Ellie, but tell her I'm taking her to the…um…into Galway for a new pair of school shoes. Her old ones are worn out.'

'OK, Mam!' She's all delighted again.

We leave the house and pull up outside the Munroes' ten minutes later. The girls are waiting for us, sitting on the wall of the driveway, Ellie looking like death warmed up. My older daughter crawls into the back seat and sits with her head slumped against the window, not meeting my eyes. Kate scrambles happily in behind me.

'What are we doing in the shop, Granny?'

'I, ah…' Mam clearly hadn't thought that out. 'I need to change the stock around in the storeroom so I can find things easier, love.'

'No problem,' Kate says, oblivious to the awkward atmosphere in the car. She prattles away about school, and Mam keeps asking her things until we get to Marie's Boutique and I let them both out.

'We might go to the hotel for tea and a scone when we're finished, Mags,' calls Mam as she unlocks the shop.

'Righto, Mam, I'll ring you later. Have fun, Kit Kat.' I wave and smile as I pull away. Ellie is still in the back seat staring out the window beside her.

I stop in the garage and get a can of Coke – something I don't normally buy for my girls, but it is good for a hangover – and a packet of paracetamol.

'Take two and drink that,' I say. 'And get in the front.'

Ellie moves into the passenger seat without a word but takes two tablets and washes them down with the Coke.

I drive on, out of the village, and after a couple of kilometres, I turn right to join the motorway to Galway. Ellie has yet to speak. Three more kilometres, and I take a left turn and drive down to Glasheen Lake, a beauty spot where swans and ducks gather and families have picnics in the summer. It is cold now, so apart from two joggers, we see nobody. I cut the engine and we stare out at the grey lake. A flock of Canada geese that winter in Ireland are flying low across the gunmetal sky, heading for home. Rain isn't far away.

The clock in the car is the only sound. Despite being digital, it makes an annoying clicking sound. What bright spark came up with that, I'd like to know? As if someone would get a lovely nostalgic warm glow from a digital clock ticking in a car? I feel a disproportionate anger towards whoever did it.

'I'm sorry.' It's just a whisper, and it is accompanied by a fat tear down her cheek.

'I would imagine you are,' I say, nowhere near ready to forgive and forget.

'I...I never should have agreed. Jess said she wanted to go, and I should have stuck to the plan of going to Cat and Trish's, but...'

'You didn't.'

'No.' More silence, more irritating ticking. Plus now there's the sound of her picking her nails; she always does that when she is worried.

'What alcohol did you drink?' I'm in garda mode, I can hear it in my own voice, but it's the only way I can handle this.

'Cider, I think it was. Jess is going out with this lad – he's from Oughterard – and he gave it to us.'

'Did you take any illegal substances?'

'No!' She's horrified enough for me to believe her, and I'm thankful for that. 'Mam, I swear on my life, I never took drugs. I never drank before last night – it was my first time.'

'Why am I supposed to believe you about that when you lied to me and your dad about going to the twins' house? And let us drop you off there?' I ask, and I hate the coldness there, but I need to know and I need her to tell the truth.

The tears are flowing in earnest now. 'I didn't drink anything before, Mam. I swear I didn't. I...I'm so sorry... I know you'll never forgive me...and you hate me and you're right to...'

I'm not anywhere near smiling yet, but honestly, the histrionics of teenagers. Ellie was always one for the dramatic language.

'I'm very angry,' I say firmly. 'And I'm humiliated because I was forced to arrest my own daughter. And you understand that you'll have to be treated the same as everyone else, don't you?'

She nods miserably, then whispers, 'I read it online today that you can go to jail for trespassing. Is that true?'

She's terrified, I can see, and as tempting as it is to let her stew, I find I haven't the heart. 'You won't be going to prison.'

She exhales, relieved now that the fear of incarceration is off the table. Maybe I shouldn't have reassured her after all.

'But you will still have to face a judge and pay a fine, and do community service, and maybe have your name in the paper.'

'Oh.' Water brims in her eyes.

'Which I can assure you is going to be a lot more embarrassing for me than it is for you. Oh, Ellie, I'm so disappointed in you, I really am. I never thought you'd be so deceitful or so stupid as to do anything like this. I thought you were so much better than this. Has Dad spoken to you yet?'

'No.' A tear escapes and runs down the side of her nose. 'Not really.'

Good. Even if Kieran hasn't had a proper go at his precious daughter, it doesn't look like she's had a lot of sympathy from that department.

'Does Granny know?' she whispers, picking at her nails again. She looks even more wretched than she did an hour ago. Emotionally and physically. Kieran must have got her up early this morning, and it was probably 2 or 3 a.m. before she got to bed. I doubt she's slept.

'Yes, Granny knows, and she is shocked,' I say brutally. 'It was all over Mass this morning, and she was defending you to Joanna Burke, saying it couldn't possibly be true of you. So not only have you made a town joke out of me, you've made a liar out of your granny as well.'

More tears, stormy ones this time, and I start to feel a small spark of sympathy. This is a harsh lesson to learn, so many awful consequences stemming from one act of bad judgement.

'Is that why she gave...gave the storeroom job to Kate instead of to me?'

Ah. The spark of sympathy winks out. She isn't crying for embarrassing her granny; she is crying for her Saturday job. The same job she made me feel so guilty about getting for her is suddenly something she doesn't want to lose to her sister.

Afraid I'll start shouting really cruel things at her if I open my mouth, I start the engine and drive home.

Kieran is in the kitchen; I can see his broad back as he stands at the counter making a sandwich. Presumably Kate is still with Mam.

'Go to your room.' I say to my daughter in the hall, pointing up the stairs. I want to speak to her father alone.

She nods and stands before me, hoping for a hug.

I turn and head to the kitchen, leaving her there.

# CHAPTER 12

'So,' I say, as I take a seat at the kitchen table.

He carries on making his sandwich, roughly slicing a tomato to go with the several layers of ham he's piled onto the bread. He doesn't get out more bread, doesn't offer to make me one. My heart sinks. He is still angry with me.

'Can we talk about this, Kieran?'

He glances at me. His mouth is tight, and there's no hint of a smile even in his eyes.

Kieran is a good man. He's a great husband and father, he works hard and is good to the people who work for him, and he's universally liked. He's kind to his parents, though they drive him daft most of the time, and he and I have a mostly harmonious relationship.

Magazines would tell you that it's critical to 'keep the spark alive,' or to 'connect emotionally' with your partner, but honestly, I don't think that's really true. I do fancy him, of course, and him me, I suppose, but it's not like we're ripping the clothes off each other all the time. It's different, maybe not as exciting or as urgent as it once was when we were young, but it's better, I think. More meaningful or more comforting or something.

As for the emotionally connecting, well, he's like most Irishmen in that regard. He's allergic to what he calls 'big chats', telling me he feels hijacked and that he, or any man, can never win or even compete with a woman in a war of words. We have, according to my husband anyway, 'all the words for that stuff' and we seem to win just because we're better at talking about it. I kind of see his point, but sometimes I do wish he could be more open. Like I might ask him something about how he feels about his work-life balance or something, but he feels it's a loaded question and an opportunity for me to criticise. It really isn't, but that's how he sees it. He often says he thinks women wish men were deeper, thought more about things, but he isn't like that. He is content with his life, he loves me and the girls, he likes his job, we have enough money, and as far as he is concerned, that is all there is to it. Life has been kind to him. He has good parents who looked after him...well, until the current impasse, but hopefully that will get resolved. Though with Nora digging her heels in and Kevin being as bad, it's hard to see how at the moment. What I'm saying is, things have for the most part always fallen his way, and so to him, picking at the minutiae of who feels what is a pointless exercise.

I've long ago given up. And most of the time, it's grand. If I'm upset about something to do with him, I talk to Mam or Sharon. Both of them love him, so I'm safe. I'd never give out about him to anyone who might store it up and use it against us later.

I could talk to them now, but I don't want to. This is different – this is between us.

I want him, my husband, her father, to help me navigate this bit of the parenting thing. There's no manual, and for every parent, the next hurdle is – for them and for the child – their first time. I've never had my daughter lie to me, get drunk and get arrested before. This is new territory, and I need help from the one person on earth who loves her as much as I do.

'Kieran, we have to talk.'

He puts down the knife on the counter. He doesn't turn to face me; he just looks at the cupboards in front of him. 'There's no point in talking about it,' he says.

I have to make him see my side. 'But –'

He cuts me off immediately. 'No. You're not going to talk me round this time, Mags. I'm not going to let you.'

'But –'

'No. You've done a wrong thing, Mags. You've chosen to apply the full force of the law on kids we know, our neighbours' kids, kids whose parents I do jobs for. One of them being our kid, if you haven't noticed.'

My heart thumps, but I manage to speak calmly. 'Oh, I've noticed. But she and the others broke the law, and they have to face the consequences.'

He scoffs, slamming the other slice of bread on top of the loaded slice. 'Do you think I don't know how you turn a blind eye to plenty of other stuff, Mags? Martha and Annette? Jerome's family?'

He's right. I do. But only when it's harmless and not affecting anyone. I know for a fact that if I went up to Martha and Annette's, I would find cannabis growing. Illegal, one hundred percent, but I also know it's for their own use and it gives Annette great relief from her arthritis, so I ignore it; they're not harming anyone.

I don't routinely prosecute the Travellers for having no road tax because I need them on my side, and that said, if I spot the tax is out on a settled person's car, I will only mention it, give them time to sort it out instead of fining them. That's just common sense. I will always try the easiest and least aggressive route first, only resorting to the harsh reality of prosecution if people refuse to play ball.

'Kieran, what was happening at Horsehead wasn't something unimportant affecting nobody else. Those kids were getting out of hand, thinking they couldn't be touched because they were juveniles. They were damaging private property, drinking underage. There were drugs involved, Kieran. And not just marijuana, though that's bad enough. You might think weed is harmless fun...'

This is a loaded comment, referring back to when I came home from work one day to find my sister Delores, who was over from the States, introducing my husband to the wonders of weed. I went mental, nearly murdered Kieran, pointing out I should be arresting them both and how it would look to the rest of Ballycarrick if they knew I was letting them off because I was related to them. Come to think of it, maybe I shouldn't be as surprised by his current attitude as I am.

'But whatever about adults, Kieran. Weed is terrible for growing brains – it can cause psychosis. This isn't just about law-breaking. These drugs are actively dangerous, and I had to take a stand. Some of the resin they were smoking is even laced with heroin. I had it analysed' – I don't say by who – 'and it's very dangerous and addictive. You can easily overdose on it.'

He's startled. This is news to him. Of course it is – it's the first time we've talked.

'Did Ellie take any?' His guard is down a bit now; he looks stricken.

I hurry to reassure him. 'She says no, and I believe her. I don't think she'd lie to me about that. And it was also her first time drinking. That's what she said, and I believe her about that as well...'

I stop. The look on his face is telling me something. 'What is it, Kieran?' I ask.

'Nothing.'

But there is something, I know it. All my instincts as a wife, mother and guard are tingling simultaneously – not just tingling, they're twanging.

'Kieran, this is our daughter, mine as well as yours. It's important. If you know something I don't, you need to tell me.'

And fair play to him, he tells me. He hates doing it, but he does.

Horsehead wasn't the first time she'd been drinking. A few weeks ago, she came home from what she told us was a trip to the cinema with her friends, but Kieran smelled drink on her when he picked her up. I was working evenings so wasn't there. He said he gave out to her but never told me. She swore it was the first time and she'd never do it again. He claims he didn't want to worry me, which is total crap and he knows it. He was just happy to be in her good books for once, never mind where that left me.

I call Ellie downstairs then, with both of us in the kitchen, and she confesses that it wasn't the first time but swears blind it is the last.

Tears and sobbing follow, which means, of course, that Kieran ends up hugging her and soothing her as she plays him like a fiddle.

I, on the other hand, tell her that I don't believe her, that I can't trust her any more, that she is grounded indefinitely. School and home, those are her only locations. I cancel her youth theatre because she's using her acting skills for the wrong purpose – barefaced lying. I cut off her pocket money. I confiscate her phone. I also ring Mam and tell her to give the Saturday job to Kate, which causes even more howling. It's not ideal for Mam. Kate is too young to leave in charge of a shop. In fact she's too young to be employed at all officially, so she'll just be there to fetch and carry and take a bit of the weight off, let Mam sit down and have a cup of tea and a chat with the customers. Which is something, but it's still a shame, because now Mam won't be able to escape the shop entirely for a couple of hours, which is what I really wanted for her.

Ellie weeps and wails. She begs and grovels. She can't believe I'm being so harsh. And Kieran's body language makes it clear he agrees with her, even though he's got enough cop on not to challenge me in front of her. Kieran is too soft, and I will not be made a fool of by my own child. Actions have consequences, and she needs to understand that. Words are meaningless. It's all tears and sorrys and I love yous, but as I point out to my husband and my daughter, Limerick Prison is full of people who are very sorry. Sorry doesn't cut it in a court of law, and it doesn't cut it with me either.

I hate being the bad cop, literally, but someone has to be.

# CHAPTER 13

On Monday, I'm in a foul mood and spend the whole day writing reports of the events of Saturday night for the courts.

It's a nightmare, and I hate doing it. The only good thing about it is that at least I'm not at home. It's a relief to be out of the house.

I'm now officially the worst mother in the world, and Kieran is the best dad. All day yesterday and this morning, Ellie kept hugging him and asking his opinions about things, but when I said anything to her, she would answer in a cold, polite voice, using the fewest words possible, mainly just yes and no. Poor Kate is in a state. She wants to help her Granny in the shop, she wants to show she loves me, she loves her dad, she wants her sister to love her – she's doing emotional cartwheels.

As for Kieran, I've never known things to be so frosty between us. We were kind of talking over breakfast, but in that way you do when you're married for what feels like a century and you just functionally talk. We arranged dropping and collecting of the kids from school, we discussed what to have for dinner tonight, we told each other of our work schedules – but that was it. Last night we went up to bed at different times, and normally we cuddle up, but for the first time, he slept on his side and I on mine.

All this is killing me, but I'm not going to cave. I'm not just playing a game to scare Ellie; I'm genuinely frightened for her. I hate doing this, but I can't back down.

So that's how things stand at home.

I'm working away at my desk when my heart sinks at the sound of a voice in the public office. Duckie Cassidy. Michael is on the front desk, and I hear them talking. I need Detective Sergeant Cassidy like I need a hole in the head right now. The derision and sexist remarks I can just about take, but since his promotion, he's graduated to ultra patronising and even higher heights of condescension.

I put down my pen. If I go out to him, at least I can decide when the audience is over. If I don't, he'll come in here and I'll be stuck with him for ages. Wearily and without any enthusiasm whatsoever, I get up and open the door connecting my office with the public one.

'Why don't women need watches, Mike?' I hear him snigger. Michael mutters something. I know he has aspirations for the detective unit, so he can't afford to get on the wrong side of Duckie. Despite being a complete cretin, the man is well connected and comes from a long line of Cassidy men who were high up in the force.

'Because there's clocks on stoves now!' He guffaws and then sees me standing in the doorway.

'Aha, Mags, there you are now,' he announces, like he's just found the Holy Grail.

'Hello, Detective Sergeant Cassidy. How are you?'

'Ah, no need of that. Call me Donal. I'm the same man as I was before the promotion.'

Unfortunately, that's true. 'How are you, Donal?'

'And you know, I was happy enough where I was, same as you, but we have to go where we're needed.'

The idea that any department of the entire Irish police force needed or wanted Duckie Cassidy is laughable, but I maintain my composure. 'I'm sure you're a great asset to the detective unit these days.'

'Ara, we've both been around the block plenty of times, Mags, and for some 'tis the bright lights of the commissioner's office. But you know' – he points at me – 'without the rank and file flat-footing it around the country, we'd have nothing to investigate. Never underestimate the important policing work you do here. I know some people see you as only dealing in the trivial stuff, but that's important too.'

I want to punch him, the patronising fool.

'Oh, that's us all right, all dog licences and bald tyres.' I laugh. I won't let him see he's annoying me.

'And raids I hear, using the full force of the riot squad to catch a load of kids having a few cans?' He winks at me.

Of course. He's here about his son, Tom.

'And destroying property and setting fires and smoking weed, some of which was probably laced with heroin.' I raise my eyebrow slightly, urging him to challenge me. For all his braggadocious nature, he is a coward really. He's shown his true colours time and time again.

Michael is dealing with someone who needs a passport application stamped, so Duckie sidles over to me. His aftershave is overwhelming. He must have soaked in a bath of the stuff, and the pong almost makes me cough. His voice lowered, he murmurs, 'C'mere, Mags. My young fella was there. He was there with your young one, I heard, and school friends of his as well from St Colm's. They're all from good families, so it might be best to let it rest, you know? The courts haven't time for it anyway, and sure they got a fine fright, fair play to ya – I'm not arguing against that – but I'd just let it go now.' He pats my shoulder and goes to leave. 'I'll let you get back to it, but we'll hear no more about it, right?'

He says it like it's an order. I feel the fury rise up.

'You will hear about it,' I say calmly, 'because it will be heard in the District Court at the next sitting. Every single one of those involved will be prosecuted – yes, including my daughter – so I'm afraid you'll have to tell your son that there is nothing you can do.'

He stops and turns, his face flushed. He looks like a big overweight pug, his face kind of squashed and rolls of fat bursting over his collar.

He used to dye his thinning hair a weird plum colour, but now his head is shaved.

'Mags,' he says, like I'm a particularly senile inhabitant of a nursing home, 'come on now, don't be silly. You know how this will look. You'll be a laughing stock, and the Western People will be sure to make it known that your kid is one of the prosecuted. Why would we do that to ourselves, hmm?'

The raised eyebrow, the smarmy tone make my blood boil.

'Because it's the law,' I say quietly but with conviction. I'm happy that my voice at least isn't betraying the emotions I feel. He'd love to be able to act like I am hysterical.

'Ara, Mags, will you stop?' He gives a supercilious smirk. He's buried his hands in his trouser pockets, and I see his belly straining against the buttons of his shirt. 'The law, my arse. Why don't you leave catching the baddies to us detectives and stop playing silly games, wasting everyone's time?'

'Was that all you wanted?' I ask coolly.

'Look.' Now he's starting to lose his temper. 'I've told Tom and his friends we'd let this go. Don't make me go higher with this. You'll only end up looking even more foolish than you do already.'

I wonder, does he owe one of those kids' fathers a favour or something? His son goes to the fancy fee-paying private school on the edge of town and mixes with the pampered offspring of the rich. Duckie has probably made out he has more influence than he has, like he's a detective inspector or something, when in fact he is a detective sergeant and his rank is no higher than mine, despite the plain clothes. I can just see him up in the golf club, someone powerful having a quiet word in his ear, and Duckie saying, 'Oh yeah, no bother, I'll make it disappear.' Acting the big man. Well, as if I needed any more reason to progress with the prosecutions, I have it now.

'Go as high as you like, Donal. I'm only doing my job.'

He narrows his piggy eyes and jabs his finger at me. Good Lord, he's ugly. 'Do you want to hear a few home truths about your tearaway teenage daughter? Because you will if this goes to court...'

I stare at him, confused. Surely he doesn't know something I don't, something even worse about Ellie.

'Throwing herself at my Tom, flirting with him, chasing him,' he snarls, 'calling him Superman.'

Tom Cassidy, Superman? On what planet? I feel gross, violated at the thought.

The supercilious smirk is back; he knows he's got inside my head. 'See, if it wasn't for your Ellie flirting with my Tom and leading him on, there's no way he would have been there at that party. He's an innocent victim in my eyes.'

'I've to go, so if that's all.' Before waiting for him to reply, I go back into my office, close the door and lean against it, blinking back the tears of shock. His Tom and my Ellie? No, it's not possible – he's awful. In all my worries with her about the drink, I never thought of boys for a moment. And as for Tom Cassidy...

My head is wrecked.

My phone pings. A text from Sharon. *Samovar 1 p.m.?*

Normally, lunch in the local pub with her would cheer me up, but not today. Today I have no appetite at all. Today I need to be alone.

*Sorry, swamped. I'll give you a buzz later. x*

I get a GIF back of SpongeBob SquarePants doing eight jobs at once, sweat pouring off his yellow self.

I look out the window to see Bertie Mahony's wife, Maura, crossing the street towards the station, looking nervous but determined. Rachel, her daughter who was arrested on Saturday night, had three little bags of weed in her pockets. Three bags each containing around three grams of cannabis worth about a hundred and fifty euro. She says they're not hers, and I'm sure she's right – they probably belong to her drug-dealer boyfriend – but if I wanted to press possession for sale or supply, I could.

Bertie must have ordered Maura to confront me, the poor woman, and I really don't need Mrs Mahony in here in tears pleading the girl's case. I duck out the back door and take the keys of a patrol car on my way. As she enters the station, I'm halfway down the street.

# CHAPTER 14

*I* turn right at the end of the town and head east. I'm just going to drive around for a while. I don't want to go home.

I'm going to have to ask Ellie about Tom Cassidy, and it makes me feel sick. The thought of her having anything to do with a son of Duckie Cassidy...ugh. It literally turns my stomach. I pass St Colm's private school, where Tom attends, and I grip the wheel so tightly, my hands hurt. I wish it were Duckie Cassidy's throat.

Beyond the school fields, I pass Drumlish halting site, and on a whim, I drive in, the patrol car sending all the young ones scattering. Even now, with their own cousin Delia working as a guard, they are wary of us. The nice thing for me, though, is that none of them were at Horsehead on Saturday night, so I won't have to hear from any parent here about why their kid is perfect and how it was everyone else led them astray.

I get out, but not before pulling a wine-coloured hoodie over my uniform shirt, and I leave my hat on the seat. I deliberately don't lock the car as I walk to Jerome's caravan. To lock it would be to suggest I don't trust these people. I'm only half sure nothing will happen, but I have to give the benefit of the doubt. I wouldn't lock it if I pulled into anyone else's driveway, so I won't do it here either.

Jerome's caravan is the biggest and is home to him, his wife Dora, Delia and her brothers, Gerard, Paddy and the youngest, Pecker – nobody calls him by his real name. Four children are not many for a Traveller family, but Dora almost died having Pecker, so the doctors made sure she didn't fall pregnant again. Delia told me one night how her father had insisted on it; he wasn't taking any chances with his wife's health. The other men had jeered him behind his back, but never to his face – they wouldn't dare. There is a strange version of masculinity among Traveller men. They are all able to fight, and it is a very patriarchal society. Women stay at home, have babies, cook and clean, while the men go out, if not working, then doing their own thing. Not many will employ a Traveller man, so they tend towards cutting trees, laying tarmacadam, things like that, with varying degrees of competence and integrity. As far as I can see, Jerome made his money in horses, breeding, buying and selling, and his sons all work with him, even little Pecker, who should be at school but who never went, as far as I know.

I knock on the door, and a moment later, Dora opens it.

'Hi, Dora, how are you? Don't worry, nothing's wrong,' I say quickly. This is something I learnt early on in my career – people always assume we are bringing bad news to their door, and in most cases, they're right. So when I'm just making a social call or stopping by for something trivial, I am quick to say it.

I see her visibly relax. 'Ah, Mags, howreya keepin'?' she asks, the broad vowels and sing-song accent unique to the Travelling people strong.

'Grand, Dora, grand altogether. And yourselves?'

'Ara, fine. Jerome has me minding this dog. I swear we never minded the kids as much as he has me minding Gyp.'

'Is she sick?' I'm instantly concerned. Gyp is a lovely dog, a brindle, short-haired terrier of some kind, the sort they call a Heinz 57, a bit of everything, and she's been here forever. I remember her being always around Dacie McGovern's caravan.

'Ah, Mags, the poor old thing is deaf as a post now, and one of the young lads drove in too fast and she never heard him, and she got hit by the car. The vet had to amputate her leg, poor thing. They suggested we put her down, and we know she's old, but she was Jerome's mother's since she was a pup and we're fierce fond of her, so we are. Jerome is sure there's life in her yet. He's feeding her up with Guinness and bread.'

She stands back so that I can enter the caravan. It is decorated nicely and spotlessly clean. Gyp's basket is in the kitchen area; she is fast asleep in an awkward position, as she has a cone on her head to stop her licking her stitches.

A glass cabinet stands in one corner full of crinoline ladies, and in the other corner, a matching one with framed family photos. I smile when I see the one of Delia the day she passed out of Templemore Garda College.

'Did she tell you what happened at her cousin's weddin'?' Dora asks wryly, seeing me looking at the photo. Since she finally accepted me a few years ago, she has become a different woman around me. She used to be wary and not say much, but now she chats away.

'No, she didn't?' I look at her inquiringly.

'A fella tried grabbin' her,' Dora says, and there is a hint of devilment in her eye.

Grabbing is a horrendous practice where a young male Traveller will literally grab and manhandle a single girl at a social function, dragging her away from the group and physically holding her hostage until she gives him a kiss. Given that Travellers marry young, sixteen or seventeen, the grabbing can go on from fourteen or fifteen onwards. Girls don't like it, Delia tells me. It's a lose-lose for them. Virtue and purity are paramount for a Traveller girl if she wants to marry; when it comes to them, there is no tolerance for sex before marriage. And if a girl is grabbed, often she becomes less attractive as a wife. The practice is one of the reasons they marry early with parental approval – no time to get a bad reputation – but nothing is done to stop the grabbing. You won't be astonished to note that the same rule doesn't apply to boys; if anything, the boys are positively egged on by their peers and older male relatives.

'And how did that go?' I ask, guessing by the glint in her eye at the answer.

'Well, her daddy's vexed, or he says he is anyway – 'tisn't the way for a girl to be goin' on – and we're getting some quare looks since, but the lad who tried ended up with his arm bent up behind his back, pinned to the wall of the pub, roarin' like a donkey.' She laughs heartily.

I chuckle, picturing the scene. Delia McGovern is well able to handle herself and any assailant who comes her way. ''Twould be a brave boy would try anything with our Delia,' I say.

Dora nods as she puts the kettle on, but she looks serious now. 'She should be married though, Mags. Like, she's coming up on twenty-two years. That's too old, and she'll be left, and what good will the country people and their ways be to her then?'

Dora is worried for her daughter, and I can see why. Country people, what they call those of us who live in houses, are all well and fine, but we aren't them and they aren't us, and I've never heard of a successful marriage that crossed the divide. Darren Carney and Delia McGovern are going out, but though Dora and Jerome tolerate Darren now, even secretly like him, he isn't one of their own. He's a settled man, and they still hope the relationship will end.

Meanwhile, the whole Travelling community knows of Delia and Darren's relationship, so as far as most of them are concerned, she is soiled goods, which is another burden for Dora to bear. She is afraid her daughter will fall between two stools, neither a country person nor a Traveller, and married to neither.

'I don't think she'll be left, Dora. I think she'll marry Darren. She and he are very solid, though they have no plans immediately, as far as I can tell.'

'And his father and mother would accept my Delia as a wife for their boy, would they?' She raises a sceptical eyebrow, and we both know it's the truth. 'They would not, Mags, and well you know it. She's a foolish girl for all her brains, and he's a foolish boy if they think different. No, they won't be marrying.'

She's right about the lack of acceptance. I sincerely hope the two sets of parents don't feel as disgusted by the thought of Delia and Darren together as I do at the idea of Ellie having anything to do with a son of Duckie Cassidy, but neither family will be thrilled with the match, and that's the truth of it. But Delia and Darren are their own people and strong-willed, so they probably stand as good a chance as anyone else.

'They might accept her one day.' I like and admire Dora too much to patronise her by pretending there's no problem. She knows well how people feel about them.

'And pigs might fly,' she says darkly.

'What about yourselves? Does Jerome still prefer her to have a Traveller husband?'

Dora nods. 'He has cousins over in England. Over there they're not so fussy as we are here, so he could probably find a match there for her if he thought she'd take it, but she won't. He's fierce vexed over it, Mags. Clattering your man at the weddin' was just more of it.'

'But surely he's proud of her for putting the boy in his place?' The whole thing is so contradictory.

She brings me a mug of tea, setting it on a lacy coaster on the coffee table beside me. 'He is, very proud, and it made him laugh, but at the same time, my man is a Traveller through and through to his bones, and he wants things to go on the way they always did. He's proud of Delia and her being in the guards and being so clever and strong, but all the same, he'd prefer to see her married and with a few babies on the rug.'

Gyp the dog gives a little whimper, and Dora rushes over to her basket to soothe her, gently rubbing her coat.

'*Ar munya dil*? Hush, hush…'

I recognise the words as Cant, or Gammon, the Irish Traveller language, spoken rapidly between themselves usually and generally when in company of settled people.

The dog calms again and returns to sleep, and then the door opens and the enormous figure of Jerome McGovern appears. The van sinks beneath his weight as he enters. Dora automatically stands and goes to the stove to make him tea.

'Howreya, Mags? Don't get up...' He shakes my hand. Over the years Jerome and I have become friendly. I loved his mother, Dacie, and the bond has kind of transferred down to him. He is a ferocious-looking man with the tattooed hands, the gold rings and the heavy bracelet, all pure gold, you can be sure. The black leather coat and the full head of dark hair, swept back and curling over his collar, are all part of the look of the head of a Traveller family, but he is a gentle, considerate person underneath all of that.

I smile up at him. 'I was just telling Dora how impressed we are with Delia,' I say. 'You might have heard about Saturday night at Horsehead – she did a great job.' I'm tempted to say how relieved I am that none of his own brood were there – more than I can say for myself – but I don't, because I don't want to come over like I'm surprised they weren't.

'We're proud of her too,' says Dora firmly.

Jerome glances at his wife, who delivers him a mug of tea as he sits down opposite me.

'*Whist,*' he says, the one word silencing her. Dora, unlike other Traveller women I've seen, is not afraid of her husband, and I know he would never hurt a hair of her head, but his word is still law and his authority unquestioned, even by her. '*Bug, dashe the sooblik.*'

Dora leaves the van then, having been dismissed by her husband. I can't speak their language – it is too difficult, only verbal and delivered at lightning speed – but I know *sooblik* means boy and *bug* means to go or to leave, so I assume he has instructed her to go and mind the youngest.

It is a source of fascination to me how the Traveller women are so subservient to their fathers and husbands when they are utterly fearless in the face of the gardaí, or anyone else for that matter. A bunch of Traveller women are a much more intimidating prospect than a group of their men, yet they do as their men tell them without question.

I see he's thinking about saying something. 'Is there anything I can do, Jerome?' I ask.

He exhales and looks down at his huge hands. He's enormous in the small space. 'I'm tormented over Delia. She's showing no signs of settling. I know she's all about the shades' – he smiles; he didn't mean to use the Traveller name for us – 'and 'tis a right job I'll have to get someone for her, being the way she is, but...'

'Dora told me about the lad who tried to grab her.'

He sighs. 'That's the kind of thing I mean. We don't like it, Mags. I know your kind do, but we just don't. The word is out she's got notions, that she won't be told, but if I rein her in now, maybe the cousins in England can help.'

'Jerome, I...' I need to tread carefully, because firstly, it's not my business, but secondly, I need to be careful that what I say doesn't sound like a criticism. 'I just think Delia won't ever go that road, marriage to a Traveller boy, giving up work to have a big brood of babies and all of that.' I know for a fact that's true. Delia's told me numerous times that she wants to marry Darren and have maybe one or two children, no more, while keeping on with her career in the gardaí just like I do, but she's never been able to tell her father. She's asked me to speak for her if he ever brings it up with me – apparently, he listens to me – and I feel I have to try to make him understand at least.

'What will she do so?' he asks, bewildered. I wonder, does he still think she just joined the gardaí and did all that training to pass the time until he found her a Traveller boy willing to overlook her short-comings, after which she'd leave her job for life in a caravan with a load of kids? Clearly he does.

'Delia has a career planned, Jerome.' I deliver my words gently, and I feel a bit of a fraud. Two years ago, when Delia applied to join the gardaí reserves, I knew Jerome only allowed it because she persuaded him it was just a nice thing for her to do before settling down, and I didn't disabuse him of the notion. But you can't take a person to the parapets, show them the kingdom and expect them to go back to work happily in the dungeons. The freedom, the life she can have, are too much of a pull for her now. She'll never go back, not as a stay-at-home wife and mother. Delia will always be a Traveller, not just by her heritage but in her heart and soul. She's fiercely proud of her ethnicity, and she loves her family and wouldn't want them any differ-ent. But she can't go back.

'And who'll take care of her?' he asks, and I hear the deep tender worry there. His girl, his only daughter, without a man to protect her.

I smile. 'Well, she'll take care of herself. She's going far, Jerome. She could be the Garda Commissioner yet.'

'But who will she marry? Not that young lad she's with?' He knows Darren now and likes him, but it's still too much of a stretch for him to imagine his daughter marrying a country man. I feel a pang of sorrow for him; everything he thought he knew is crumbling before his eyes.

'She might, and he's good, Jerome, kind and decent. But Delia doesn't need Darren to look after her. Even if they break up, she will be fine. She's tough, she can earn a living, and she's nobody's fool. You'll just have to accept that, I think.'

The big man twists his gold rings, staring at the floor. I know he's gazing into Delia's chosen future and finding it cold and sad and pointless. I know he's already missing the daughter he thought she was. I know he's mourning the horde of tumbling babies, the little boys he would have shown how to mind the dogs and chickens and horses, and the little girls he would have cared for with all his gentle strength, ready to murder with his bare hands any man who touched a hair of their heads.

'I've no choice, I suppose, do I?' he says at last, and to me at that moment, he's a bigger man than he's ever been before.

* * *

ELLIE IS AT HOME, watching the World Cup with Kieran; some men in silver and blue are playing another lot in orange and black. Soccer is something Ellie has no interest in at all, no more than myself, but she knows it's a sure-fire way to her daddy's heart, and at the moment, she thinks Daddy is all she's got.

'Ellie? Could you come in the kitchen for a minute?'

'Ah, Mags, it's gone to extra time,' complains Kieran. 'Don't drag her away now.'

'Ellie.' I know she doesn't care who wins, and this is a good chance to talk to her without her sheltering behind her father.

With an angry expression, she gets up and follows me into the kitchen, where she leans sulkily against the counter. I remain standing by the table.

'I need to ask you a question, Ellie, about something Detective Sergeant Du – Donal Cassidy said to me today.'

She looks at me cautiously. I get the feeling she doesn't know what I'm talking about, but at the same time, I haven't forgotten what a good actor she is.

'About his son, Tom.'

'Oh. Spider-Man.' Her voice instantly drips disgust.

'Spider-Man?'

'Hands everywhere. He's such a creep. None of the girls can stand him. What about him?'

I feel wild laughter bubbling up inside my chest, but I mustn't crack up in front of her; we're not at that stage yet. 'Nothing,' I say in a slightly strangled voice. 'Go and watch the soccer.'

'Seriously, Mam, what did you drag me out here for?'

'Ellie, go and watch the soccer with your dad. He wants to believe you're a fan, so if I were you, I'd keep up the act, or he'll be disappointed.'

Shooting me a foul look, she storms back into the living room.

As soon as she's gone, I allow the giggles to come.

Oh, Duckie, you big eejit. Not Superman. Spider-Man.

# CHAPTER 15

Three weeks later, a motley crew of teens are brought before the juvenile District Court, and I am delighted it is Justice Seán Linehan, a stern, no-nonsense kind of man but infinitely sensible. He is also very funny in private, and I like him a lot. Some of the older judges are as daft as the crows, but not Seán.

He fines each child a hundred euro for the court poor box that gets divvied up by local charities and warns them that the court will not be so lenient if it ever claps eyes on them again, and he makes each of them promise that the hundred euro will come from their own labours; the bank of Mammy and Daddy is not allowed to pay. They get a long lecture about public order and public safety and are ordered to attend a seminar on the dangers of drugs and alcohol to be held at Ballycarrick youth club. The youth leader, Declan Barrett, will take a roll call, and the court will hear about anyone who doesn't turn up.

Then he calls me to the stand and asks me if there is any public project that these young people can do to make up to the community for being such a nuisance. His clerk had texted me, asking the same a few days ago, so I am prepared.

'Well, Judge, the council is going to be housing a number of

Ukrainian women and their children in Horsehead from next week' –
I know this from Foxy – 'and though some of those in court today
have cleared up the rubbish left by the party, it would be lovely and
welcoming for our Ukrainian friends if the whole house is thoroughly
cleaned, floors scrubbed, windows washed and the brambles cut back
around the garden and yard. There's a team of council workers
coming down next week, and as it's the Easter holidays and many
hands make light work, I suggest these teenagers are put at the
disposal of the team foreman.'

I'd contacted all the parents to explain it would sit well with the
judge if their child made amends before the court case, and I'd fixed a
Saturday for it and supplied bin bags and rubber gloves, wire brushes,
rags and white spirits to the ones who turned up, including my own
daughter, and they'd cleaned up the remains of the bonfire and mud
and graffiti. And I had Kieran fix the broken window and the door
that was off its hinges.

Not all the kids had the sense to join in the clean-up, though.
There were too many parents out there like Duckie, reassuring their
precious offspring this wasn't their fault, they'd been led astray, they
weren't responsible for their own actions and needn't get their hands
dirty trying to fix the mess they'd made.

I've already decided not to name their names to the judge, but I'm
damned if they're going to get away with it. I haven't said anything
else to their enabling parents, but I'm going to make sure the council
foreman knows exactly who the slackers are who haven't lifted a
finger yet. The likes of Tom Cassidy, for instance. His Spider-Man
powers should come in useful for washing a lot of windows.

'Ideal.' Seán perches his glasses on his long thin nose, and with a
completely straight face and in sonorous tones, he sentences them to a
week of community service, starting at nine next Monday morning
and working at Horsehead every day that week until the council
foreman is satisfied the house is fit for human habitation.

'Failure to present yourself will be judged to be contempt of court,
and a bench warrant for your arrest will be issued.' He gazes at the
miserable gang before him, his pale-blue eyes cold. 'Be sure to be

there and to follow the foreman's instructions to the letter. I do *not* wish to see any of you before me again.'

He bangs his gavel, and it is over. All in all, it is a good outcome, and they are chastened boys and girls, which is the intention. Hopefully there will be no more destructive behaviour, underage drinking and dangerous drugs in Ballycarrick, at least for a good while.

The kids are taken out by the side door to be formally discharged, while I head out into the corridor to wait for Ellie. Kieran is already standing there, in his best suit. He shoots me an uncomfortable look when I go to stand beside him. 'Do you mind waiting for us in the car, Mags, please?'

I leave without a word. I'm really hurt. On one level, I understand why my husband doesn't want to be seen with me in this setting, not in front of all the other parents, his friends, his neighbours, his customers, all of whom have just had their Easter holiday plans ruined. It must be mortifying for him. But does he think it's any easier for me?

When they come walking through the car park towards the car, my husband has his arm around my daughter's shoulders and she's sobbing. And when she gets into the back of the car, she immediately starts having a go at me about how unfair it is that she and Jess and the others who cleared up the mess are having to do the exact same community service as the ones who didn't, and how Jess is so upset because she had all sorts of fun things planned for her Easter holidays and now she can't, the poor thing. 'It's horrible for me, Mam. I hate you being a guard. I wish you'd stop and stay at home like a normal –'

'Ellie, don't talk to your mother like that,' says Kieran quite sharply. I'm pathetically grateful for his support until he adds, 'Or I'm not giving you back your phone.'

Silence in the back.

I would love to leave it that way, silence all the way home, and I'm sorely tempted to, but I have to say it. 'I don't remember agreeing to give Ellie back her phone, Kieran. And after that outburst, I'm certainly not agreeing to it now.'

So instead of a pleasant silence for the rest of the ride, there's outrage and weeping in the back and stony faces in the front.

* * *

ON MONDAY, I drop a glowering Ellie off at Horsehead, dressed in old clothes, and leave her to the mercies of the council foreman, a taciturn man called Tadgh Milligan, along with all the other gloomy young ones.

Kieran is the white-knight parent who gets to rescue our daughter later that day, but when she walks into the house, splattered in mud and paint, she seems in a slightly better mood. She's still not talking to me unless I ask her a direct question, and then she only answers in monosyllables, but when Kate starts prattling on about her day in the shop, Ellie says, 'Call that work, nattering to Granny all day? You should see what I was doing.' But she doesn't say it in a mean way. Later she even plays a game of Monopoly with Kate, because she's bored senseless without her phone.

On Tuesday she arrives home still gossiping to her father about how some of the kids are hard workers and how she and Jess despise the slackers. 'Tadgh, he's the foreman, it takes half his time chasing the lazy ones. Like Spider-Man was washing the windows, and he was taking hours and they were still dirty, so Tadgh took the cloth off him and showed him how it's done. Tadgh is grumpy but he's fair, and he says it's important for a foreman to be able to do everything anyone else can do, but better – that's how you gain respect. And then he stood over Spider-Man, making him do it the same way until everything was gleaming.'

Kieran is in heaven. He never expected to have a daughter interested in anything to do with construction. I think he's even beginning to dream of Ellie joining his roofing business, and the way she's sucking up to him, I wouldn't be surprised if she floated the idea herself – she's that desperate to get her phone back.

On Wednesday she's looking proud of herself. 'Tadgh had me and Jess cleaning off the old paint in the kitchen. He said I was a proper hard worker, so tomorrow he's going to show me how to paint a ceiling.' By this time, she's sort of including me in her news bulletin. She's not talking to me directly, but she's not turning her shoulder either, though before the evening is out, I hear her begging Kieran about the phone again and him apologising to her for not being able to do anything about it, which really bugs me as we're supposed to back each other up.

On Thursday I drop down to inspect the work at Horsehead, and the place is already starting to look more habitable. I am surprised to see the avenue is now wide enough for not just a car but a van or a truck; the council workers must have their hedge-cutting machine with them. The house is shining in the sun, cracks freshly plastered. The brambles have been cleared from the surrounds, and the windows are clean and shining.

Tom 'Spider-Man' Cassidy is sitting on the top step in the sunshine, though when Tadgh Milligan appears around the corner of the house, he jumps up and tries to look busy. Everywhere, other teenagers are working, carrying rubbish out of the house, helping to mix cement, sorting the slates that will be used to fix the hole in the roof. None of them seems unhappy; they're all very focussed.

I find Ellie inside. She is on a stepladder painting the kitchen ceiling, with Jess holding the ladder.

'Hi, girls. You're doing a wonderful job,' I say cheerfully.

And Ellie, caught off-guard, says, 'Hi, Mam...' But then breaks off with a worried glance at Jess; she's uncertain if she's allowed to acknowledge my existence on this earth.

But Jess says, 'Hello, Sergeant Munroe,' with quite a nice smile, and Ellie relaxes, and we all have a chat about the work. Both of them have a moan about the slackers and what a waste of time some of the lads are especially, that the girls are way better.

As I drive back down the avenue, I feel like bursting into song. Ellie is talking to me again. It's like all the hard physical work is doing her good, doing all of them good. Maybe I'll let her go back to working for Mam in the shop after this. It will mean she can pay off the court fine all by herself, and it will be good for Mam too, which is the main thing, and it will make Joe happy.

The last time I saw Joe Dillon, a couple of days ago, he was standing on the step of his shop as I passed by on my usual stroll up and down Main Street, and we had another conversation about how he wants Mam to slow down, relax, enjoy life a bit more. 'While she still can,' he added, rather ominously.

I'd laughed. 'Sure there's plenty of life in her yet.'

But instead of laughing with me, he hesitated. A shadow crossed his face, and I could tell he was weighing something up, whether to tell me or not.

'Joe? What is it?' I asked him calmly.

'Nothing... Ah, it's nothing, Mags. I just wish she'd take it a bit easier, you know?.'

'Are you sure that's all? You seem worried?'

'Ah yeah, it's grand...' He brushed off my concern and just side-tracked about the weather and how he couldn't believe it was predicted to rain all the coming Easter bank holiday weekend. You'd think he hadn't been brought up in the west of Ireland.

Tourists to this country marvel at the green, how lush and fertile the whole place is, how in the spring and summer the countryside is a riot of colours from flowers and trees, not to mention the fairy tale-looking patchwork of fields. But let me tell you this – we pay a price for that. Rain. And not the nice rain you see in films, dramatic down-pours where women are always caught out in it, and their dresses cling gorgeously to their perfect figures, and with hair that actually looks even better wet. Oh no. We have soft, sideways sometimes, wetting rain that is relentless and soaks you right to your underwear even if you've a coat, makes your hair stick to your wet rosy cheeks, slides down the back of your neck and into your shoes.

In the old days, the garda uniform was wool. Can you just imag-ine? In Ireland? A wool coat that takes months to dry. I'd say they were just resigned to the coat being wet from October to March.

Listen to me. Here I am sidetracking my own thoughts. That's rain for you. Endlessly fascinating. They say the Innuit people have fifty words for snow; well, we're not far behind them with descriptions of the rain.

Right, I'll talk to Mam about maybe lifting the curfew on Ellie and allowing her back to the shop. Kieran will approve, so I'm looking forward to discussing it with him. It's time he and me broke the ice. We need to get back to talking properly again and being united. Besides, I want to hear about his own family issues. I've kept out of the Munroe thing for the last few weeks, mainly because of how things are between me and Kieran, but whatever is going on there is taking its toll on him. On top of the Oliver thing, his father had his hip operation a couple of weeks ago. He's at home recovering now, and I know there's a truce between him and Nora; there's too much water gone under the bridge of their marriage for her to turn her back on him when he needs her. But although she cooks for him and brings him to the toilet, she's still not much company for him, so Kieran, Orla and Gearoid are trying to be there for their father as much as they can. Which means on top of the frostiness between us, Kieran's also been out a lot of evenings recently.

My phone pings. I glance down, see my husband's number and pull over.

Before Horseheadgate, Kieran would text me at least once a day, just checking in. But he's stopped sharing all but the most perfunctory bits of information, so a text from him is a rarity.

*Can you check PULSE for an Oliver Murphy please, born in 1965?*

I'm astonished. This is asking a favour, so you'd think he'd at least have the good grace to be more than curtly polite. It's also a favour he knows I can't do for him.

PULSE is the gardaí's internal system where citizens' information and personal data is stored and accessed as necessary in the policing of the state. Under data protection legislation, the public can technically request to see what information it has, except in cases where information would identify another person or if the information is being used by ourselves to investigate or prosecute an alleged offence.

Kieran knows I would never do something like this. Apart from anything else, I could be prosecuted myself for misuse of confidential information. I'm shocked he'd even ask. Only last year two gardaí were sacked and prosecuted for giving information from PULSE to a private investigator. Kieran had laughed, saying that he bet we all did it, looked up old boyfriends or neighbours, but I told him that we genuinely didn't. It was wrong. He hugged me then, saying I must be the straightest guard in Ireland.

My fingers hover over the keys, about to text back, but this is ridiculous. He's my husband, my Kieran. We need to put an end to this cold war, and texting is not the way to do it.

I ring him.

'Hello?'

I'm momentarily thrown; that's not Kieran's voice. 'Hi, Kieran?'

'Oh, Mags...sorry...I...eh...he left his phone here this morning, went away without it. This is Kevin here...'

'Right.' My mind is whirring. 'Kevin, did you just text me from Kieran's phone?'

'Er...I...ah...I...'

'Kevin?'

'Yes, I... Look, I'm sorry, Mags. Maybe I shouldn't have asked, but we're getting nowhere. All we have is his name, and that's probably been changed, and I just thought you might be able to –'

'I definitely can't. It's totally illegal and unethical. But why didn't you ask me yourself? From your own phone?' I'm annoyed now as well as astonished. The man doesn't say boo to a goose for years and now this.

No response.

'Kevin?' I ask, seething now.

'I'm sorry, Mags, I should never... I just...don't know what else to do...'

I realise Mr Stoic is crying again.

'Look, I can't use garda resources like that,' I say, a little more gently, 'but I do have investigative skills, so maybe there's something I can do to help?'

'Kieran said we were not to ask you to do any more, and we've drawn blanks everywhere. I hired a private investigator, but he got nowhere either. Kieran and Gearoid and Orla genuinely tried, and Aoife even went to Dublin to some records place but found nothing. They seem to be able to give up, and Catriona's no help, and Nora is against it anyway, but I just can't stop. He's my son, Mags. I have to find him.'

I exhale. I wonder, did Kieran tell Kevin not to ask me for help because he doesn't want to compromise me? Or is he just still so angry with me that he doesn't want to be around me more than necessary?

I need to sort this out before I do anything else.

'Did Kieran mention where he was working today before he forgot his phone?'

'He didn't forget it, Mags. I took it from his pocket.'

For God's sake! What kind of a family have I got? These people are ridiculous.

'Right. Do you know where he is?' I repeat.

'He's up at the industrial estate. He had to price a job for the window place up there – they're expanding or something.'

'Fine. I'll speak to you later.'

I hang up and don't care if I've come over as rude.

The industrial estate is about five miles outside Ballycarrick, a big sprawling mess of buildings with no charm whatsoever. It would give you depression to work there every day, I often think. Grey steel and glass everywhere. I know the glass place, so I drive straight there and am relieved to see Kieran's van. At least I don't need to chase all over the country looking for him.

Luckily too he's sitting in it having a coffee, so I park behind him, get out and surprise him when I open the passenger door and sit in, shoving a file and some boxes of nails to the floor.

'Mags?' He looks panicked. 'Is everything all right?'

'No, Kieran, everything is far from all right,' I say grimly, slamming the door behind me.

'Are the girls OK?' he asks, but I see him relax. He knows this is a 'me angry' rather than a 'me frantic' meeting, so that's good, or better at least.

'We need to talk properly, figure out our differences over Ellie, then we need to talk about your parents. Your father stole your phone, by the way, and asked me to check the PULSE from it so I'd think it was you and do it.'

'What?' He is shocked. 'Why would Dad think –'

I hold up my hand. 'Not your parents first – us first.'

'Here?' he asks, confused.

'Might as well. Nobody around, so we can talk.'

'OK, but every time we do, we end up fighting,' he says, but I detect a note of sadness in his voice rather than belligerence. So I give in a bit. That's actually what marriage is, compromising, all the bloody time.

'Look, I know all this was hard on you, the court case, not just because of Ellie but your customers' children and everything. And I'm sorry, but I couldn't back down, not unless a whole bunch of kids – including our own – were going to end up in even worse trouble. They had to feel the effects of what they were doing, and it's done her good, Kieran, even you must see that.'

He nods reluctantly. 'She seems to enjoy the work, all right. She talks to me about it.'

'She even spoke to me today when I went to check in on what they were all doing.'

He smiles slightly.

'So I'm thinking we might let her go back to the Saturday job with Mam,' I say.

He brightens even more. 'And her drama group?'

I relent. 'I suppose so. It is educational, even if she does love it.'

'And her phone?'

I roll my eyes. 'Kieran, hold on right there. We can't give in on everything just because she's said two words to her mother without being hostile. You're too soft, and she won't learn anything from that.'

He looks deflated. 'OK, but she is trying hard, I know she is, and I just hate seeing her upset about not having her phone. If someone else caused her to be upset, we'd do something about it, but we're the ones doing it and I just hate it...'

'*She* did it, Kieran,' I say, but gently. 'Ellie is not a little girl any more. She's a great kid, but she made some bad decisions, and we'd be terrible parents if there were no consequences for that. Our job is to prepare them for life, and she needs to understand that if she messes up, there's a cost. We have to teach her that, no matter how hard it is.'

He's silent and thinking, and I know him well enough to know I need to wait for him to speak.

Eventually he exhales. 'OK.'

'Really OK, or begrudging OK and the cold war continues?' I ask with a small smile.

He rubs his stubbly jaw with his calloused hand, and I see how tired he is. It must be so hard for him, with everything else going on in his life and then, on top of everything, coming home to Ellie telling him how heartbroken she is about her phone.

'Really OK,' he says.

He takes a sip of his coffee and offers it to me. We take our coffee the same way. That sounds so romantic, but it isn't really; it's just in a busy house with two smallies, we'd both end up drinking each other's, and so it kind of just became milk, one sugar, and now we share.

I receive it gratefully and take a sip.

'You're a great mother, Mags. And look, you're right, I know. I'm too soft. We'll do it your way. Let the phone wait.'

'And you see why I had to prosecute Ellie?' I know I'm pushing it, but we need to clear the air completely.

'I suppose so, but please tell me a small bit of you regrets not mentioning the coming raid over dinner?'

I laugh. 'Do I wish my own daughter wasn't out of her head on cider in a derelict house? Do I wish I didn't have one of my officers put her in a patrol car? Yes, Kieran, I wish that, for so many reasons. Of course I do.'

He looks properly at me now, for the first time since we started talking, and I feel a surge of love for this good man who always tries his best.

There's another pause, and he faces forward, his eyes fixed on the gunmetal wall of the wholesale glass place. 'I know you had to do it.'

'I did.' I reach over, with no triumph in the victory, and hold his hand. He squeezes mine back. I feel myself relax. We're OK.

'Right. Now your parents – what's going on there? I thought Oliver might be on a bit of the back burner, but it seems not?'

'Yeah, Dad is still at it, though she's as tight as a clam.'

'He said he even paid a private detective?'

'He told you that? Yeah, we all chipped in to pay for it, except Catriona, who's totally on Mam's side now. But nothing came of that. The guy didn't string us along. He tried for a couple of days, then said he could see it was going to be impossible so he couldn't take any more of our money. These days it's just Dad fighting with the internet trying to find things out. She said about them giving him the surname Murphy on the birth cert – that was common practice, it seems. The nuns deliberately did things to make reuniting very difficult for both parties. So I'm sort of resigned now to the mystery never being solved.'

'And how are you about that?' I ask.

He gives a deep sigh that feels like it carries the weight of the world. 'I honestly don't know. Like, I'm bewildered as to why she won't help us get started, say a word about where the convent was or his exact birth date or anything, and in another I'm not. You know how she is. And if she heard that bit of gossip about someone else, she'd nearly burst with the excitement of telling us. I suppose she thinks everyone in the world is as small-minded and as gossipy as she is.'

I'm surprised to find myself thinking he's being unfair on Nora. That long-ago teenage girl learnt a very hard lesson at a very young age about being respectable at all costs, and it's hard to unlearn survival mechanisms born out of trauma.

'But apart from your mother not saying, how does it feel to know you have an older brother out there somewhere?'

'Weird. Like, I'm the eldest, that's who I am in the family, so now what? But I suppose I'm interested. I definitely want to meet him, out of curiosity if nothing else, but I don't know beyond that. Like I said, I'm kind of resigned to it never happening.'

'Do you think they will end up divorced over it?' I ask gently.

He shrugs. 'I don't know. For sure, the way things are between them isn't sustainable. Something has to give. I've learnt some interesting things about Dad, though. It's not all bad.'

'Go on.' I'm intrigued but no longer surprised to hear there are more hidden depths to Kevin Munroe.

'Like last Sunday, there we were visiting Dad at the same time, myself and Orla, and Mam was off in her room with the door closed as usual. Orla picked up Oliver's baby picture – you know Dad keeps it framed on the cabinet by his bed now. Anyway, she said how strange it was Mam called this first baby Oliver when all the rest of us had real Irish names, couldn't be anything else, yet she chose Oliver for her first born.'

'Oh yes, I didn't think of that...' It had never occurred to me before that the Munroes all had Irish names. Or I suppose it did, but it didn't register. I know loads of Aoifes and Catrionas and Kierans. But it is definitely saying something. Nobody can accuse you of having notions of upperosity with names like those. So it is strange, because if anyone has notions, it is Nora.

Kieran nodded. 'And then Dad said quietly, "That was me," and we all looked at him, and I asked him, what did he mean? And Dad explained Mam wanted fancy English names for all of us, names like James and George and Felicity and Elizabeth. But Dad wasn't having it. He told Mam that they were both Irish and their children would have Irish names, and none of this nonsense pretending to be something they weren't.'

I'm amazed. Based on what I've seen of his parents' relationship, this is a revelation. First, that their father had once been capable of an independent thought not filtered through the queen bee, but also that Nora had actually done as he said.

'And then Orla asked Dad why he thought she liked the name Oliver,' Kieran says, smiling slightly, 'and he said he had no idea except Mam made him take her to *The Pirates of Blood River* in the pictures about five times, and Oliver Reed was in that – she even told Dad she

146

liked what she called his "brutish good looks" – so maybe our Oliver was named after him.'

All my conceptions about Nora and Kevin Munroe are being rattled. The idea that Nora had a crush on any actor is hard to imagine, but if she did, I'd have thought she'd like someone smooth and well spoken, Cary Grant or one of those lads. Oliver Reed had been a hellraiser and a drinker and definitely a bit on the rough end of things, but maybe Nora really did have a dark side – who knew?

And it seems Kevin Munroe is actually capable of winning an argument with her when he's really got his heart set on something. Maybe he'll even win this one, and she'll end up telling him what he wants to know about the location of the convent and the exact dates, in which case we could be in a better position to track him down. Which reminds me.

'Why did you tell your dad not to ask me for help?'

Kieran thinks, then shrugs. 'It's not your problem. You had enough to deal with, and I didn't want them blurring the lines, you know? Like I hope you knew straight away it wasn't me asking you to check PULSE – I'd never do that. So I was right – they would cross a line. My father is like someone possessed. I've never seen him like this.'

'I might be able to help, though. Not as a guard, but I can bring some skills to investigating if you'd like me to?'

'Would you?'

'If you want me to, of course I will.'

He smiles and runs the side of his finger down my face, and I kiss it when it reaches my mouth.

'I'm sorry I've been such an eejit,' he says. 'I hate fighting with you. My whole world is wrong if things aren't right with us.'

'You aren't an eejit, and I'm sorry too.'

He leans over and kisses me then, a long, lingering kiss, and I breathe in the lovely smell of him. Familiar, safe, loving, home. Whatever happens, he's right. Together we can get through it.

# CHAPTER 16

*A* week later in SuperValu, picking up some steaks on my way home from work, I notice a beautiful blond woman buying a large bag of rice, like those catering bags, and lots of vegetables that are in the close-to-sell-by-date basket. She is dressed in a fashionable raincoat, belted and brown, rather like ones you see in pictures of women during the war, and a silky yellow and blue scarf. She has a girl with her, obviously her daughter, who is around Kate's age, maybe a little older, also nicely dressed in a smart woollen coat, with long, shining almost white-blond hair.

'Hello,' I say to the woman as I lean in to get a bag of organic baby carrots.

She smiles back but says nothing, and the girl looks scared. As they move on around the shop in front of me, the woman puts six loaves of the cheap sliced pans and a three-litre carton of milk into her trolley. I choose a fresh-baked wholegrain loaf. Skimmed milk, because I'm pretending to watch my weight. It's easy to watch – you can't miss it. The slim little girl selects a big pack of chicken thighs and wings, but the woman checks the price and murmurs something and puts the bag of meat back on the shelf. I find four ribeye steaks, streaked with fat, Kieran's favourite. So much for the skimmed milk.

As the mother and daughter pass me again on their way towards the till, I glance into the trolley. It's half full, but everything in it seems to be the cheapest available. Six tins of own-brand beans in tomato sauce, six tins of chopped tomatoes, a big bag of onions, a big bag of potatoes and a large tub of cooking margarine. The girl is walking very close beside her mother, holding her coat like she's afraid of losing her, and even though she's so young, she seems careworn.

Intrigued, I watch them as they approach the till, wondering who they could possibly be.

Anne Marie, who manages the shop, must be short-staffed again – it's as hard to find shop workers as cleaners these days – and she's having to man the checkout herself. She says nothing to the mother and daughter, just bips their shopping through, which surprises me because she's normally very chatty and friendly.

Since Covid, nobody has cash; everything is contactless. So I'm also surprised to see the woman take a brown leather wallet from her pocket and count out some notes, then go to a coin pouch and painstakingly extract some coins. She has no shopping bag, but Anne Marie gives them some brown paper bags, and the woman and the child carry their shopping in their arms as they leave and head away, walking down the road. They don't appear to have a car.

I grab my last few bits and make my way to the checkout.

'Did you ever see those people before, Anne Marie?'

She glances after them as she scans through my items. 'No, but, Mags, listen to me. A really similar-looking family came in yesterday.' Her voice becomes hushed and anxious. 'Two women that time, three little boys and a girl as well, all in nice clothes but very little money, and they couldn't speak English either. They're staying out the coast road, according to Elsie Flanagan anyway.'

'Oh, you mean Horsehead!' I know from Ellie that the council workers had cleared a pathway through the woods behind the house to make it a shorter walk from there to the town. 'They must be the Ukrainian refugees. I didn't know they had arrived already. God love them, the poor things. No wonder they look so terrified.'

Anne Marie's face clears, and she beams in relief. 'Oh, that's it! God

149

love them is right. That Putin is a lunatic and a dangerous one at that. If I'd realised, I'd have given them those chicken pieces they were looking at for free.'

'That's a nice idea.' I put down a twenty-euro note. 'If that woman comes back, give her some meat or whatever she wants, and take it out of that but don't say who it's from.'

Anne Marie smiles and nods and tucks my money behind the till, and I head on home with my fancy steaks.

* * *

'MAGS!' Kieran calls me from the kitchen where I'm testing Kate on her Irish spellings before bed. 'Come in – I want you to see this.'

I leave Kate and go into the sitting room, where he and Ellie are watching something on TV. I recognise Ray Lonergan, a famous talk show host, frozen on the screen where Kieran has paused it. Ray Lonergan is like Marmite – you hate him or love him. Nora loves him, but he drives me a bit mad because he's so sycophantic to his guests, and Kieran can't bear him at all, so I wonder why he's got him on.

Kieran unpauses the TV and we watch. It turns out this isn't Ray's talk show after all; it's the news, and he's being interviewed rather than doing the interviewing.

'...my own personal story,' he is saying. 'My instinct was not to discuss it publicly, but when I discovered that my birth mother was one of Ireland's leading campaigners for the rights of mothers and their children born in such places, I felt I needed to speak up.'

The off-screen interviewer asks, 'So you're here today to launch a very important initiative. Can you tell us about that?'

'Yes. The problem of lack of information, lack of support and lack of legislation around the babies born in the Church institutions from the 1920s right up to the 1980s is compounded by the remnants of shame and embarrassment that these places engendered. So given my public profile, I propose a nationwide initiative, called Operation Spotlight. The campaign will be launched on *The Nightshow* on Saturday the fourteenth of next month, where other high-profile people in Ireland who had dealings with the mother-and-baby homes will be on to tell their stories. You might be surprised at a few of the faces.' He smiles his dazzling-white grin.

'And what message do you want to send to people affected, be they women who gave birth, or the babies themselves, or even the adopting parents?'

'Look, I'm not dictating to anyone, and every story is different, but I just think if those of us in the public eye can get the ball rolling, tell our stories, then hopefully around the country, people will see it and maybe feel a bit empowered to do the same themselves.'

'And how would they set about doing that, Ray?' asks the disembodied voice.

'Simply this. If you were in one of those places, if you had a baby in one of those homes, if you adopted a baby from one, legally or not, if you were that baby, we encourage you to tell us your story.'

'And there's a number people can call?'

'There is. There's a helpdesk, and someone there will take your details, and then at a time convenient to you, you can come in person, or by phone or by email, and tell your story. A whole team of people is on hand to collate that information, and hopefully together we can build up a fuller picture of what happened, bit by bit.'

'And what would you say to someone who is at this moment thinking, "I've kept the knowledge of that baby or the story of my birth to myself for thirty or forty years. Why would I tell everyone now and open myself up to ridicule?"' the interviewer presses him.

Ray turns to face the camera. 'I'd simply say this. You are not alone. There are thousands of us, and we'll support you. All of us. This is a national trauma that we have suffered as a people, and while just like with any trauma, it is easier in the short term to keep it buried, in the long run, you have to deal with it in order to be truly happy. And let's do it together. Let's tear off the cloak of secrecy, under which only shame and guilt can flourish. There is power in numbers, power in all of you who were so traumatised. So take courage, and let's not hide in corners any longer, fearful and ashamed, but rise and walk out into the sunlight, holding hands. Be brave, and I promise you, you'll find nothing but love, understanding and support from us, and hopefully from your own family too.'

'Thanks, Ray. And now back to the studio for a look at today's sporting action...' The voice has a catch in it, and I'm irritated to find that I also am touched. Ray Lonergan is so good at pressing all the right buttons.

Kieran switches off the telly. I look at him. He looks at me.

And Ellie looks from one to the other of us. 'Hey, what is everyone looking at each other for?' She gasps dramatically and claps her hand to her mouth. 'Oh, don't tell me, you were in one of those places, and I have a brother or sister somewhere I don't know about? Mam, Dad, why didn't you *tell* me?' She is both horrified and excited and confused all at once.

'Don't be silly, Ellie,' I say a bit sharply. 'I'm not that old, for goodness' sake.'

She giggles and says in a perfect imitation of Ray Lonergan's voice, 'Mam, be brave, and I promise you, you'll find nothing but love, understanding and support from us...'

'Ha, ha, ha.' I throw a cushion at her as she peals with laughter and forgets the whole thing about the looking at each other.

# CHAPTER 17

*T*he station is blissfully quiet, and I avail of the momentary peace to make a coffee and ask Delia if she wants one. Between Kieran's troubles and the court case, it's the first time I've had the time for a proper chat with her in weeks, and I miss her company.

Since her grandmother Dacie McGovern asked me to take her as a reserve officer four years ago, I've had a connection with Delia. That, and the fact that she saved my life when a human trafficker shot me.

She joins me in my office, and I make us a cuppa.

'I was talking to your parents the other day,' I tell her. In Ireland 'the other day' is a handy measure of time that covers anything from a couple of days ago to sometime in the last century.

'Oh yeah? They didn't say that. What were they talking to you about? Don't tell me, time is ticking on, I should be married...'

'Something like that.' I smile and offer her a biscuit.

'They know nothing else. They're Travellers, and I am too, and proud of it. But I've no notion of marrying for years if I ever do, and I'll be marrying who I choose if the humour takes me, but trying to tell my daddy that...'

'I think they're worried you'll be left on the shelf.'

She laughs. 'Wait till they hear myself and Darren are going to move in together – they'll blow a gasket altogether. But we're adults and we want to, and Mammy and Daddy will just have to try and understand. We're actually after applying for a mortgage, and we're hoping to buy one of the new houses up behind the church.'

'And you won't get married?' I ask gently. It's not my business, and if Ellie or Kate told me they were going to marry their boyfriend at age twenty-two, I'd go mental. But as much as Delia eschews some of the Traveller ways, she is still one of them, and living in sin with a man not her husband and not a Traveller will be a bitter pill for her parents to swallow.

'Darren says we can if I want, but I don't want to – it's not for me.'

I blow on my coffee and say nothing. I completely understand her right to do this, but it will be a savage blow to Jerome and Dora.

'You think maybe I should get married for their sake?' Delia is sharp-witted; she can read people like a book.

I take a cautious sip. 'It's not for me to say what you should or shouldn't do in your personal life, Delia.'

'I know, but I'm asking your opinion. What do you think, Sarge? What should I do?'

I try to imagine what Delia's paternal grandmother, Dacie, would say. She was a wonderful woman. The first thing she would ask is if Darren is a good man – would he be kind to her, look after her? And he would; I'm sure of it. And the next thing is, would it last?

For Travellers, divorce isn't an option. They marry and stay married, no matter what. I've had women battered black and blue by their husbands, but they won't testify against them. I've heard of cases where a married woman, mother to a tribe of kids, is shamed for getting pregnant at thirty-five because she's already a grandmother herself, as if she got herself pregnant. If a Traveller man goes to prison – and a much higher proportion of that community are incarcerated as compared with the general population – his wife is not just expected to wait for him but to stay at home and wait. Don't be out and about. It's a man's world for sure.

Still, I suppose if she doesn't marry Darren in the traditional Traveller way, then maybe the traditional Traveller rules won't apply and she won't have to be stuck with him if it all goes wrong.

'On balance, I think you should, Delia,' I say honestly. 'If you love him and he loves you, and you're willing to live together anyway and you're tying yourselves to twenty-five years of debt together, then you are committed anyway. And it would make life easier for your parents among the rest of your community if at least you were married.'

'Even to a country *feen*?' She chuckles.

'Even to a country *feen*.' I smile at her use of the Traveller word for a man.

'So you recommend marriage, do you, Sarge?' She takes a mouthful of her latte.

Delia looks very like her mother, though fair rather than dark, and she is handsome in that way Traveller women can be. Wide face, strong jaw, blue eyes, fair skin, athletic and curvy. I can see why Darren is mad about her. She is incredibly bright into the bargain and is her own woman.

I think back on the past turbulent month of my own marriage. If Delia and Darren marry, then nobody from her community can advise her; it would be so far outside their experience. And I know she looks up to me, so I feel a responsibility to be honest.

'I do, Delia. I wouldn't change a thing. But I'll tell you something. There will be long periods where it's not so great. I love Kieran and he loves me, but sometimes it's hard. Two people tied together, by love for sure, but also debt and kids and elderly parents and extended families. And sometimes it's boring. You've heard all his stories. He's heard yours. And sometimes it feels unfair that one person is bearing more of the responsibility for the house or the finances or the kids or whatever, and sometimes you'll wonder what on earth you hitched your wagon to this fella for – you'll think that you'd be much better off alone. Nobody tells you that about marriage, but it's true. It's not like that all the time, or if it is, you should pack your bags, but if you go into it, then go in with your eyes wide open. It starts with passion and love and all of that, but that's nature's trick to get us to procreate, why we're here. Otherwise who in their right mind would sign up for it?'

She laughs. She and Darren are still in that stage for sure.

'Seriously, though, nobody,' I say. 'So once the passion wears off, and that's quicker than you think, it's just two imperfect people, trying to make a life together. And there are great days and there are terrible days, and you hope that on balance there are more good days than bad.'

'Did you ever think of writing romance?' She chuckles and I smile.

'I'm telling you the truth.'

'OK, and so while we're truth telling, is childbirth really terrible or is it true you forget it? I'm not pregnant, by the way, but my mam would never talk about things like that, nor my aunties either, and I just wondered.'

'It's terrible, the worst pain you'll ever feel in your life, and you don't forget it, but it kind of blurs, I suppose. But it's also the best feeling you'll ever have when they put that baby in your arms. That's the truth.'

Delia reaches inside her garda shirt and pulls out a chain, on which is a ring with a diamond.

'Darren gave me this, with no pressure, he said. He told me to put it on if I ever want to get married, but I don't have to ever if I don't want to. He gave it to me the morning we were going to the bank about the mortgage. No Travellers get mortgages, and I had such imposter syndrome, terrified your man the bank manager would have me thrown out for having the cheek to even ask. Darren told me we'd arrest him for discrimination if he did.'

It's my turn to chuckle. 'Abuse of garda powers there.'

'Anyway, I put it on this chain. Like I'm committed to him, and I do love him, and I can't ever imagine being with anyone else. By country people's standards, I'm young to marry, but by Traveller standards, I'm well and truly over the hill.' She takes a deep breath. 'I suppose I'm scared his family will be disgusted.'

My heart breaks for this brave, kind girl. 'The Carneys would be a very, very lucky family to get you, you would be such an asset to their family. If she can't see that, then that's her loss. You do what you and Darren want, Delia, and don't mind anyone else.'

'You sound like my nana,' she says, and I know it's the highest of compliments.

'I feel like a granny some days.' I smile ruefully.

The door opens in the public office, and Delia leaves to see who it is. A minute or so later, she's back.

'There's someone here to see you, Sarge. She doesn't have an appointment, but I said I'd see if you were free.'

'Who is it?' I ask.

'A blond woman, broken English. She has a little girl with her.'

I get to my feet, pulling on my garda jacket. 'And is she in need of us for some reason?'

'Not that she would tell me. I don't think she has much English, but the girl has a little. She says her mam wants to see the big police-woman. I guess that means you, Sarge.'

'Oh God – "big"? Am I really that fat?'

'I'm sure she just meant important.' Delia grins, and I hope she's right.

When I go out into the front, it's the woman I saw in the shop yesterday, with her daughter who looks around Kate's age. I smile at them. 'Hello, ladies. Welcome to Ballycarrick.'

'*Privyet.*' The woman smiles back, while the child clings to her side. I assume *privyet* is 'hello' in Ukrainian.

'And how can I help you today?' My first thought is that Anne Marie told them I paid for the chicken, even though I told her not to.

Glancing down at her daughter, the woman says something in what I assume is Ukrainian, and the girl looks at me and says in a high, trembling voice, 'My mother name is called Klara Shevchenko. Tatiana in Samovar bar say you don't have cleaner. Please ask and my mother will clean station.' She swallows, relieved she got the sentence out.

I'm delighted. It's not about the chicken at all; it's about a cleaning job. Well done, Tatiana, for sending Klara this way. Klara must have gone to her first, and Tatiana knows I've been looking because I asked her about her own cleaner, but she was flat out already. I make an instant decision.

'Yes, we would like a cleaner. Two hours every morning between nine thirty and eleven thirty.'

Mrs Harris usually started earlier, but school begins at nine twenty, so once Klara has her daughter enrolled in the local school, she'll be able to drop her off first.

'We pay seventeen euro per hour. Is that all right?'

The child looks confused. If she's only learnt English in primary school, she's probably struggling with my accent. I open Google Translate and say the whole thing over again, and the app must have worked, because when the woman reads it, she beams and nods and says, 'Thank you, thank you.'

I return the smile and we shake hands, and she says something to her daughter, who asks solemnly, 'When she come?'

'Can your mother start Monday?' I ask her, very slowly.

This time she understands me and translates, and Klara looks delighted.

'Yes! Monday! Thank you!'

I wonder if I'd be as grateful under the same circumstances. We've seen on the news the Russian bombing of Ukrainian cities. The idea that these people have had to leave their homes, their families, their businesses, and come here to a place that most of them had never even heard of is bad enough, but I know for the vast majority of the women, they've left their men behind, often elderly parents too. I can't imagine if Kieran had to fight to repel invaders of Ireland while myself and the girls went to the other end of Europe where we couldn't speak the language. My heart goes out to this woman and her daughter, who is clearly traumatised by it all but is putting a brave face on it.

'What is your name?' I ask the girl, thinking I must invite her around to play with Kate.

'Alina,' she says, blushing.

'And how old are you?'

'I have eleven years.'

'Brother? Sister?'

A shadow crosses her eyes, and she shakes her head. 'No. Just mother. My father is in Mariupol. He must fight.' There is a stoic strength to how this little girl delivers the news, as if by saying it, she is toughening herself against the horror.

I open Google Translate again and say into it, 'I'm sorry about your country, Alina. You're very welcome here. If we can help with anything, please tell us. Your father is very brave.' It is clumsy and inadequate, I know, but I think it's always better to try rather than stay silent.

The girl reads what I've said and nods, then shows it to her mother, who smiles and brushes away a tear, so hopefully Google Translate has conveyed what I mean.

After that I show Klara where the cleaning cupboard and hoover and stuff is, and the overalls that Mrs Harris bequeathed to us when she retired – she was shorter than Klara but also a lot wider, so they're big enough. I'm about to give her Mrs Harris's keys to the various offices when I realise that I am trusting a total stranger when maybe I shouldn't. I've asked her nothing about herself.

I glance at Delia for her opinion, but she is showing the little girl something on her phone. The girl has a broad smile, much more relaxed now. Delia is good with kids. Good with people. She's showing no signs of worry about this pair, and I decide to trust her instincts and go with my own gut as well, and I hand Klara the keys. Still, I should ask her something about herself.

'So you are a cleaner in Ukraine, Klara?'

She calls to her daughter in Ukrainian, and after I repeat the question to Alina, the child says, 'My mother teach biology in our country. Here, she clean.'

I feel myself blush. The woman is a biology teacher for goodness' sake, and here I was wondering if I was right to give her a cleaning job.

Klara gets ready to leave. It's the end of my shift, and between Alina's primary school English and Google Translate, I manage to offer Klara and her daughter a lift back to Horsehead. It isn't far off my path, just a quick detour for me in the car, while for them it is quite a walk, even if they go the way the council cleared through the woodland.

The avenue up to the house is rutted with potholes that are full of water, but I skirt the car around them. There was thunder and lightning last night and rain like you wouldn't believe, but it feels like it's blown itself out, for now at least. After the bend, the house comes into view, and I see a lot of bedding draped across home-made clothes lines.

'Rain came in house,' Alina informs me.

'Oh dear.' I glance up at the roof. I thought the council had replaced the missing slates, but they must have blown off again, though I can't see where.

There are lots of little children playing outside among the draped bedclothes, about twenty of them, though it's hard to tell with the billowing sheets. They must be delighted that it's warming up a little bit and the dreaded grey rain is gone for now. I remember when my two were small, the relief when they could get out in the garden and run off some energy after days of being stuck in the house.

As I pull up, I see an older woman with muscled arms at the side of the house, slicing some felled branches of alder into small logs with a chainsaw. She turns as I park, stops and stretches her back and lays down the saw. Klara and Alina thank me, then say, '*Privyet*,' and a few other words to the woman before they wave and go into the house.

I decide to introduce myself and get out of the car. The strong woman suddenly looks very worried and takes a step back. It's my own car so not a garda vehicle, but I am still wearing my uniform, and this seems to have alarmed her. '*Privyet*,' I say with a big smile, hoping I haven't got the word wrong.

She gives a little bark of laughter, clearly surprised by my impressive grasp of Ukrainian. Or maybe by my dreadful pronunciation. 'Good afternoon, officer. Has someone complained about me? I can prove to you, I have the council permission.'

It's my turn to be surprised. 'No, I'm not here to complain about anything. I was just giving Klara and her daughter a lift home. So you speak English?'

'Five years in America.' She is smiling a little now; she has perfect teeth.

'Good, that's good.' Life is going to be much easier if at least one person in this community has fluent English, because then they will be able to ask for my help if they need it. I extend my hand. 'I'm Sergeant Mags Munroe. I run the local police station, and Klara is coming to work for us as a cleaner.'

She steps forward and grips my hand firmly, saying, 'Daniela Bondarenko.'

'Nice to meet you, Daniela. I hope you have everything you need, enough food for all the children.'

'We are managing, thank you for asking. Today your supermarket gave us a present of five chickens and enough sausages for everyone for a week.'

'I'm glad to hear it.' Well done, Anne Marie.

'We are all very grateful. But don't worry, we will soon have jobs, I hope, and be able to look after ourselves.' She isn't dismissing me, she's not being rude, she's expressed her gratitude for the free food, but I can tell it is wounding for this woman to rely on charity, and I wonder what high-powered job she had in her own country.

'Alina told me that Klara is a biology teacher. And you?'

She smiles faintly. 'I work as manager in sustainable forestry. That is why' – she indicates the perfect pile of small logs – 'I happy for council to fell alder to make a path. I try to explain this to the man who came earlier, but he was very cross. I think maybe something is wrong with him.'

'What man?' I ask.

She shrugs. 'I forget name, foreign names too hard for me to remember.'

'Did he say what he was doing here?'

'He say he is an important politician, but I think he not, very stinky and dirty.'

I try to keep my face impassive. 'Ah...' Ronnie Atkinson, the Green Party counsellor. I could cheerfully swing for that eejit.

'He is shouting a lot about pine martens, many rude words. I think maybe he does not know I speak English.'

'I hope he didn't frighten you?'

She laughs again, that short sharp bark. 'No, I have chainsaw. And I tell him, leave. But he says he is going to the police, so when I see your uniform, I am worried he is an important man after all.'

'Don't worry, he isn't. And don't let him alarm you. I will talk to him for you.'

'Thank you.' She looks relieved. She might be a strong woman with a chainsaw, but of course she is in a foreign country and has no idea how the system works – maybe we do have delusional madmen at the top of government, who knows? I for one couldn't possibly comment.

'If you have any further problems with the same man, come straight to me.' I take out my notebook, scribble down the station phone number and hand it to her.

'Thank you, but I will be fine.' Still polite, but the pride is back.

I nod. 'You are clearly all very skilled, and I'm sure you will soon be self-sufficient, but until then, don't hesitate to ask us for anything you need. My husband is a roofer...' I look up at the roof, still expecting to see some missing tiles.

'Thank you, but Natalia has already fixed the tiles. She is a roofer by trade.'

Good Lord, these women are Amazons; they put us Irish women to shame. 'That's amazing.' I can't wait to tell Kieran there's a qualified roofer in town, though come to think of it, maybe I won't tell him if she's as stunningly beautiful as the rest of them. 'Right then, Daniela, I'll be off. Glad to see you're settling in. I doubt you'll have any more trouble, but if you do, please give me a shout. We'll be out to you as soon as we can.'

'Thank you, Sergeant Munroe.'

'Mags, please.'

We shake hands again, and Daniela returns to her work as I walk back to the car. The children stop their games, and several little boys come to look at me. Little boys especially tend to love the cops – they like uniforms and handcuffs – and I smile at them. *'Privyet,'* I say, and several of them shout it back, so my pronunciation can't be that bad.

As I start the engine, Sharon texts me.

*G & T at six, just the one ;-)??*

I shouldn't really, but it's Friday and Kate is with Evie. Ellie will be at home, but Kieran is there – he needs to do his VAT returns today so is working from home.

I send a quick text. *Hi, love, can you and Ellie manage if I meet Shar for a drink? xx*

*No, we'll starve to death and probably burn the house down.*

I laugh. Then my phone pings again.

*Why not make a night of it? Go for dinner in the Samovar? I'll collect you so you can have a drink?*

He's so kind, encouraging me to go out and have fun.

I text Sharon. *Better again, G & T first, then dinner in the Samovar? K on driving duty?*

Her reply is instant. *Yay! See you at 6.*

I text Kieran again. *You're a star, thanks. xx*

I park my car at the garda station. It wouldn't be a good look for me to leave it outside the Samovar all night. I'm in the town's bad books as it is, thanks to Horseheadgate. Although to be fair, things have improved a bit on that front. The likes of Duckie and Bertie the butcher will never forgive me, and nor will Elsie, who has stopped coming to the neighbourhood watch meetings mercifully, but several of the parents have actually thanked me for the workshop on the dangers of drugs, and for teaching their children that hard work can be rewarding.

Even Holly came up to me in the street to tell me how Jess enjoyed 'helping the Ukrainian women and children', as if Jess was some sort of saintly volunteer rather than there on a court order, doing community service. For Ellie's sake, I just smiled and nodded along. 'Ellie really enjoyed it too,' I said.

Which is true, as it happens. I think it's made her friendship with Jess more equal, because they've had to work as a team, and she's acquired new friends, and it's helped her understand her father's job better as well. She's back working at the shop on Saturdays, though Mam still hasn't left her in charge, but hopefully that will come, and apparently, she's already letting Ellie do things her own way a bit.

Like last Saturday, Ellie was telling me and Kieran over dinner that Mam let her change one of the window displays. She'd added in some wide-leg cargo pants with cropped V-neck jumpers and chunky runners to one mannequin and a Gym+Coffee hoodie and ripped jeans to another, which she'd got Mam to order.

'And Granny didn't mind?' This didn't sound like the Marie I knew. She's always been such a control freak when it comes to that place, and Marie's Boutique is strictly for over-forties and little kids; Mam is nervous of teenage fashion.

Ellie nodded happily. 'She was delighted. Especially because I made her mark the trousers up sixty percent and the jumpers forty percent on the cost price. People have more regard for things they have to spend a bit of money on. The Gym+Coffee hoodies are seventy euro online, so we dropped them to sixty-five to get people in, so she made a nice profit too.'

'Ah, look at our little capitalist,' Kieran said with a fond chuckle as he speared another sausage. 'Fair play to you, love.'

'Yeah.' She was so proud of herself. 'Galway is too far to go for just a top or a pair of pants or something, so the teenagers are delighted to have somewhere to buy a bit of new gear in Ballycarrick. Granny said she was wrecked at the end of the day, all the young ones coming in to check out the new lines. Like, I told her they'd fly out the door, and they did.'

I sat there smiling. It felt so nice, just to be at home with my family, Ellie being in such good form, chatting with Kieran and me and Kate about her successes in the retail trade. Though I did feel a bit worried about Mam. My idea of her employing Ellie on Saturdays seemed to have made more work for her rather than less.

I have a few minutes to kill until Sharon can get to the Samovar, so I pop into the station to say a few words to Darren and Michael about maybe arranging a youth club fundraiser for the Ukrainians.

Just in time, I spot Ronnie Atkinson at the counter and stay where I am, in the doorway.

He is explaining to Michael and Darren in his boomy voice how the Ukrainians up at Horsehead are ruining the wildlife, and how they are violent and should be evicted.

'Mm, mm,' Michael is saying, writing in his notebook. 'Violent, is it?'

'Out of control,' he spits angrily, randomly placing air quotes around the word 'control'. And he explains at boring length and with much numbering on his fingers how he went there, one, out of the goodness of his heart to offer his help as their local government representative and, two, to explain how they mustn't disturb the pine martens and, three, to make sure their children didn't run about in the woods making noise, only to find a Ukrainian person in the act of chopping down trees for – air quotes – 'firewood', and this person, one, threatened him with a chainsaw and, two, ordered him off the land.

I notice Ronnie keeps saying person, even though Daniela is clearly female. I suspect he doesn't want Michael and Darren to know it was a mere woman who saw him off.

'You're saying this person attacked you with a chainsaw?' asks Michael politely, his pen poised.

'Well...' Even Ronnie can't quite bring himself to lie that badly. 'Not directly, but the point is, there are habitats in those trees. It's utterly unacceptable!' His voice rises again. 'Obviously in Ukraine there's no such thing as' – air quotes – '"sustainable forestry". I mean, look at Chernobyl...'

Ronnie's grasp of politics apparently doesn't extend to knowing that Ukraine was not an independent country when the Russian nuclear reactor melted down.

'Clearly they have no concern for the environment! They have cut a whole path through the woodland. I will go to court on this matter – I will be seeing my lawyer in the morning...' His voice gets even shriller as he snarls and threatens, as if anyone gives a monkey's what he does with his mornings.

165

'You certainly can do all of those things, Mr Atkinson,' says Michael politely, and then spots me standing there listening. I put my finger to my lips, but despite Michael's best efforts to stay poker-faced, Ronnie must have seen his eyes flicker in my direction, because he turns and pounces.

'Sergeant, I'm glad I caught you,' he announces. 'I need to make you aware of a development up at the Horsehead place. There's a belt of native oak up there, and the Ukrainians obviously don't understand nature – they'll have them all down given half a chance. So I'm going to apply for a Tree Preservation Order. And I'm not alone in this, Sergeant. Let me tell you, there are plenty of right-minded people who are not keen on this level of destruction to our native forests, and our voices will not be silenced!'

Oh, for the love of... I force myself to stay looking neutral. 'Well, as far as I understand it, the council made the path themselves through the alder trees to enable access for the residents to the village without having to go around the very dangerous main road, and there was no intention to fell the oaks. The residents have the council's permission to use the already felled alder wood, so it's very unlikely any protection order will be issued.'

'Sergeant Munroe...'

I try not to wince at his patronising, mansplaining tone.

'Sergeant Munroe, it was very *unlikely* that Ireland would rid itself of colonial invaders. It was very *unlikely* that slavery would be abolished. It was very *unlikely* that you ladies would get the vote. But nonetheless all those things happened, thanks to good people getting together and protesting. We wouldn't be much good to future generations if we didn't protest, just because the desired outcome was *unlikely* now, would we?' He raises a hairy eyebrow at me. It seems he needs an answer.

I sigh. Sharon will be at the Samovar by now, and my G & T is calling to me. 'It is your constitutional right to apply for the order, of course, and even to gather people to protest in the event it is not granted. However, I will warn you that should such a protest trespass on the Horsehead property, or if you personally go confronting people in their home, I shall be obliged to intervene.'

He moves a foot closer to me, and the aroma of damp dog assails my nostrils. I've never wanted to take a power hose to a person as much as him. He seems to have something stuck in his teeth, and I guess it's peanut skins based on the open hemp bag of nuts stuffed in his pocket. He's also wearing sandals, which is just ridiculous considering it's about five degrees outside. And anyway, nobody should have to look at his hairy toes and gnarly toenails. I know, this doesn't sound very professional, but honestly, he's a total dose.

'Oh, don't you worry.' He waggles his finger at me. 'I will apply, Sergeant, and I'm more optimistic than you, let me assure you. I am, after all, a member of the council myself, in case you have forgotten. Maybe we're not feeling very hopeful given the state of law enforcement in the country, but we must persist and try harder, mustn't we?'

Argh. I want to punch him. I really do. 'Well, I'll let you at whatever it is you're doing, and remember, do not go up there again. This matter is now closed.'

Before he can ask me what we plan to do to stop him, I leave, and I stomp up the street, furious.

# CHAPTER 18

*S*haron is settled in the panelled-in little corner of the bar, the snug as it is called, traditionally the only place the ladies were allowed to sit, but in recent decades, the only place for a confidential chat.

'Well, either the worst of the South American drug lords has turned up at bingo in the church hall or your mother-in-law has invited you for one of her interminable Sunday roasts? Which is it?' she asks after she calls for two G & Ts.

'Neither, just a long day.' I sigh, squishing in beside her, my knees nearly overturning the table. Irishwomen must have been a lot skinnier than me back in the day to fit more than one of them into this tiny space.

'You sure?' She raises an eyebrow. 'Is something after happening?'

I can't tell Sharon police business – it's a constant bone of contention between me and Kieran, and I can hardly make an exception for my best friend – so I change the subject. 'Just the usual. Don't worry about it. Now, what about the job hunt? How did the interview with Brown Thomas go?'

Sharon's been trying the fashion retail route again since our last conversation.

'Don't ask,' she says bitterly, and I don't pursue it. She's obviously having no luck and is too annoyed and frustrated to even want to moan about it, and this time it's she who changes the subject. 'Do you and Kieran want to come over to us on the fourteenth for Trevor's birthday? Don't worry, I'm not cooking. It will be a take-away – that's my birthday treat to him – along with lashings of red wine.'

A distant bell dings at the back of my mind. There's a clash of dates here; I just can't remember... Then I do. 'Oh no...'

'Problem? I know you're busy, that's why I'm booking you so far in advance. We can make it the Friday if you prefer?'

I smile gratefully. 'Yes, that would be great, thanks.'

At this point a beautiful young blond woman appears beside us holding two menus and indicating to us to follow her. Tatiana might not have needed a cleaning lady, but she seems to have scored herself a Ukrainian waitress, which is great. She's been run off her feet trying to do two jobs at once, serving behind the bar and in the restaurant.

After we're seated at our table, Sharon grabs the wine list and asks, 'So what's on the fourteenth? Camogie? Drama group?'

'No, nothing to do with the girls for once, though I'm warning you, when Sean hits his teenage years, you'll find you're nothing but a glorified taxi service. Not even glorified, come to think of it. No, I know this sounds pathetic, but there's a programme on that Kieran really wants to watch on Saturday night.'

She looks surprised. 'Can't he record it?'

'He wants to watch it live.'

'What is it?' Sharon makes a face. 'Surely the only thing on live telly on Saturday night is that clown Ray Lonergan and *The Nightshow*.'

Kieran hasn't sworn me to secrecy and Sharon will be discreet if I ask her to, so I decide to confide in her. It's tiring for me, not having anyone to talk to about Oliver except for the Munroes themselves, who are too invested to be rational. I've tried my best, promised Kevin to do what detecting I can while sticking to garda rules, but I've hit the same brick wall over and over again, the same as the guy they hired privately. To be honest, unless Nora comes around, nothing is going to change.

'That's what he wants to watch,' I say. '*The Nightshow*.'

'What?' She laughs incredulously. 'He hates Ray Lonergan!'

'I know, but this one is a special show about people who were put into mother-and-baby homes, about people coming forward and telling their stories and trying to piece the whole thing together, you know?'

'I heard something on the radio during the week. Lonergan himself was born in one or something and adopted?'

I nod. 'Yeah, and he's decided to do a special where people come and tell their stories, hoping it will encourage others and eventually hoping they will fill in the gaps where the religious orders either don't know or won't say what happened.'

'I get that.' Her brow furrows as she takes a sip of her drink. 'But what has that to do with Kieran?'

I take a deep breath. She knows Nora and how I feel about her, so this is going to be a juicy bit of information. She is also fiercely protective of me, though I'm well able to mind myself, and she takes Nora's slights against me very seriously, more seriously than I do, to be honest.

'OK, but this is strictly between us, OK?'

'Did Kieran get someone pregnant years ago and now he's trying to find his child?' She's fascinated and half delighted with the scandal of it all, I can tell.

'No, you eejit.' I laugh at the idea. 'It's not him, it's his mother.'

I watch the news sink in.

'What? No way. Nora? Nobody's-good-enough-for-the-Munroes Nora? You're joking.'

'She got pregnant back in 1965, and she had a baby boy in one of those places. She gave him up of course, she had no choice, and so –'

'Fur coat and no knickers, Nora Munroe?' she splutters. 'And she had the cheek to tell me that I was lucky that Danny Boylan was paying me maintenance, the nosy old wagon!'

'Shh…' I warn her. The snug can lure you into a sense of security, but nothing is private in Ballycarrick, where everyone seems to be blessed with supersonic hearing.

Sharon drops her voice to a whisper. 'All right, but go on, tell me everything. Now she wants to find him? And what did Kevin say? Nothing, I presume?'

Kevin Munroe's silence is legendary, not just in his family but throughout Ballycarrick. One night, years ago, Kieran and I were only going out a short while, and he wasn't long back from America. He was living at home, and we all went out to the Galway races, drank too much, and he told everyone they could stay at his place. I barely knew Nora at that stage, but even then I guessed the idea of a load of drunk young people crashing on her immaculate sofas would send her into a spin.

Sharon was wearing a white linen suit – it was the '90s, in her defence – and she didn't want it creased, so she took it off and slept on Nora's cream leather couch in her underwear. Poor Kevin arrived into his sitting room the next morning to find Sharon standing topless, because the underwire of her bra was sticking into her so she took it off. And even then, he didn't say a word. Sharon was offended that even the sight of her pert young boobs wasn't enough to get a word out of him.

'Well, that's the thing,' I say. 'Kevin isn't being silent at all. He's been shouting and demanding answers.'

'No...' Sharon hisses in astonishment. 'That's not possible! Is he really angry with Nora?'

'He is.'

'I can't picture it...'

'The thing is, you see, the baby is his, and Nora never told him.'

'What are you on about?' Her eyes are as round as saucers.

So over drinks and then a delicious dinner of char-grilled chicken, sweet potato mash and sprouting broccoli, I tell her the whole story: Kevin's uncharacteristic burst of emotion, the fruitless search that has been going on for months and now this thing coming up next month, Operation Spotlight.

'Kieran is going to try to get his mother to watch it on the fourteenth. That's the day of the big reveal, when lots of important people in Irish society are going to come on and talk about their own experiences with the homes. Maybe that will give her the courage to look properly. And we need her to do the looking. It's really hard for birth mothers to get information, but if anyone else tries, almost every door is closed. The information is so sensitive – this is peoples' lives we're talking about – so the groups who do this, who find people, won't share whatever they know with anyone but the mother or her child.'

She's still shaking her head; she can't get past the snobby-Nora thing. 'Oh my God, Mags, I'm so amazed. Nora, and how Kevin's parents thought she wasn't good enough for their precious boy, and then she did the same thing to you. I know I should feel sorry for her, but I don't truthfully. She's a stuck-up cow, and even now she won't help her husband and kids to find his son, their brother.'

'I don't think it's as simple as that, honestly, Shar. She is so ashamed and fears being judged. Those times really traumatised her. She was told she was dirty and stupid and sinful and –'

'Like she'd judge someone else, you mean?' Sharon is a bit black and white about things.

'Well, yes, but… Anyway, that's why Kieran wants to watch on the fourteenth, up at his parents', and I'm going along as moral support or something, though what good it will do, I don't know. She's adamant she won't change her mind.'

'Well, she loves Lonergan, doesn't she?'

'She does. His family are well-got – I forget why now.' I sigh.

'His father is Jeremiah Lonergan, that owns Brackenlough Stud.'

'Oh yeah.' I remember Nora telling me now, informing me all about stud farms. She wouldn't know one end of a horse from the other, but to hear her, you'd swear she was best mates with the Aga Khan.

We're offered desserts, but Sharon waves the menu away. She never eats dessert, and I shouldn't so it's a blessing that she never even looks. Kieran always has dessert, and though I don't order one, I usually end up eating half of his.

'Funny if it turned out to be Lonergan who was her son.' Sharon grins. 'I bet that would bring her out of the bedroom. She'd be dying to claim him. She'd probably turn around and disown all the rest of you.'

I laugh as I take a last delicious sip of Tatiana's mysteriously good coffee, then signal to the young Ukrainian waitress for the bill. We had a brief chat with her when she delivered the food, and she's called Olga and was a computer technician in her previous life. 'Well, apparently, gorgeous Ray already knows who his mother is, but yeah, I get your point.'

# CHAPTER 19

*K*lara is a marvel. The entire place is immaculate, and it's such a pleasure to work somewhere that smells so nice and clean all the time. I offer her hours in our house as well, and she is happy to do it. Selfishly, I dread the day the war is over and she can go back to being a biology teacher in her own country... No, of course I don't mean that, and I shouldn't even joke about it. Of course I want her to be able to go home to her loved ones, her husband who is a doctor at the front and her elderly parents who are trapped in Mariupol, a city that would frighten you to look at now that Putin has tried to flatten it. I just mean it's really nice having her around. She's a lovely woman.

Alina is still coming as well, despite it being term time. Klara hasn't enrolled her in Ballycarrick school yet. I don't think it's because her mother doesn't want her to go to school; I suspect it's because Alina is afraid to let her mother out of her sight in case she loses her, like she has already lost her father and her grandparents.

Delia has been wonderful to Alina all week, showing her around the police station, bringing her for a ride in the garda car, telling her what it's like being a guard. She is really patient, and the girl is rapt.

She's picking up new words rapidly between Duolingo and talking to us as her mother works. She's like a sponge.

But there's only so much amusement to be had in a little rural garda station.

'Delia, it's all quiet on the Western Front, so why don't you take Alina to show her your dad's puppies?' I suggest when Friday comes around. 'If her mam doesn't mind?'

Klara doesn't mind at all, but Alina is reluctant to leave her mother's side until Delia shows her pictures of Jerome's new pups on her phone; they are red setters, gorgeous. When she and Alina come back an hour later, Alina is flushed and happy and chatting away in Ukrainian to her mother, who looks slightly taken aback by what her daughter is saying. Klara keeps shooting me worried looks after that, but when I ask Alina what the matter is, the child just grins and rolls her eyes. It's great to see her coming out of her meek, traumatised shell, but it's not much of an answer.

I don't find out what the problem is until the end of Klara's shift.

I'm in my office, and there is a knock on the door. It's Klara, with her daughter.

'Hello?' I put down the report I'm writing.

Klara comes to stand beside me and shows me a picture on her phone of what at first I think is a very colourful Travellers' halting site, but the text is in English, and I read that this is a picture of Ukrainian Roma.

Once she's sure I've understood that, she looks at me questioningly and then points to Alina.

I look at Alina. 'What is it?' I ask slowly.

Alina looks embarrassed, like she'd rather not answer, but at Klara's prompting, she blurts out, 'My mother afraid of Roma. She say, how can police have Roma father.'

I drop my eyes to the desk, unwilling to meet Klara's gaze. I don't know what to say. I'm surprised and disappointed in her, annoyed, to be honest. We've taken in these refugees, and now they're complaining about who else is in Ireland? I swear, when Alina went off with Delia, it never crossed my mind to warn her mother that

Delia's family are Travellers and live in a caravan. I mean, that would be like discrimination.

I have to admit, though, if Klara had been a blow-in from Dublin or something, there's no doubt I *would* have said something before I sent her daughter off to hang out on a halting site. I'd have warned her the McGoverns were Travellers, but then I would have explained it was fine, that they've lived in Ballycarrick for generations, and that Delia's father, Jerome, is the head of the family and a gentler soul you couldn't meet.

So why didn't I tell all this to Klara, using Google Translate?

It's daft really, but I suppose I didn't expect Klara to be so like a settled person in her views. I mean, to me, the Ukrainians are sort of like the Travellers themselves, dispossessed, socially vulnerable, facing discrimination and, at the same time, a bit exotic. It seems Klara doesn't see herself that way. It seems Klara thinks she's a settled person, and she needs my reassurance.

It's not too late to fix things, I decide. After offering them a lift home, I drive very slowly past the McGovern site, and as I was sure she would, Alina shouts, 'Puppies!' very excitedly. With an apologetic smile at Klara, I stop the car. Alina jumps out and rushes over to Olivia McGovern, who is holding one of the puppies in her arms.

Martha and Annette's son, Finbarr, is there too, and he gives Alina the furry baby he is holding himself, beaming. With another encouraging smile at Klara, I get out of the car and go to admire the puppies that are wandering bandy-legged around a straw-lined pen, watched by their sleepy mother. As I lean on the rail, Gyp comes limping over to greet me, and I bend down to pet her. She seems much recovered and getting around fine on her three legs.

'I was wondering how you were getting on,' I say to her, smiling into the little terrier's trusting half-blind eyes.

'Oh, Gyp's grand.' Olivia beams. 'Uncle Jerome is giving her Guinness and bread to build her up like.'

'It's good for dogs, Jerome says. Not too much – we don't want her drunk, though,' says Finbarr earnestly. 'She was Nana Dacie's dog,' he explains to me, and it's sweet how he refers to Olivia's grandmother as if she were his own.

'I know she was, Finbarr. I remember her there when I'd visit Dacie. She'll be looking down on her little pal now and glad you two are minding her.'

After a while, Klara climbs out of the car. She stands there hesitantly, and I beckon her over and introduce her to Olivia and Finbarr. She smiles a little and strokes the puppy Alina is holding. Then Jerome appears, and she looks worried again. Of course, he is a huge man with a mop of oiled-back black hair and tattooed arms and hands that would frighten you if you didn't know him. But after I've done the introductions, with much pointing and sign language, he calls to Dora to make tea. Dora invites us into her lovely, neat caravan, and after a while, I see Klara relax, because she can see with her own eyes that this is a safe, friendly environment. She even gets out Google Translate so she can chat to Delia, who has arrived to join us.

And for the next half hour, we all sit around in Dora's caravan drinking tea, as if Ukrainian refugees, Irish Travellers and members of the police force get together for social chats every day of the week.

# CHAPTER 20

Over the next week, Alina spends a couple of hours a day at the site. She's become a great pal of Finbarr's, and Klara thinks maybe soon she'll have the courage to go back to school for a full day. A lot of her friends are already enrolled, and Ellie and Kate tell me the other kids are making them very welcome in school.

Ellie and her friends invited two Ukrainian girls to go to a youth disco in the parish hall with them 'for the craic'. Which is an Irishism to do something for the fun of it. The girls went home with the request to their mothers, and when Google translated it to 'crack cocaine', the poor women were terrified that their daughters were hooked up with west-of-Ireland teenage crack dealers.

Ellie roared with laughter when she was telling us, and Kate giggled as well and said, 'Or with west-of-Ireland teenagers who got caught drinking cider.' Ellie went bright red, and Kieran smothered a smile.

'Too soon, Kit Kat,' I said sternly. 'Much too soon.'

Language barriers or not, it's great how the adult Ukrainians are fitting in as well.

Anne Marie at SuperValu now employs three of the Ukrainian women as shop assistants and shelf stackers, and I've told Kieran about the female roofer, though he's still getting his head around that idea. He says he feels awkward at the idea of employing a single woman in a gang of men.

'What, like the way it was when I started off in the force?' I ask.

The four of us are sitting around a table in Luigi's, having the sort of family date we should have been having when Ellie was off partying at Horsehead. 'What was it like, Mam?' asks Kate.

A moment ago, she'd been all chat about the county final next weekend and how if Chopper McCarthy who trains them saw her scoffing pizza this close to the game, he'd have a canary. Chopper is intense about underage camogie on a level you won't find at the Premier League, but he has brought a lot of glory to the Under 12s in Ballycarrick.

But Kate has forgotten about Chopper and is looking at me.

'It was like being in a '70s sitcom, love, a bunch of blokes sitting around thinking I'm hilarious just on the strength of me being female. Not laughing at my jokes, mind you. No, women weren't supposed to be able to tell jokes in those days...'

'Seriously?' She is round-eyed, like I'm telling her about the Stone Age.

I pat her hand. 'Things are better now, thank goodness, but there's a long way to go. And, Kieran, how will you get Ellie to take over your roofing business unless you set a good example by employing a woman?'

'Oh, ha, ha, ha,' says Ellie, who has dropped all the acting about being interested in the roofing trade since she got her phone back, although to be fair, since her Horsehead experience, she's stopped being dismissive about it at least. 'But, Dad, she's right.'

'OK, OK.' Kieran sighs as he covers his pizza in chilli oil. 'I'll talk to this woman.'

'Good for you,' I say, and I mean it. The thing is, I've met Natalia now, on another trip to Horsehead dropping off Klara, and she is not the dainty blond I thought she might be but a strong woman in her forties, with a buzz cut, wearing the same kind of trousers Kieran favours, with lots of pockets and loops to hang things from.

179

Luigi, real name Leonard, arrives down to the table to take our order and brings a bottle of Rioja and two cans of Fanta. He knows us of old.

'Thanks, Luigi,' Kieran says as Luigi pours us each a big glass of wine. He doesn't bother to go through the rigmarole of asking either of us to taste it; we always get the same one.

'And how are the *principessas* today?' Luigi asks in his broad Offaly accent. He's called my two the *principessas* since they were tiny.

'Grand, Luigi, thanks,' Ellie answers. Since the drinking and the community service incident, I swear she's matured. No more eye-rolling and heavy sighs; she's actually such a pleasant kid to be around now. Maybe that awful thing was for the best.

'Ellie, I wanted to say something to you. I was talking to our new waitress' – Luigi has also hired one of the Ukrainian women– 'and she tells me the house they're living in is lovely. She knows how hard you all worked on it. The man from the council – Tadgh Milligan, is it – told her all about it, and she says thank you all for doing it.'

Ellie blushes to the roots of her hair. 'Well, we kind of had to do it, but I'm glad it's OK...' she manages.

'We all make mistakes, love, even grown-ups. That just means you're human. But making up for it, doing a good thing, that's a great sign of a person. I'm proud of you.'

Ellie wells up. She's known Luigi all her life, ever since he abandoned his florist shop in Offaly for a west-of-Ireland woman and the bright lights of Ballycarrick. He gives her shoulder a squeeze before taking our order and moving on to the table behind us.

'We're proud of you too, pet,' I say quietly, and she wipes her eye with her sleeve. After she'd finished at Horsehead, Ellie and I had a heart-to-heart, and she'd told me that the worst part of it all – and it was all terrible – was embarrassing me in front of everyone and seeing how hard it was for me that day in the District Court. And how it was the cause of a fight between me and her dad. We hugged then, and I told her that nothing she could ever do would make me not love her, that I might want to choke her, but I would always love her, no matter what. That's life, isn't it? Never plain sailing, but rupture and repair. Constantly.

* * *

IN THE MORNING, Kieran goes off to Horsehead to chat to Natalia and I drop Ellie to the shop. I say hi to Mam, who is carrying boxes into the back of the shop. She looks tired, I realise, so I make her sit down and let Ellie carry the boxes, despite Mam's protests that my daughter is only a slip of a thing.

'No, I'm not. You should have seen what I could do at Horsehead, Granny,' says Ellie. 'I've got muscles now. Just tell me where you want these.' And she sets to with a will, in between putting the kettle on to make her granny a cup of tea.

Then I bring Kate to Orla's nice detached five-bedroomed house to play with her cousin Evie, and me and Orla have a cup of tea in the kitchen, sitting on stools at the marble kitchen island, and discuss the plan to watch Ray Lonergan on the fourteenth, which is now in two weeks' time.

'How is your mother about the idea?' I ask Kieran's sister. 'Does she know we're all congregating to watch it in her house?' I feel a bit nosey asking, but then I'm being dragged along to watch as well, so I want to know what I'm getting into. Kieran is so weary from this whole saga, I don't like to keep pushing at him to talk about it.

'I did tell her, and I told her why – well, Gearoid and I did it together, or we tried to anyway. She just started crying again, so that was a disaster. I've never seen her cry so much, really at all, ever in my life. She's so fearful of the scandal, but we explained that Dad is going to keep searching anyway. But I don't know. She says she won't watch it but she can't stop us.'

Although I like Orla, we've never confided in each other about anything important before. Nora's tagline for Orla is 'always immaculate', which in her case is true, and to be honest, I don't fully trust someone whose house is always spotless. Today, though, I get the feeling she wants to talk at a deeper level than just how the girls are doing at school and what new washing machine to buy and things like that.

'How are you feeling about all of it?' I ask gently.

Orla sighs as she shakes out some biscuits onto a plate. 'I haven't really thought about how I feel, to be honest, Mags. I'm more worried about my parents. Mam's cooking for Dad and stuff, but in between she's still doing her recluse act, staying in her room. I don't know. It's ridiculous, neither willing to see the other's point of view. Decades of being a total doormat, and now Dad is digging his heels in, and nothing is going to stop him. And Mam is just as stubborn. She's still refusing to even consider the thought of looking for Oliver. It's a full-scale cold war up there.'

'The irresistible force meeting the immovable object.'

'Yeah, that.'

'It's a lot, for sure. I know Kieran is struggling with it too.'

She sighs, her elbows on the marble surface of the island, absently massaging the back of her neck. 'Part of me wishes it had never come out, bad as that might sound. Another part of me wants to find him, to meet him. And a really big part of me is scared at what that scenario might look like. You know, Mags, I love Ballycarrick. I love my family the way it is. And a lot of the time, I understand how Catriona feels – I'm cautious of anything throwing a grenade into my comfortable life. But then the idea that we all have an older brother wandering around someplace, knowing, or maybe not knowing, that he has another family... Now that we know about him, I don't see how we can just leave it, so I just really hope Mam comes around.'

My phone rings, and I glance down at the screen. It's Ellie, and for a moment, I think of not picking up; I've never had a conversation like this with Orla before. But you never know when it's going to be an emergency.

I pick up.

It's an emergency.

# CHAPTER 21

*J* sit with Joe on either side of Mam's bed in the hospital, while she tells us, 'I don't know what all the fuss is about. It was just a small blockage. They've put in a stent. There's nothing wrong with me at all now. I'll be out of here in no time.'

All the while she's saying it, she's grey in the face and lilac under her eyes and around her mouth. I feel sick. I know I'm fifty-one years old, but losing my mother is not something I can even consider for a second. And I know from the doctor she won't be out of here in no time. The cardiologist has booked her in for a full set of tests, Holter monitor, echogram, EKG, the whole works, and they're not going to let her go until she's in the clear of having another attack any time soon. 'Shh, Mam, please get some rest.'

'Yes, Marie, love, please, close your eyes,' begs Joe.

'Oh, stop mithering me. You're like two old women. I'm not one bit...' But before she even manages to finish the sentence, she's drifted off.

I get up and go into the corridor, and Joe follows me. He's shaking and in bits. My poor Ellie is consumed with guilt – she thinks it's all her fault for getting in the new teenage gear and running Mam off her feet – but Joe feels even worse because he thinks he should have known.

It turns out Mam wasn't feeling great all day Friday, very tired, and then in the evening, she'd had a bit of back pain between the shoulder blades. But then in the morning, she insisted she was grand for work, and Joe assumed it had been a muscle twinge or something and didn't make her go to the doctor.

'Thing is, Mags,' he tells me as we stand in the corridor outside her ward, 'I had a small bang myself about five years ago, but I knew what was happening because I got a bad pain in my left arm and something that felt like indigestion. I just knew then, that's a sign of a heart attack, and sure enough it was. I had the stent, got enough of a fright, gave up the cigarettes, cut the pints way back, and no more fried food. But your mam, she lives pure healthy, and I never knew tiredness and a bit of back pain between the shoulder blades meant anything in a woman...'

I hug him. 'Joe, stop blaming yourself. You're not a doctor. And you know what she's like. She's stubborn, like you said before.'

'If it hadn't been for that Ukrainian woman...'

'I know. Stop.'

It doesn't bear thinking about, what would have happened if the Ukrainian doctor hadn't come into the shop that afternoon. She'd called in looking for work as a shop assistant – Anya Kurylenko was her name – and Mam explained how the shop only made enough for one full-time wage and her granddaughter was all the help she needed, but she said she'd certainly keep Anya in mind if things changed and asked her would she like a cup of tea before she went... but then Mam seemed to take a turn.

As Ellie told it, Anya Kurylenko, noticing Mam didn't seem well all of a sudden, took my mother by the arm and touched the back of her hand to her cheek. 'Have you a pain anywhere?' she'd asked in very good English.

Marie looked confused and pulled away. 'I'm fine. I'll just have a sit down...' she'd started saying, but then she seems to get a sharp pain and fell, that was when the woman turned to Ellie and said calmly but insistently, 'Call emergency services now, and tell them to send an ambulance to this address. Tell them your grandmother is perhaps having a heart attack.'

And she'd made a protesting Marie sit down in the back room, and she'd sent Ellie rushing to the chemist for a bottle of uncoated aspirin. She forced my mother to swallow the lot. How she'd made Marie do it, I don't know, but the doctors in the hospital already told me and Joe that by thinning my mother's blood with the aspirin, Anya Kurylenko had stopped Mam from having a second, potentially fatal heart attack.

It's a lot to take in, that my mother's life was saved by such chance.

'And the first thing she said to me when I got here,' Joe says, with tears tumbling down his cheeks, 'is, "I'm not giving up my shop, the end."'

'She's ridiculous.' I'm almost more cross than concerned now. 'That's insane. She needs to retire, take it easy, before something worse happens.'

'I might as well be talking to the wall.'

'Right,' I say. 'Leave it with me. I'll fix this and get her out of that bloody shop if it's the last thing I do.'

'Mags...' It's Sharon, hurrying up the corridor with an armful of flowers, very anxious at the sight of Joe's tears and my thunderous expression. 'How is Marie?'

'She's...she's Delaney's bloody donkey,' I say fiercely, and while Sharon looks puzzled, me and Joe collapse in hysterical sobbing laughter.

# CHAPTER 22

*I*t's Wednesday morning. I've been with Mam since eight listening to her complaining about being stuck in hospital when she's perfectly fine, thank you very much, so now I'm late. Klara is already in my office, cleaning furiously with a blank expression on her face, dusting and dusting a bookcase that definitely doesn't need any more dusting.

'Klara, what's wrong? Are you all right?'

She looks terribly upset, and I wonder if she's noticed some of the unpleasant tweets circulating on Twitter about Horsehead. I wouldn't have seen them myself if Ellie hadn't shown me.

#horsehead #ukraine #refugees #theanswertowarisnottodestroy-wildlife #pinemartens

It was bloody obvious to me who'd sent that one. His Twitter handle is @Icare. I'm surprised he didn't use an air quotes emoji, and I would like to strangle him. Ellie reported the tweet as hate speech – not on my say-so, as I have to stay neutral – but it's not been taken down. Apparently, it doesn't violate Twitter's rules to falsely accuse victims of war of destroying the environment.

Also these, and I'm amazed the author – Twitter handle @lovegolf – even knows how to use Twitter.

#horsehead #keepthewarout #wildlife #pinemartens

Bloody stupid Elsie Flanagan, who's never played a game of golf in her life, just inexplicably dresses in golfing clothes.

I know it's her, because she came storming into the station on Monday accusing the Ukrainians up at Horsehead of shooting the wildlife. Apparently, her precious son, the one who got arrested at the Horsehead rave, happened to be in the vicinity and heard gunfire.

'It's a crow banger, Mrs Flanagan. It's not a weapon. They are using it to keep the crows off the vegetables they've planted.' Delia tried valiantly to calm her down.

Delia knows it's a crow banger because I was so impressed by it, I've told her all about it. One of the women in Horsehead is an engineer, and the last time I was there dropping Klara off, Alina took me to see it. We went around the back of the house, through the old farmyard and outbuildings, and she opened a gate into a little vegetable garden, roughly twenty metres by thirty. The veg had been planted, and green shoots were poking up. In the middle of the patch was a crow banger on a tripod. It was a home-made one, with a cylindrical piece of pipe attached to a barrel of propane, and fixed to one of the tripod legs was a black box. It looked like a telescope. Within a few seconds, it emitted a loud bang, like a shotgun blast, and a few seconds later, the cylinder spun around and fired again, and finally it delivered a third bang in yet another direction. Incredibly resourceful.

'Do you think I'm thick stupid? Is that what you think?' Elsie's voice rose in volume and pitch. 'I want to see Mags this minute, this very minute! That place is giving me ulcers. Ask Dr Mulcahy. I'm actually on tablets, and that bloody Horsehead is the cause, if it's not you lot overreaching yourselves over nothing, then turning a blind eye when something really serious is going on.'

I got up from my chair in the office and went out into the public area. 'Mrs Flanagan, how can I help?' I smiled.

'Ah, Mags.' She turned from Delia. Her ensemble was more bizarre than usual. Black and white harlequin-patterned trousers, a cerise pink half-zip top and inexplicably one of those sun visors, though it was grey and fairly miserable out. 'You're who I need. The immigrants above' – she rolled her eyes and thumbed in a vague direction – 'have a gun, and they're shooting the wildlife.'

'As Garda McGovern said –'

'Mags Munroe, do you think I came down in the last shower? Seriously?' Her hands were on her pudgy hips; she was like a terrier. 'I am making an official complaint. It's a gun they're firing, not a crow banger, and 'tis lucky poor William didn't get in the line of fire – he could have been killed. I want it investigated. If you won't do it, Mags, I'll have to go over your head.'

This kind of thing used to drive me daft before, but now it's like water off a duck. At the same time, though, I was getting fed up with the way she is always threatening to complain about me, and I wanted to put an end to it for once and for all.

'To whom?' I asked pleasantly.

'What to whom?' She's waspish at the best of times, but she was really cranky then.

'Who would you like to report me to? For dereliction of my duty?' I was still sweet as can be.

'Your superior, of course.' She was indignant, and her cheeks were pink.

'And that would be…?' I kept smiling. 'I just need to know so that I can answer the charge you're levelling. Because to make such an accusation, and indeed to be the subject of something like that, is very, very serious, and I'll need to know who to direct my GRA representative and legal team to. And obviously your solicitor and presumably your barrister as well, because an accusation of this nature couldn't be heard in the District Court. It would have to go directly to the Circuit Court and possibly the High Court.'

She was flustered. 'Ah, Mags, will you stop talking gibberish about courts and barristers and go up there and take that gun off those mad women before we're all shot dead and the place looks like the Battle of the Somme?'

'So you're not going to proceed with your accusation?' I asked innocently. 'Because I must take very seriously threats and accusations against me or any member of the force, so before we discuss Horsehead and what your son was doing on the grounds, I need to be clear...'

'No, of course I'm not. Look, Mags, don't mind about that...' She tried to wave her threat away, but I wouldn't let it go that easily. People like her think the gardaí work for them personally and are there to do her bidding, and if she doesn't get her own way, she throws a hissy fit. Well, no. Just no.

'Oh, but I do mind, Mrs Flanagan. I mind very much when someone makes an unfounded allegation that I'm not doing my job properly.' I stared her down then and did not break eye contact. If Elsie thinks she can bully me, she can think again.

'I didn't say that...' she mumbled.

'Well, what you said was that I was derelict in my duty and that you would need to report me to someone who outranks me.'

'Well, I didn't mean it...' She had turned puce red.

I waited.

'Look, Mags, I'm sorry, all right? I just...this whole Horsehead thing has me at my wits end, and that's the truth. But you and the rest of the guards here are doing your best, and it's very hard...'

OK, we could proceed.

'Will you step into my office? We can discuss it easier there.' I opened the door and let her walk past me, giving Delia a small wink and a smile.

In the office, Elsie sat down but I stayed standing.

'So, Mrs Flanagan, what is it about that place that's causing you such upset?'

'Like I told you, them immigrants, Russians or Ukrainians or whatever they are, have a gun, and even if it's a crow banger like you say, they shouldn't be doing it – it's frightening the wildlife.'

'Mrs Flanagan, firstly, they are Ukrainian citizens displaced from their country by an illegal and illegitimate war being waged by Vladimir Putin and the Russian government and, as such, are welcome here to seek asylum. Secondly, it's council land, and they have council permission,' I said as patiently as I could, 'to live there, to grow what they like, to chop timber, to try to make the best of a very, very, bad situation.'

She snorted. She'd definitely been spending too much time with Ronnie. At that moment, I had a horrible epiphany. They are both single, unsurprisingly. Dinjoe Flanagan died years ago, and nobody was ever blind or deaf or smell insensitive enough to have anything romantically to do with Ronnie. Maybe they were having a fling... No, please, that awful cesspit of a beard – surely Elsie Flanagan wouldn't stoop that low.

'I'm serious, Mrs Flanagan. They have a right to protect their vegetable patch, like every other farmer in the land.'

'But it's not *their* land, Mags, it's *ours*. They've no right to be digging things up or cutting trees down or disturbing the poor little pine martens, doing stuff in our country. There'll be caravans next –'

'Mrs Flanagan,' I interrupt sharply, 'maybe if you just stop obsessing about what the Ukrainians are doing, let them live their lives and get on with your own, you'd be happier and able to come off your medication?' I know it sounded patronising, but honestly, this woman is an absolute punish. It also annoyed me that she mixed the Ukrainians up with Travellers, though I know I haven't got a leg to stand on when it comes to that one. 'And by the way, please inform your son William that trespassing is still against the law in this country.'

Elsie's lips went white. She gripped her handbag and leapt to her feet, her visor askew. 'That's typical of you, Mags,' she hissed. 'You'd sooner defend a bunch of strangers who shouldn't even be here than look after your own.' And she stormed out. And the next thing, she was tweeting.

So now I think maybe Klara has seen Elsie's silly tweet and is worried.

'Are you on Twitter, Klara?'

She shakes her head furiously, still dusting.

'What is wrong?' I say slowly.

'No wrong.' Her English has been improving but is still very weak.

I open Google Translate on my phone and hand it to her. She shakes her head some more, but I won't give up. I take her duster away and just stand there, and finally she takes the phone and speaks into it and hands it back. The written translation reads, *My mother is hurt, bomb is break leg.*

She is pale, with tears running down her cheeks. I can tell there's something worse. I've been here too many times in police work.

'Your father?' I ask gently. She mentioned she'd left her parents behind because they were too frail to travel. I hand her the phone again, but she waves it away. She has the words for this. They're common enough.

'He is dead.' And at that she collapses into my arms, and I stand there, holding her, with not one single word of consolation for her.

Delia puts her head around the door to see what's happening, then leaves and reappears with a cup of tea and a box of tissues.

After Klara has sat down and drank some tea, and wiped her eyes and regained her usual astonishing stoicism, we discuss through the app what can be done to get her mother out.

'Your husband? Is he nearby?'

'I don't talk from my husband now eleven days. His phone finish. He at front, far, far away. I don't know where is he.'

'Could the Red Cross help? Or one of the other aid agencies? I'd be happy to try to contact them for you? Or Ukrainian police? Maybe I could make a request for information as a police officer here?' I am racking my brain for a way to help her.

She keeps shrugging. 'Too far from border. Too far. I go now... collect Alina to tell.'

Delia and I watch helplessly as she gathers her coat and handbag, our hearts going out to her. I can't imagine the terror of my mother injured in a war zone and not knowing where my husband is, or having to collect Kate from school to tell her that her grandfather has been killed by a Russian bomb.

'This is terrible,' says Delia softly.

'I know. I can't believe this. One of these women actually saved my mam's life on Saturday, and now we're standing around like dummies, like there's nothing we can do for Klara's mother.'

'Maybe I'll talk to my father.'

I look at her, confused. 'Jerome? Why? What can he do?'

'He was talking the other day, how Alina is so traumatised by leaving her whole family behind. The women here are in touch with others who are trying to get out. They can get to the border, but apparently, it's chaos there. He was even talking about just taking the van and going to get them all, or if he couldn't, bringing them supplies or something. Mam was very disapproving.'

'She didn't want him to go?' I'm surprised; Dora is such a kind person.

'She was savage about it.' She shakes her head.

'Why so?'

'She thinks he has an eye for Klara.'

'Ah, what nonsense. Jerome is as faithful to her as the day is long.'

'I know, Mags,' agrees Delia, with an expression of youthful horror at the very thought of her parents being interested in anything sexual. 'As if my dad would look at a woman at his age. Sure he's too old for that. Do you mind now if I go to talk to him about what has happened?'

'You do that.' Maybe Jerome taking a trip to the Polish-Ukrainian border isn't such a wild idea. It's got me thinking. There's the money raised by the youth club – that could be used to pay for diesel or something. No doubt some people on the board will object to giving the McGoverns money, but hopefully Derry the chairman will over-rule it. I won't offer until I know it will happen, because I don't want to hurt Jerome's feelings.

As Delia leaves, I settle down to try and catch up with my paper-work. I'm compiling the reports for the court of people on bail or temporary release who need to sign on at the garda station every day. This includes at least four of the Carmodys, the Traveller family up the Tuam road whose wild young bucks are constantly blotting their copybook, despite their grandfather's best efforts to calm them down.

The next moment, Darren comes bursting into my office. 'Sarge, problem!'

I sigh, putting down my pen. 'What's the matter now?'

'A disturbance up at Horsehead. Anya was on the phone. She says there's a load of people outside the gates, carrying placards and things. She doesn't know what they're at, but they have a loudspeaker and they're shouting about the land belonging to them, and the children are scared...'

Instantly I think of Ronnie Atkinson. He threatened to hold a protest about the pine martens – he must have rounded up a load of environmental evangelists. I jump to my feet in a fury.

'Come on.' I grab my hat and high-viz as well as stab-proof vests for both of us. Public order offences up to recently meant a fella drunk and roaring in the street, but these days you need to be more careful.

Nicola is off today, and Michael is in court. I call Delia to tell her there's trouble at Horsehead and that me and Darren are off to sort it out, that it sounds urgent, so will she come back and mind the station.

We jump into the squad car, and within minutes we arrive, parking parallel to a line of up to twenty cars.

Turns out it's not Ronnie and a few annoying crusties protesting on behalf of the pine martens. It's far, far worse. It's a protest of fifty, maybe sixty young men, none of whom I recognise – some are only teenagers – chanting and shouting outside the gates of Horsehead. Home-made signs saying 'Close the Borders' and 'Enough Is Enough' and 'Not Our War' are being waved aloft, and the rabble are being orchestrated by a big fella with a shaved head and a megaphone, standing on an orange crate, who keeps bellowing out slogans, including, 'The answer to war is not to destroy the environment!' and 'The answer to war is not more shooting!' and 'Our land, not their land!' So even though Ronnie and Elsie aren't here, you can see where this came from; they've been feeding red meat to these people whether they meant to or not, the pair of stupid eejits.

Darren goes to get out of the car, but I stop him.

'It's their right to protest on a public roadway, so they're not committing an offence. We need to just observe. Besides which, there are only two of us and many more of them. Call Michael, ask him if he's on his way back, and if so to join us. See if you can get hold of Nicola as well. It's her day off, but if she's prepared to come in, I'll find overtime for her. And call Ballinasloe, see if they can send anyone.'

Then I ring Anya. I have her number, since I went up to Horsehead on Sunday with an absolute sack of vouchers for SuperValu and the butcher's and Teresa's and the chemist's and all the local shops. People are so good, and they feel for these poor women, so they just want to help. When word got out that there was a gathering of vouchers – there wasn't really, but it kind of just happened – they all came up trumps. As I'm always saying, most people are really decent and kind and compassionate. But unfortunately, the ones who aren't tend to also be loud.

Anya answers after two rings.

'Is everyone OK up at the house?' I ask.

'Yes. We can hear the loudspeakers, but we've closed all the doors and windows and drawn the curtains. The kids are all in the kitchen, which is downstairs at the back, so they can't hear what's going on.' She sounds calm but frightened.

'All right. We're here observing, and we're not going anywhere. It's these people's legal right to protest on public property, I'm afraid, and until they break the law, we can't intervene. But we'll be watching carefully and have called for backup.' I pause. 'And, Anya, none of these people are locals. The people of this village support you all.'

'We thought that, Sergeant, thank you.'

What I don't tell her is that the backup so far is pretty thin; it's Michael and maybe Nicola. I can hear Darren on to the garda station in Ballinasloe. It doesn't sound very promising, and even if they do have a spare car, they're forty minutes away. The local station at Carragh was closed recently in the latest round of budget cuts, and the one in Toorbawn is only open four hours a week so they'll be no good either. I'll have to call this into Galway. I'll need backup fast if this escalates, and the rabble look a bit riled up.

'Oh, Sergeant Munroe.' Anya hesitates. 'My children are in the secondary school, but I can't leave to get them and I don't want them walking back into this, or any of the other children from the primary either.'

'Don't worry,' I reassure her. 'I'll call the primary school to keep the Ukrainian children back. And my husband is collecting my daughters from secondary, so I'll get him to pick up yours, and you can collect them at our place whenever these people disperse.'

'Thanks so much, Mags. They know Kate – she was Danika's buddy last week, and she helps with the hurling training of Sergei's class – so they'll be happy with that.'

'Grand. She can have a puc around in the garden with him.'

'Thank you so much –'

'Anya, stop thanking me. I owe you more than I can ever say for saving my mother's life. And I wish I could disperse these eejits. I've never seen them before in my life. I've no idea where they came from, but as I said, they are entitled to express their views unfortunately. We'll just hope they get bored soon.'

I end the call and consider my options while texting the school secretary to hold onto the Ukrainian kids and texting Kieran to pick up Anya's children. Several of the protesters are eyeing us now, and though the patrol car is sturdy and fortified, it's not armoured. I examine the nearest protesters for signs of weapons. It's cold for the time of year and they're all in bulky jackets, so it's hard to tell. I wonder where they sprung from.

'Did you get Nicola?' I ask Darren.

'She's gone to Donegal to see her aunt.'

'Is Michael finished in court?'

He shakes his head. 'Got put back. A defendant failed to appear, judge issued a bench warrant, so they're gone to find him.'

'Right.' That's that option out of the question so.

I pick up the radio to contact Galway, because if this escalates, Darren and I won't be able to do much, and they promise to be on standby if it does. Then I call Delia at the station on our TETRA system, the new inter-garda communications system that is actually secure, unlike the analogue system we used to have, which was a disaster.

She picks up. 'Hello, Sarge?'

I explain the situation, ask her to lock up and come down with the other garda car.

After that Darren and I just sit and watch as the young men parade up and down, shouting about how this is their country and Ireland is for the Irish, and Ireland is full, and no one will replace them. 'Go Green or Go Home!' reads one banner, which strikes me as oddly familiar...

'This is terrible, isn't it?' Darren is upset. 'I hate to see stuff like this. I thought we were better than this, kinder. But these people here... I don't know, Sarge, it feels like...like we're turning into a nation of people I don't recognise.'

I'm feeling the same way, looking at them. Ireland isn't like this. Not even Ronnie Atkinson, not even Elsie probably meant this to happen. On the whole we like to welcome people, and most of us don't have such short memories that we forgot how we went all over the world and were accepted.

'They are such a tiny minority, though.' I try to reassure him. 'And not one of them is a local, so that's encouraging. Most people realise that these women and children would much prefer to be at home with their men and their parents, but Vladimir Putin saw fit to destroy their country, and kill civilians in the process. Most decent-minded people here and around the world want to help. Even Jerome is talking about going over with a van of stuff and maybe picking some people up. Look at how much money was raised by the youth club. Look how well the kids are settling in school.'

He nods, but I see he's disillusioned. That can easily happen in this job. You see some stuff that would put your hair on end, and it would be the easiest thing in the world to believe the whole of humanity is going to hell in a handcart. But it's just not true, and you need to keep reminding yourself of that. I learnt it when I was a young guard on the border, and it's important that those under my command learn it too.

Darren and I have always got along really well, especially since I stood up for his and Delia's relationship to Delia's family, so we have some history of personal chats.

'Listen to me now, Darren. This is important.'

He looks at me quizzically.

'Because we meet people when things are going wrong, when they're either the perpetrator or victim of a crime, because we're the ones that need to go in when some man is battering his missus and kids, or take the computer off some creep who's downloading child porn, because we have to go to court and testify against people who make a living selling drugs and destroying lives, and yeah, because we have to watch and listen to bigoted, racist, cruel people like these who think it's OK to terrify little traumatised kids, we could easily get to a point where we think the whole world is gone to the dogs. But, Darren, it's not.'

I smile and he does too. A faint one but it's there.

'It just isn't. It's the biggest problem in any police force – morale. Because we see the worst of humanity – that's our job – it can colour your whole world view. And the longer you're in the job, the easier it is to believe everyone is bad, everyone is devious, a liar, mean, cruel, whatever. But they're not. If anything, as a species we're getting kinder. That's why injustice bothers us so much. Back years ago, they thought nothing of cruelty to kids, to animals, to anyone even a tiny bit different. You didn't dare to go against the rules. You had to stay in the herd and do as you were told. But nowadays we think differently.'

I hope he doesn't think I'm lecturing him, but it's important he understands.

'Very few people slap kids now, for example, where before everyone did. It's an offence to hurt an animal. If you said that years ago, they'd have laughed at you. Gay people, trans people, people of colour, people with a disability, Travellers – the discrimination was universal and accepted, not hidden. I'm not saying it's gone – we both know it isn't – but it's recognised as wrong now, and most decent people don't do it. The point is, the world isn't fixed, nothing close to it, but we're moving in the right direction by acknowledging that being unkind or discriminatory against people because of their gender, their ability, their colour, their sexuality is not OK. So that's progress. And we're supporting that progress. So yes, we need to deal with the drugs and the drunks and all the rest of it, but we're enforcing the slow but steady change towards a kinder world.'

'Lord hear us.' He winks and gives me a chuckle.

'Lord graciously hear us.' I give the traditional response at the end of a sermon.

Outside, the group of young men are drawing closer together, lowering their placards. The shouted slogans have stopped, and the man with the megaphone has jumped down off his soapbox and is mingling among the others. Hopefully they've decided to call it a day. Behind us, a car pulls up. Delia. Darren glances in the rear-view mirror with a wider smile. 'Ah, Sarge, I know, and I suppose you're right. Like, the idea that Delia would be a guard, a Traveller and a woman, was unheard of in the past, but here she is and well able.'

'And she's a very clever woman and a great asset to the force.'

'You won't believe this, Sarge, but my mam asked her down for the weekend. My parents' wedding anniversary is on Sunday week, and they're having a party at the golf club. Delia has been to visit once or twice, but this is a big family party, all the extended families and everything. I'm working on the Saturday and the party is on Sunday, but Delia's off all weekend, so Mam texted her to ask if she'd come down and help on Saturday to get the place ready and all the rest of it. Aine is going too and Barry's wife as well.'

'So she's in?' I grin.

'Like Flynn,' he confirms, and I can tell he's delighted. His family were dismayed to find he was going out with a Traveller girl, one who lived on a halting site in a caravan, but Delia has just been herself, and now it looks like they've finally warmed to her, despite Dora's fears.

'What's more, they've invited Jerome and Dora to the party,' Darren adds wryly, knowing the impact his words will have on me.

'Wow.' I'm not sure what to say about this. Delia is a true Traveller girl, but she knows how to dress like a settled person. Jerome and Dora definitely look like Travellers. They won't be changing their style for anyone, and I feel a bit wary on their behalf. Darren's parents and siblings might be all right about it, but the idea of Jerome and Dora in a fancy golf club down the country is a scary one. The potential for embarrassment is huge, because the sad truth is that if the McGoverns turned up somewhere like that without an invitation to a private party, they wouldn't be allowed in. It's how it is. I might have just been waxing lyrical about progress and kindness and how Ireland and everywhere is getting so much better, but the fact is, whole towns will shutter their pubs and shops and everyone will retreat behind closed doors when the Travellers arrive.

It would be easy to say that everyone is racist and that their ideas are based totally on prejudice, like these fellas parading up and down in front of Horsehead right now, but I always try to see the two sides to every story. Not all Travellers cause trouble, but some do. Not all publicans are racist, but if you've had your place smashed up in a Traveller fight and nobody will compensate you, can you blame them for locking the doors the next time? The trouble is, like in every place in the world, I'm sure – including in Ukraine, as I recently found out – Travelling people all get tarred with the one brush, even though like settled people, they're all different. The Carmodys are mostly fine, although there's four of them on remand right now. The McGoverns are never in trouble; they live by the law and get on with their community. But people just see Traveller and that's it.

'Will her parents go, do you think?' I ask.

He shrugged. 'I've no idea. Delia said it to her mother, but Dora says she'll have to wait for Jerome to decide.'

I smile. Yes, Jerome will decide and Dora will follow. It is how it is. I wonder if Delia will be so biddable if and when she and Darren get married. I doubt it somehow.

'Sarge!' It's Delia on the radio from behind us. 'I think they're on the move!'

'Call Galway for me!' I answer quickly, because she's right. I was so involved in talking to Darren, I've missed the slight giveaway movement, the turning of shaven heads towards the avenue. Before Darren's even had time to throw the car into gear, the escalation has begun, and that big thug of a leader is racing up the avenue towards the house with his nasty little followers streaming along behind him.

I call Anya. 'Stay inside and close the curtains. Do not come out or open any doors or windows.'

I'm afraid of flying glass inside the house if these people start throwing things. I can see some of them stooping for stones and fallen branches as they run. Darren drives after them, and Delia is behind us. I get on my police megaphone. 'Disperse, disperse. You are on private property. You are committing a criminal offence. You will be arrested under the Public Order Act. Leave at once, leave at once!'

A couple of them turn, making taunting gestures, and a big stone hits the windscreen. Although the glass is very tough, cracks radiate across it, and Darren swears and swerves, bypassing the two men who stopped to throw the stones, and the men pelt the sides of our car with more stones.

Up ahead is the house. The raging mob is nearly at the top of the avenue, and in the distance, I can see two women standing on the steps – it's Daniela holding a hatchet and Natalia wielding some kind of roofing tool. My heart is in my mouth. I get on the phone to Anya again. 'Tell Daniela and Natalia to get inside immediately. They're going to get killed if they try to defend the house like this!'

'I begged them not to do it, Mags –'

'Get them inside!'

As Darren screeches to a halt, I leap out of the car. 'Drop your weapons! Place your hands on your heads!' I shout into the megaphone.

None of them are paying any attention. They're lining up in a row, looking at the women on the steps, figuring out who is going to tackle them first. Upstairs, I see Klara's face peering out, and little Alina beside her. One of the young men hurls a stone. It hits the wall beside the window, and Klara and Alina flinch back and disappear before the next stone hits and shatters the glass.

'You're all under arrest!' I shout pointlessly as Darren and Delia take up positions on each side of me. I am the only one with a taser. I'm going to have to use it, though God knows what good it will do.

It crosses my mind that we could come to serious harm here, and I think of Kieran and the kids, and Mam and Joe, and everyone...

I step forward, taser in hand.

I barely have time to register the shouts and the thundering of hooves before a sulky comes charging around the side of the house at breakneck speed. Jerome must have come the back way, the way cleared by the council. He stands with his feet planted apart on the floor of the sulky. He is huge and dark and glinting with gold like a magnificent charioteer of old, holding the long reins of his horse in one hand and with the other flourishing a long whip that he cracks over the nearest shaved head. Within seconds, the protest is in chaos, as what looks like all of the McGoverns and quite a few of the Carmodys and an entire menagerie of ponies and horses, traps, sulkies and three motorbikes circle and charge. They have come from both directions, up the avenue and down the new path behind, their owners shouting and yelling and generally being intimidating, young bucks who are only too delighted to get involved in a bit of hellraising.

Normally such messing draws my admonishment, though they only do it every so often and usually on country roads with no houses, but today I am delighted to see them all. And while I'm not saying I know how those young Travellers knew to come up here today of all days with the Wyatt Earp act, I confess I suspect the hand of Delia. Jerome has turned and gone now, leaving the young bucks to it, and if I see him, I know he'll deny he was here, with that big gold-glinting smile of his.

I indicate to Darren and Delia to draw back behind the cars, out of the fray. No need for us to do anything. The protesters are trying to regroup, but I see Paddy Carmody and his cousin Wayne Ward jump bareback onto two enormous, venomous-looking horses, who rear up on their hind legs, hooves flailing dangerously, while their cousins turn their sulkies, sending gravel flying, and flank the horses, charging straight at the attempted gathering, sending the protesters scattering once more. Expertly the Travelling lads round them up like sheep and drive them back down the avenue to the road, and then I can hear their whoops and raucous laughing as they depart. They won't hang around for me to have any issues with the tax on their motorbikes or the fact that four of them were supposed to sign on at the station this morning as per the terms of their bail agreement and never showed.

On the steps, Daniela and Natalia lay down their weapons.

My phone rings, and it's Alina. 'We're hiding. We're scared. Is there more going to come?'

'No, everyone's gone,' I say with a smile. In the background, out in the road, I can hear car engines starting. 'They're leaving for good, don't worry. Jerome and his family saw them off.'

'Jerome came to help us?' she asks incredulously.

'Looks like it,' I say.

'Mama, Jerome came to help us!' I can hear her saying to Klara in English, before breaking into Ukrainian.

Anya then comes on the phone. 'I heard what you said to Alina, and now Daniela and Natalia are here – they're telling us all about it. The Irish Roma came and saved us! They are magnificent. You know, in Ukraine the Roma are fighting the Russians? Nobody expected them to do so, but they are. Maybe these Roma are their brothers.'

I've been listening to a podcast about Ukraine Roma, and they're nothing to do with Irish Travellers. The Roma are a people who came from India originally, and Irish Travellers are indigenous to this country. But I don't correct her. 'They have their moments,' I smilingly agree.

'Will they be back, though, the protesters?'

'I doubt it, not after that reception. I'll do some digging, see if I can find out who they are. I know we have dedicated units looking at the rise of this kind of thing. They seemed well organised, and I didn't recognise any of them. They're not from Ballycarrick, so it wasn't local people.' I really don't think Ronnie and Elsie meant this to happen. 'Leave it with me. I'll try to find out who we're dealing with. I'd say they're heading back to where they came from with their tails between their legs right now.'

'Do you really think it's safe? We're all a bit rattled in here.'

'Let me take a spin around, make sure they're gone. Hold tight for another little while. I'll ring you shortly.'

Darren turns the car, and we drive down the avenue, followed by Delia. The cars that lined the road outside when we arrived are all gone, and there's no sign of anyone, protesters or Travellers.

I text Anya. *Coast clear. No rush to pick your lads up. Stay there if you need to.*

She texts back. *Thanks, Mags. I'll just stay for a short while. People very upset.*

*No bother. My husband working from home this afternoon, and Kate will be delighted to have them to play with.*

As we're driving back to the station, I say to Darren, 'So how's your faith in humanity coming along?'

And he grins and says, 'Not too bad, Sarge, not too bad.'

# CHAPTER 23

*R*onnie's constituency office is on Main Street, past the turnoff to the Market Square. He's here – his car's outside. He's had it customised to look like it's covered in leaves, and emblazoned down both sides is 'Go Green or Go Home'. It's the same slogan as was on the banner outside Horsehead. It was definitely his Twitter account that set this ball rolling, inadvertently or not.

I've already had a stern word with Elsie. I went to her house first thing this morning after the school run and told her all about the nasty little organisation she brought down on Horsehead. I'd already checked with the dedicated unit, and the young men who turned up in Ballycarrick are from a very unpleasant ultra-right-wing organisation that has been wreaking havoc at refugee centres up and down the country. Two of their leading members are facing charges for grievous bodily harm of a young black student, while another is banned from Twitter and Facebook for hate speech.

Elsie is closing her Twitter account, and I'm glad to say she seems genuinely ashamed and embarrassed. She's frightened herself, I think, with the power of her words. She's always been one to throw around accusations and complaints without a thought that they might land somewhere and do serious damage, and normally they don't land hard, not in Ballycarrick, where everyone knows her, but Twitter is a different matter. On Twitter, things multiply and multiply, and accusations that seem of little weight can turn into wrecking balls.

When I walk into Ronnie's office, he looks up with a self-satisfied smirk. 'What can I do for you, Sergeant Munroe?'

'You know what you can do for me, Ronnie?' I say coldly. 'You can stop going on Twitter making libellous accusations about a community of refugees who deserve all our compassion.'

'I...I...' He turns puce and tries to talk over me, but I talk over him instead.

'You may call yourself Mr "I Care" on Twitter' – I make air quotes, though I'm sure he won't get the reference; people never recognise unflattering portraits of themselves – 'but your tweets have brought some of the nastiest men in all of Ireland to our doorstep. You've endangered the lives of innocent women and children, not to say my own life and those of my officers.'

'I...I... What do you... I had nothing to do with that group, and I certainly didn't –'

'Not deliberately maybe, but people like that latch onto the kind of nonsense you've been spouting. They take it and run with it, and before we know it, people who desperately need a bit of kindness and compassion shown to them are terrified.'

'But what can I do? I didn't want that to happen, of course I didn't, but –'

'What can you do?' I ask, deliberately misunderstanding him. 'Well, I would begin with removing that slogan from your car outside, because it is now associated with the most racist right-wing group in Ireland today. And if I were you, I would go about scrubbing my social media accounts of anything that could look like incitement to violence.'

'I have never done anything violent in my life!' He manages to get a word in, because I've had to pause for a fraction of a second to take a breath. 'I am anti-war! I am anti every kind of violence! I haven't a racist bone in my body, so don't you dare come in here –'

'Oh, talk to Elsie,' I say bitterly, deciding not to waste my breath explaining things all over again.

'Elsie?' Again, he flushes puce, but in a different kind of way, embarrassment rather than anger this time. It's a horrible thought, but the epiphany I had the other day, about him and Elsie being an item, looks horribly like it might be true.

I need a cup of tea to settle my nausea. I make my escape.

Next stop, the McGoverns, where hopefully Dora will make the tea.

* * *

JEROME LOOKS up from the chicken coop as I swing the car into the site and come to a halt. He straightens up to his full commanding height, his expression a bit uncertain. He's wondering will I give him a hard time about what happened at Horsehead yesterday.

I touch my finger to my garda hat in a mock salute before pulling the cap off my head like I always do and tossing it onto the passenger seat beside me.

As I climb out of the car, Olivia runs over to greet me. 'Uncle Jerome is going to Poland. That lady Klara's mam is there, and she wants to come here to be with Klara but she can't 'cause they've no way of getting here. So Uncle Jerome is going to drive our van over to get her and bring her back.'

'Isn't he very good to do that?' I say, and Olivia beams with pride. My heart breaks a little for her. Traveller kids so rarely are given reasons to be proud of who they are and what they do. It isn't right. Ballycarrick might be better these days than other places, but still there is a terrible stigma against them.

'So you're definitely going to the Polish border with Ukraine? Is that right?' I ask him as he comes over.

'He is.' Dora is standing on the steps of her caravan with her arms folded, looking stern and not at all in a tea-making mood.

'You don't want him to go?' I smile over at her.

'What I want don't have nothin' to do with it. He'll do as he pleases,' she says, and turns and stalks into the depths of the caravan, bristling.

Jerome winks at me. 'She thinks I have an eye for your one Klara,' he says, without guile.

'And have you?' I ask, with a trace of a smile.

'Ara, Mags, my days of chasing *beores* are well behind me.' He grins back at me to reveal a gold tooth.

'That's not a no, Jerome,' I say admonishingly. 'She has a husband over there, you know?'

'She has. And there's not been a word from him. Maybe the Russians got him.'

'I hope not.'

He grins again. 'Sure, I'll go anyway.'

'And you better reassure Dora that you're not putting your eye on young Ukrainians, or she won't be happy.'

He laughs, a deep rumbling sound. 'Ara now, Mags, don't be at me. It's only that Klara has her mother over there, hurt like, from the bombs and that, and I'm fond of the little girl, so I'll do her mother a turn for her sake. There's more than the mother there. Some of the other women up in Horsehead have relations trying to get here too, so I'll have a van full with the help of God.'

I smile and give up on him. 'Well, it's very kind of you. There's money in the youth club fund for diesel, and they say you can have whatever you need for the trip – ferry tickets, that kind of thing.' I've checked, and the youth club committee, which is chaired by the former primary school principal Derry McLoughlin, one of the most sensible people in the village, has agreed to support Jerome's mission.

'And they'll give money for safekeeping to the likes of us?' he asks, and I see it in him as I see it in Delia, though with her less often now, that mix of belligerence and vulnerability.

'They will.' I nod. 'It was a fundraiser for the refugees here, anything they want or need, so surely bringing their family members here to join them comes under that umbrella?'

He shrugs.

'Oh, and, Jerome, Derry was saying that a contact he has at the

Polish camp near the border explained how there are lots of women with babies and young kids there, their husbands are fighting and they don't want to be too far away from them, so we thought maybe bringing medicines, baby supplies maybe? '

'We'll bring whatever he wants us to bring,' the big man agrees gruffly. 'Sure, it doesn't have to be just the van. We've a couple of jeeps too. Maybe there's others we can bring back.'

'Who else would drive?'

'Myself, Billy and Jimmy. We'll leave Pecker – he's too small yet. We've two jeeps and a minibus.'

'Right.' This sounds promising. 'Will you call to Derry so, and he'll arrange the stuff? And the tickets and the fuel card and whatever else you'll need. You don't need me to help – you and Derry can work fine together.'

'Grand.' He speaks gruffly, but I can tell he's pleased to be part of the town.

* * *

BACK AT THE STATION, Klara is just leaving. She's on her way to another cleaning job, at Lavinia Moran's house. Lavinia thinks she's a saint, employing a Ukrainian woman even though 'she hasn't a word of English, the poor creature'.

'Did you manage to contact your mother to tell her someone is coming to pick her up?' I ask her, through Google Translate.

'Yes, but impossible for Jerome to go in Ukraine. She need to reach border. But it is many days in bus from her apartment and leg in cast. And so sad – my father.'

'Poor woman. And any word of your husband?'

I'm dreading the answer, but her face lights up. 'Yes. He injured, not bad, clinic at front getting big boom.'

'A bomb?' I ask.

'Explosion, patients die, very bad, but he OK, a cut.'

'Oh, Klara, I'm so sorry...' I say aloud. The poor woman. I just can't imagine.

'No, he is alive.' She thinks Google Translate has failed to get her meaning across. 'Alive,' she repeats slowly, with a big smile.

I smile back at her and nod. But it wasn't that Google Translate had got it wrong; it was just... Well, I suppose good news is relative in a war zone.

She adds, through the app, 'He not able to work as doctor for month. He lose two fingers.'

I try not to look too horrified. She seems perfectly calm about it all. I suppose what would be an absolute catastrophe in rural Ireland is a mere scratch in eastern Ukraine. 'Perhaps he can also reach the border, find Jerome?'

She nods politely. 'Yes, yes.' But I can tell she is humouring me. She doesn't believe rescue is possible. That her husband is alive with eight fingers is enough for now.

'As I say, anything we can do,' I finish lamely.

She nods and smiles and walks away down the street. She has vouchers for SuperValu, which Anya passed on to her. Horsehead is a shining example of community in action.

# CHAPTER 24

On Saturday, Kate and Kieran come strolling down the street to meet me after work. Kieran had to take my car to the garage for a service and we've arranged this, so I'm expecting them. Kate runs to hug me when she sees me, and though she's twelve now, I lean down and breathe in the scent of my child. Precious, precious child, safe and sound, and a father with all ten fingers.

'Hello, Kit Kat, how was your day?'

'Good. I got picked for the camogie team for the Under 14s for the county final on Sunday even though I'm only twelve because Ciara Kennedy fractured a bone in her foot. Isn't it brilliant?'

'Well, not for poor Ciara, I suppose, but...' I glance at Kieran, who grins.

'Ah, she's grand. She has her cousin's wedding in Lanzarote next week anyway, so she's delighted with the excuse to go to that instead. Chopper is raging, but sure he'll get over it,' Kate says airily. 'Can we call into Ellie and Granny? Like now?'

Mam is out of hospital and has declared herself cured, though at least she's agreed to let Ellie open up the shop for her on Saturdays so she can allegedly take the whole day off once in a while. I'll believe that when I see it. Mam's idea of taking a day off is going in after lunch, and poor Joe is still tearing out what's left of his hair.

'What about Teresa's? I thought we were going for cream cakes?' I'd especially arranged my shift to finish at four with this in mind.

'But Ellie and Granny want to see you, Mam.'

I sigh and allow Kate to walk me past Teresa's. She tucks her arm into mine companionably as Kieran strolls on ahead, enjoying the warm day.

'Annika and Darya in my class are able to speak really good English now. They can curse in English and everything.'

She giggles and I do too.

'I'm sure Miss Cullinane isn't happy about that.'

'She didn't hear them, and it was just when St Patrick's scored in the camogie match and we were one point ahead. They both said, "Ah, sh…" You know it.'

I nod.

'At the same time, in real Galway accents! We were all laughing.'

I suppose if those poor traumatised girls from Ukraine are exercised enough about a camogie match in rural Galway, then a few swear words aren't the end of the world.

We pass Dillon's Menswear, which is closed because Joe is trying to lead his mulish wife by example, and cross the street to Marie's Boutique.

I'm surprised to find Sharon in here; I wasn't expecting to see her. 'Hi, Shar!'

'Ah well, if it isn't little Miss Fix It,' Mam says to Kate, and my daughter beams.

'What's this all about?' I ask, wondering why my mother, daughter and best friend are looking so pleased with themselves. Ellie's beaming as well. She is leaning on the counter, and there's a row of champagne flutes there. And is that a bottle of Moët Joe has in his hand as he emerges from the storeroom at the back of the shop?

'I'm sorry, what is this?' I look helplessly at Kieran, who shrugs. He seems as genuinely surprised as I am. 'Did I miss a birthday or something? Was I in a coma for years and it's my sixtieth? Is someone getting married? Sharon, are you...'

'Nope! Not yet. Well, will I tell her or will you?' Sharon asks Mam.

'You can. I want to see her face.' Mam winks.

'Well,' Sharon says slowly, turning to face me, 'you are looking at the soon-to-be new owner of Marie's Boutique.'

'What?' I'm so confused.

'And it's all down to my darling goddaughters.' Shar beams at Kate and Ellie. She's not really godmother to both of them, only to Ellie, but she's as good as a godmother to Kate. My sister Lori is supposed to be Kate's, but she's useless. She couldn't remember a birthday if it was tattooed on her forehead backwards so she could read it in the mirror; she barely remembers Christmas.

'Start at the start. I don't understand,' I say, looking first at Ellie and then at Kate, who both giggle wildly at my baffled expression.

'You tell her, Kate. It was your idea, not mine,' says Ellie, putting her arm around her little sister. Kate glows. She'll never admit it, but she thinks Ellie is the coolest person on the planet, and her big sister's approval means more to her than anyone else's, including mine and Kieran's.

'Well, it was like this, Mam. You know how you were saying to Dad the other night, Mam, about how Granny Marie is like Delaney's donkey...'

I wince at Mam apologetically, but she just laughs. She knows herself well enough.

'And you love her so much and so does Joe, and he wants to take her for holidays and cruises and stuff as fast as he can before she dies...'

Mam snorts with laughter and tries to turn it into a cough. Joe is pure scarlet. Kieran is wiping his eyes, and I don't know whether to laugh or cry. Oh, Kit Kat.

'And also you were saying how Sharon was going for loads of jobs in fashion but she can't get one because she's not a teenager any more...'

I make big 'sorry' eyes at Sharon, who is trying really hard not to laugh.

'So I put two and two together. Sharon looks great all the time, for her age like, and she loves clothes. She and Ellie spent ages at the hospital while Granny was asleep talking about teenage stuff, like how GAA kids wear leggings and Puffa jackets and theatre kids wear those huge t-shirts and corduroy dungarees...'

'I like dungarees,' murmurs Sharon, winking at Ellie.

'And Granny Marie won't trust someone not in the family to have the shop, but Sharon is her other daughter, she always says, 'cos Sharon kind of lived in your house when she was growing up...'

Out of the mouth of babes, isn't that what they say?

'So I made a WhatsApp group and added Granny Marie and Sharon and Ellie, and I said Sharon should buy the shop and then Granny would be happy knowing that there would still be a boutique in Ballycarrick, because all the women in Ballycarrick need a place to buy clothes for weddings and funerals and dates and things. And Joe will be happy 'cause Granny can go on cruises, and Sean will be happy 'cause Sharon can pick him up from school, so it's a great idea. And they've agreed and they're doing it.'

'Are you serious?' I stare at my mother and Sharon. I'm delighted at the prospect, but this is such a big...such a... Actually, come to think of it, it's really not that big a change at all. I can be in here just as often, just with my best friend instead of Mam, gossiping and having a coffee and a cream cake from Teresa's... My stomach gives a hollow rumble at the thought.

'We sure are serious,' Sharon says happily. 'I can't wait. Trevor and I are going to move into his mam's place and sell my house – it only reminds me of creepy Boylan anyway – and we'll use the money to buy this place from Marie.'

'And are *you* sure, Mam?' I say, amazed she's agreed.

Mam is perched on a high stool at the counter, looking as well turned out as ever. That horrible lilac-grey look has gone off her skin. Her tests have all come back fine, and she's as peaches and cream as ever. The clot was a one-off, although she's taking statins now. 'Never been surer of anything. When I got Kate's messages, I don't know, something clicked. Maybe it was only then I realised how much Joe wants to spend time with me.' She smiles fondly at her husband and blows a kiss to her little granddaughter. 'You know, before I pop my clogs.'

'Well, aren't you the clever woman thinking of that solution?' I say to Kate, and my darling girl basks in the glory of her accomplishment.

Joe cracks open the champagne then, and a bottle of pop each for the girls, though they both get a sip of champagne as well, and to my pleased delight, Sharon opens a silver box of Teresa's cream cakes. I'm not going to be missing out on my Saturday treat after all.

'To Marie's Boutique!' Joe says, once everyone has a glass.

'Speech!' says Kieran, who up to now has been watching the whole thing in amazed silence.

'Speech, Granny!' urges Ellie.

'Speech! Speech! To Marie's Boutique!'

'Ah, will you all stop.' Mam smiles. 'I don't know what you'll call it, Sharon pet, but it won't be Marie's anyway. That's over now, and you know this little shop served me well.'

There is a hint of melancholy as she looks around her little empire, but she carries bravely on. 'When Milo got sick, God rest him, it gave us an income, and then when he died, it reared our girls. And like you, Sharon, I had to be around for my daughters, and this little shop gave me the flexibility I needed. I never made a fortune, but I did all right. And I thought I'd have an awful time letting it go, but no. I'm ready, and I know I need to spend more time with Joe. You've been coming into my house since you were knee-high to a grasshopper, Sharon Joyce, so I'm just thrilled it's you who'll be here now, and I wish you the very best of luck with it. I only have one request.'

'Go for it,' Sharon says with a broad grin.

'I have a wonderful Saturday girl, very capable and honest and hard-working, so I'd love you to keep her on.' Mam winks at Ellie.

'Would she happen to be my goddaughter too?' Shar asks, nudging Ellie.

'She would,' Ellie says primly.

'Well, I can't fire my own godchild, I suppose...' Sharon pretends to mull it over. 'Yes, OK, I'll keep her on, providing she keeps on coming up with the right lines in teenage fashion.'

'And you can employ her sister when I'm old enough,' Kate pipes up gleefully. 'I've got ideas too.'

'Oh, I can see the three of us sipping cocktails over in the Samovar every Saturday, plotting how to open our chain of boutiques across the west of Ireland,' Sharon jokes.

'Sounds like an excellent plan,' Mam says cheerfully.

I glance at Ellie to see how she's taking this banter. I'm nervously expecting her to pout and make some scathing comment about how no way on earth is she going to be trapped in Ballycarrick for life. But she just grins at me, and I grin back. She's so much more mature than she was before she did all that work on Horsehead. She has turned into a capable and smart young lady before our eyes, and she doesn't seem to hate Ballycarrick any more.

At the same time, and it's the other side of the same coin, I know she won't be staying here. She will want to see the world, and that's OK. She's grown so much this year. I can see the adult in her now, and it makes me less afraid for her.

Sharon checks her watch. 'Oh, it's ten to six. I've to go. Sean has his buddy Artem – he's one of the Ukrainian kids – over for pizza, and they've hurling training at half six. I'll talk to you over the weekend, everyone.' She downs the last dribble of her champagne and rushes off.

As Kate and Ellie clean up and wash glasses, and Marie tots up the till and turns off the lights, Joe murmurs something to Kieran about maybe another celebratory drink in the Samovar, and Kieran looks keen. But the girls want to go to Granny Marie's for *Strictly Come Dancing*, their weekly addiction. I can't understand it myself, a bunch of so-called celebrities doing foxtrots and cha-chas in a studio that looks like an explosion in a glitter factory, but my mother and daughters are obsessed.

Last Saturday Kate explained to me how some fella who got bronze in the Olympics did a tango, but his centre of gravity was too high and his *caminadas* and *molinetes* were off. And apparently, some woman called S, no other letters, just S, and she is an 'influencer' – give me strength – did an incredible quickstep because her *chassés* and her lock steps were perfect. It is like another language. My mother is a brilliant dancer and so are my girls. I, on the other hand, look like a wheelie bin being shoved around a dance floor, and Kieran isn't light on his feet either, so we avoid dancing at all costs.

We all leave the shop together, and Marie is the one to turn the sign on the door to 'Closed' and lock up. She lingers a while as we wait for her on the corner. She's having a private moment.

I drop off Mam and the girls to Mam's place, and then I go to the Samovar to join Joe and Kieran. I have a glass of red wine served by Olga, as her fiancé and brothers fight at the front, and I think how good it is to be alive.

# CHAPTER 25

*W*e're all gathered, Gearoid, Aoife, Orla, Kieran and Kevin. Catriona said she can't make it, and nobody is surprised. She's backing away from the whole thing. Fair enough, I suppose. Each to their own, as my mother always says.

Nora is hiding in the bedroom; she's refused to come out and watch. I'm in the loo when the instantly recognisable signature tune comes on, flooding the whole house, and I hurry to the living room.

There he is, Ray Lonergan, doing the first piece to the camera, looking all white-toothed and suave.

'So, ladies and gentlemen, you know this is a special edition of *The Nightshow*, to launch the initiative we are calling Operation Spotlight. And our aim is to do just that, to shine a spotlight into the dark – some would say the sinister dark corners of our past – and to do that with open hearts and compassion for our fellow citizens.'

I take my seat, gripped by his words. He is sincere, I can see it, and sometimes he really isn't, so it's an obvious change.

'As some of you will know, I chose to come forward and go public about my own story some time ago, though like most people affected by this, I did so with some grave reservations. And on balance it was the right choice. But this show is not about me or my story, except to say I was one of those babies. I was adopted by a wonderful family, and I did make contact with my birth mother before she passed away. She was a fierce campaigner for the rights of mothers and children. But tonight, ladies and gentlemen, I want to open the floor to you, the people of Ireland.'

The camera moves to a large call centre, showing people sitting at computers with headsets on.

'We have a full room of people willing and ready to hear your story, anonymously if you wish, but it will help more if you can give details. And so if you were affected in any way, not just the mothers and their children, though obviously they are front and centre here, but if you have any useful information that could be used to help the mothers and babies to find each other, if you delivered bread to those places, if you worked in the birth registry, indeed if you were a member of a religious order, or even a lay person who worked for them, if you took photos of the babies, processed passports, whatever role you had, please, please, come forward. I promise you no judgement, no criticism. We just need to know. Just ring the number on your screen now.'

A wide band of ticker tape crosses the screen with a freephone number.

'If you don't feel you can talk to someone in person, you can text to 55345, also for free.'

He then sits at his usual spot, and I see a panel of people, some of whom I recognise. A singer, two sportspeople – one of our national soccer team and a runner, I think – a woman who presents a farming show on TV and two other men I don't recognise, but that wouldn't mean they're not famous. I don't follow celebrity TV so don't have a clue.

As each of them tells their story, some happy, others not, we are all glued to it. Every so often they play someone who has rung in to the freephone number and is willing to go live on air, and Ray asks them their story.

There is a thread of tragic sameness, just like Nora's story. Girls whipped away at speed, by family or clergy, to some institution run by nuns, hard physical work, shame, a sense that they alone were entirely to blame for their situation, nobody else, regardless of the circumstances, babies born and then taken away, never to be found again. The searches, the alcoholism, the dependence on medication, the failures to make lasting relationships afterwards, the lies, the secrets, the fear at being found out, the dread, the longing, the pain. There is a depressing universality to it all.

One nun rings in and makes the point that they and the rest of the congregations charged with running the institutions – I refuse to call them homes as there was nothing homely about them – were not scouring the ditches of Ireland looking for pregnant girls, but that the girls were brought to them, by their fathers, their priests, sometimes the baby's father, and that they were cleaning up society's dirty secret. She claims that nobody wanted those girls or their babies, that society in general was to blame, not the religious orders.

While I agree with her up to a point, I think angrily to myself how it doesn't explain the gratuitous cruelty, the meting out of emotional, physical and psychological torture, the refusal to tell the truth, even now, all these years later. I hold Kieran's hand; he is by my side on the sofa.

The guests go on. The runner was born in a home, but her mother managed to escape with her and married her boyfriend and together they raised their daughter, who went on to become a European champion. The soccer player found his birth mother, but she didn't want to have contact, despite his adopted brother finding his birth mother and forging a good relationship. He talks about how hard that was for him and his adopted parents, the rejection twice over.

I wish Nora could hear this. I wish she would come here to watch with us.

Then something really strange happens. Ray appears to get some prompt in his earpiece, and then he says, 'As you know, we are doing this to share stories, but just because the people we're mostly discussing tonight are in the public eye doesn't mean their stories are more important or more valid. We just want to find a path for everyone affected to tell their stories. The producer of this programme is a man who is often to be found behind a camera, in the cutting room, in hair or make-up. He's a jack of all trades and master of them all. He's a veteran of the broadcasting industry and responsible for much of the quality content you've come to expect from RTÉ over the years, but he's not a person who likes to be in front of a camera. He leaves that to the empty vessels like myself.'

His annoying self-deprecating laugh somehow doesn't annoy me so much tonight.

'But he is so moved by the stories we are hearing tonight, and so behind what we are trying to do, it seems that he wants to add his voice to the hundreds who have spoken to our team tonight. Ladies and gentlemen, can I ask you to give a very warm *Nightshow* welcome to our producer, Oilibhéar MacElroy.'

The audience claps, but nobody in the Munroes' sitting room speaks or moves. Because the man who appears into the studio could be my husband, Kieran.

* * *

WE SIT in total silence as he tells his story.

'So, Oilibhéar, thank you for coming to this side of the camera. I know it's not your natural habitat.' Ray smiles, and the man looks slightly uncomfortable.

It is uncanny. Kieran had been dark, but he is much greyer now. This man is completely grey but has the same hairstyle, short on the back and sides, a bit longer on top, brushed back. He has the same straight eyebrows and wears a stubbly beard. Kieran doesn't bother shaving during the week, pure laziness, unless we are going somewhere, and his beard grows out red. This man's beard is red. Well, OK, a lot of Irishmen have red beards, but his eyes, though. Kieran looks very like Nora in the eyes, a very distinctive dark blue, and this Oilibhéar MacElroy's are exactly that same colour. He is tall and broad like Kieran too, slightly less muscular, the build of a television producer not of a roofer, but honestly, the image of him...

'I know.' The producer smiles. 'But I suppose I have a kind of rule that I won't ask people to do things I wouldn't do myself.' He speaks with the soft lilting accent of the northwest; Donegal is my guess.

'Well, Oilibhéar, you and I have discussed this topic privately several times, but for the viewers and our studio audience, can you tell us your story?'

The man takes a deep breath, as if steadying himself. 'Well, I haven't managed to locate my birth mother, despite trying. I know I was born in Bessborough in Cork, on the 15th of October, 1965. I was there until just before Christmas of that year, when I was adopted by a wonderful couple, the MacElroys, and they gave me a wonderful life. They are both dead now, but if it ever comes to pass that I find my birth mother, or if she's watching tonight' – he shrugs and gives a small smile – 'I want her to know that I hold nothing in my heart but gratitude for the life I was given.'

Clearly Ray and this man have a real connection as friends, because the compassion and support from one man to the other is almost palpable through the screen.

'And do you know anything else about the circumstances of your birth?'

'Not really. My birth certificate says Murphy for my mother and no father is listed, but as we've discussed often, there were a lot of Murphys coming out of the homes. It was a sort of generic surname the mothers were compelled to use for their children.'

'And you don't know anything else?'

'No. I went there, accessed the records, but that was all there was, no address, nothing. The only other piece of information I have – and this is something my mother, my adopted mother, I mean, thought she overheard but couldn't swear to – but she said the day she and my father came to collect me, the nurse brought another baby down by mistake. The nun in charge said to that person – my mother thought she overheard this, but as I say, she couldn't be sure – but she thought she heard the nun say, "Not that one, he's spoken for. Bring Oliver down."'

It's eerie for me, hearing someone who looks so like Kieran speaking in a Donegal accent.

'So that's why I was christened Oilibhéar, the Irish for Oliver. My parents were from the Donegal Gaeltacht –'

Kevin pauses the TV, and Oilibhéar MacElroy is frozen on screen. Nobody says anything, but Kieran is squeezing my hand so hard it hurts.

'That's my son.' Kevin Munroe eventually speaks with a deep resounding certainty, and nobody has a word to contradict him. The birth date seems right. Everything else is correct. We've found Oliver.

'Kieran, he's the image of you,' Aoife says when she has recovered.

Within seconds the Munroes are all talking together, commenting on how like Kieran he is. Gearoid, the only other boy, took after the Munroe side, more slender and fine featured, like Aoife and Orla, though Catriona looks like Kieran too, and like who seems for sure to be her older brother.

Meanwhile Kevin heaves himself up from his chair. His hip is much better, but he's still walking with a stick. Orla jumps up to help him, but he waves her away and walks heavily out of the room and down the corridor to his wife's bedroom.

'Nora,' we hear him say, not in the timid tones of the Kevin of yore but loud and firm. 'Nora, you have to come and see this.'

Silence.

He pounds on the door. 'Nora!'

Silence.

Then we hear the door unlock and open, and muttered voices, his pleading, hers flat. The door closes, though I don't hear the key turn.

We hear Kevin's feet and stick come back down the corridor, and he re-enters the room, his face expressionless.

'Dad?' asks Gearoid gently.

'She won't come.' He restarts the TV and sits, listening to Oilibhéar continue to speak. I sneak a glance at his face. I'm expecting him to look happy and triumphant, but he is ashen and grim. And I realise this is nothing to him without Nora by his side. He loves his wife. He wants her to acknowledge what is theirs.

'So what now?' Ray Lonergan says to Oilibhéar MacElroy.

'Well, like everyone else who has called in, I'll leave open what lines of communication I can. I have registered with the National Registry and have given them my details, how to contact me and all the rest of it, and now all I can do is hope.' He shrugs and smiles.

I like this man. There seems to be something very genuine about him, though maybe it's because he looks so like my husband.

He leaves the stage then, and Ray moves onto another one of the panel, a man I don't recognise with an American accent who is the head of the Central Bank. He begins his story of adoption to the United States, how his family there told him that he was adopted from Ireland, and while he was cared for, he never felt like he belonged there. So as a student he applied for Irish citizenship, got it and came to university here...

Kevin reaches for the remote control. He doesn't care about some man from the Central Bank. He wants to get in the car this moment and drive to the studio in Dublin.

'Wait, wait,' urges Kieran. 'There might be something more.' But though he captures the remote control from his father, I can't hear Ray any more. There is too much talking going on in the room about what to do next; should they phone up themselves; no, they won't be listened to; somehow they have to force Nora to watch this on playback...

I go and sit on a footstool right up against the screen, listening.

Ray has finished interviewing the banker and says, 'Well, this is a night of developments, and I want to thank you all for watching and for contributing. This certainly feels like a whole-nation effort. Now we are going to go back to another live call, someone who has rung in to our helpline. The number is on your screen now, and our operators are standing by to take your call. But right now we are going to a lady who has just contacted the helpline and would like to say something. Hello, caller, what would you like to say?'

'Hello, Ray.' The hesitant female voice is barely audible, and my heart turns over. I shush the family who are all talking over each other, but they ignore me.

'Be quiet!' I command in my garda voice, the voice of authority, and everyone stops.

'My name is Nora, and I believe Oilibhéar is my son...' We hear Nora's quavering voice in the silence.

It's Kieran who goes down the hallway first, his father and siblings behind him, and then me. They open the door of Nora's bedroom. The TV on the wall is paused, Ray Lonergan in a very unflattering pose, his mouth wide open, and Nora is sitting on the bed, her fingers holding the mobile phone white. Her other hand is gripping the duvet. She is like a coiled spring, but she is doing it.

She is claiming her son, and I am so proud of her.

# CHAPTER 26

e're back home. Mam and Joe have gone back to their place; they'd been babysitting the girls for us. Kieran calls Kate and Ellie in from the kitchen and tells them both to sit.

In a few sentences, he tells them about Nora, about Kevin and about the baby boy who seemed to have been lost to the mists of time, how miraculously he is now found and how they have a new uncle.

'What? Wait…what? Nana Nora had a baby in one of those places, and Granda is the father, but she never told him before now?' Ellie is disbelieving and I don't blame her. 'I thought those places were for girls who weren't married?'

'Nana and Granda weren't married at the time, and back then that was very shameful in people's minds that a man and a woman would have sex before marriage,' I explain.

Kate blushes at the mention of sex. Ellie is fine talking about it, and I am always very open with them about such matters, but Kate is naturally prudish. She is funny in that she says she would have been perfectly happy to live long ago when people were less 'touchy-feely', as she puts it.

'Then why didn't they get married right away?' she asks.

'His parents didn't like Nana because her family were working class. They had a fish-and-chip shop in a part of Dublin that wasn't very wealthy,' Kieran explains. 'And his were a bit more well-to-do. His father worked for the bishop, and his mother was a nurse, and so they sent him off to university. Once her parents and his found out a baby was on the way, they made sure she was whisked off to the convent before she could tell him.'

Kate's brow furrows, and I can almost hear the cogs of her brain.

'So Granda's family thought Nana wasn't good enough because her family had a shop, and they were horrible to her because of that?'

'Yes, Kit Kat, that's more or less it,' Kieran says sadly.

'Well, that's the way Nana Nora's been with Mam all the time,' says Ellie crushingly. 'And she says kind of mean things about Granny Marie's shop too, and says she hardly ever buys anything there, that's it's fine for a small town, like, but she prefers Brown Thomas in Galway.'

'And Granny Marie has way nicer things than they do,' Kate adds loyally.

I smile. Kate adores her granny, but even Mam would draw the line at saying her stock was superior to Ireland's leading designer retail outlet.

Kieran looks sad and a bit conflicted, and I wonder which way he'll jump. Defend his mother or acknowledge Kate is right? I don't know why I second-guess him; he's rarely given me reason to.

'That's true, love,' he says with a sigh, 'and I wish she wasn't that way. She is snobbish, and you're right, she sometimes was mean to Mam over the years, but will I tell you something?'

Both girls nod.

'Your granddad ran off there for a while when Nana finally told him about Oliver. He was so upset. And she wouldn't talk to me or Gearoid or any of your aunties about where he had gone. But she did tell your mam. So for all her snobbishness and dreaming up nonsense about being higher up than other people, in the end, the one she trusted the most was your mam, and that tells us all we need to know about how she feels about her.'

'Everyone trusts Mam, that's true.' Ellie says it as a matter of fact, and I am taken aback. Compliments from my fifteen-year-old daughter are still rare and to be cherished.

'But how come she never told Granda afterwards, when she was let out of the horrible place?' Kate is still puzzled. 'Like they could have got married and then asked for the baby back, couldn't they?'

I feel a surge of love for my youngest that she is so utterly confused, and I hate that it's necessary to pollute my lovely girl's perception of her country with the reality of the hard, cruel, callous nature of the society it used to be. Ireland is a very different place now. I remember watching a TV show with Kate a few years ago, and one of the characters was telling his father he was gay. She turned to me and asked, 'Why is he so worried? Is he afraid his daddy will be sad he isn't going to marry a woman and have grandchildren?'

The idea that people just wouldn't accept a person for being gay alone didn't occur to her. As I say, a different place on so many levels.

'They wouldn't let them have him back, would they, Mam?' Ellie asks, older and wiser.

'No, pet, they wouldn't. The babies were mostly adopted, and the mothers were forced to release them for adoption. And once that happened, the babies were given new identities and the nuns wouldn't tell the birth mother where their baby was if they went to find out.' I wish I could soften this for her, and especially for Kate, but I can't.

'And did Nana never try to find him?' Kate asks. 'Like maybe if she'd married someone different afterwards, I can see why she might not have said anything, but since Granda was the baby's dad anyway...'

I pause. This is the hardest part. 'No, love, she didn't try to find him.'

'So it was Granda who found him?'

'No, he couldn't do that – only the birth mother can make contact. But luckily Nana Nora changed her mind in the end.'

'Why now?' asks Ellie.

Kieran shoots me a look. I look back at him.

God forgive me, I already know Oilibhéar's tagline. He's 'my son Oilibhéar who is very high up in RTÉ'.

'Well, she just did,' I say.

* * *

'You awake?' I ask, knowing he is.

'Hmm…' he says, and I hear the rumble of sound deep in his chest as I snuggle up to him in the bed.

'Are you OK?'

It's all taking time to process. We haven't spoken directly to Oilibhéar yet, but he is going to be a part of us. Nora instantly received a message from the station that he'd love to spend time with her, that he was glad to hear from her, that he was excited to meet his siblings and, amazingly, his father. But he said that he needs a little bit of time first. He'd been expecting at best to find out just about his birth mother, so a whole family… Well, it is a lot to take in.

'He seems to have really accepted Nora is his mother. I wonder, should you do a DNA test to be sure?' It's the boring garda in me, always checking.

He shrugs. 'I don't know, should we?'

I pull back to look at him. He's lying on his back, his hands behind his head.

'I haven't a clue, love,' I say. Maybe the test isn't needed.

'I suppose we'll wait for him to get back to us. He said he just needed a few days, so we can give him that.'

I rest on my elbow and place my hand on his cheek, and he turns his head to kiss my palm.

'You all right? About it all, I mean?' I ask quietly. I know my husband is more fragile than he looks at times. It's not long since he's been back on an even keel.

He pulls me back against him, my head on his chest, and I hear his deep voice reverberate against my ear.

'It will be nice to meet him, and I hope we get along. But, Mags, he's a stranger to me. And while I'll welcome him, of course I will, you and Kate and Ellie are my family. I love my parents, and my sisters and Gearoid, but we all have our own lives now, and I've moved a long time ago from that family to this one, with you. So you needn't worry I'll go off the deep end.' He chuckles. 'I hope it works out – he seems like a nice fella – but if not, that's OK too.'

I'm relieved, and I reach up to kiss him. The kiss is slow and deliberate and so full of love, and I'm filled with gratitude for the life I have with this lovely man.

# CHAPTER 27

*D*elia pops her head around the door, beaming with excitement.

'Hi, Sarge. Daddy's home – well, nearly. He's on the road, only an hour away. Can I take my lunch early to go and meet him? He's heading straight for Horsehead, he says.'

I'm thrilled and amazed. I wasn't expecting Jerome back today.

I've been following his and Jimmy and Billy's journey on the youth club's Facebook page. The reception centre was delighted with all the baby stuff, and they had managed to find Klara's mother at the border – she must have managed the long bus trip – and also a few other grandparents of the residents of Horsehead, anxious to join their daughters and grandchildren so they can wait out this awful war together. Then the delays began...

Dora spent a good while up in a heap, suspecting her husband of all sorts, because Jerome kept texting her how it would be a few more days before he could leave, and then a few more, and then a few more... One mysterious issue after another held things up, even though Derry was convinced he'd cleared all the paperwork necessary and I'd submitted the applications to the Department of Foreign Affairs myself.

'It must be chaotic at the border, so I suppose processing everyone takes some time. They can't just have fellas showing up in vans dropping stuff off and taking people, I suppose,' Derry kept on reassuring me.

'Supposing it's because Jerome won't listen to the border guards? You know how the Travellers are about officialdom...'

'Even if he doesn't, 'tis a brave Polish border guard will try to stop Jerome McGovern getting his way in the end, whatever he's after, that's for sure.'

And Derry must have been right, because now the head of the McGoverns is on his way home.

Klara is upstairs in the station, where she is making great headway sorting boxes that were dumped up there when the station was refurbished. 'Klara,' I call up the stairs, and she appears at the top, looking at me questioningly. 'Can you come down a second?'

She pushes the duster into the pocket of her jeans and comes downstairs, seeming perplexed.

I get out my phone and open Google Translate. 'Delia says her dad is due back in about an hour. Come on, let's get Alina out of school and go and meet them!'

Klara bursts into tears.

* * *

THERE'S a crowd of excited women and children gathered on the gravel in front of the big house, and not just the Ukrainian women. Dora is there with Delia. She's been so worried; she'll be so relieved to have her husband home.

Half an hour after we get there, as hot coffee and delicious little cakes called *rogaliki* are passed around for everyone, there's a roar of engines up the avenue and Jerome pulls up in his van and the two jeeps behind him. Within minutes the whole place is filled with reunions and the sounds of tears and shouts of joy. Everyone chatters over each other in rapid-fire Ukrainian, but the language of love is universal. Tears flow as elderly parents are reunited with their daughters and grandchildren. They hug and release each other over and over.

Jerome assists a middle-aged woman down from the high passenger seat of his van. She is dressed in a fur coat and hat, much too warm for the day but I suppose it was all she had, she has crutches, and her leg is in plaster to her thigh. Klara, who has been looking around her anxiously, gives a squeal of joy and runs to hug her mother, and Alina follows, laughing with delight.

Billy and Jimmy are also hugged, over and over, by various Ukrainian women, and they lap it up. It's a happy scene.

Dora stands with her arms folded until her man comes over to where she is waiting for him. She doesn't throw her arms around him or give him any kind of a hug – Travellers are not like that with each other, at least in public, big displays of affection – but it is obvious that neither one doubts how the other feels.

I'm standing with Delia, who is not a hugger either. She looks so proud and happy. Jerome smiles at us both and raises his eyebrows, and then he nods towards the crowd, where a tall stocky man with dark brown hair that flops over his forehead and a heavily bandaged right hand has just climbed down out of the front of the van after Klara's mother. Klara's mother makes her daughter turn around to see who it is. Klara screams and then bursts into huge uncontrollable sobs as she throws herself into the man's arms.

'Jerome McGovern, you did not,' I say, hands on hips, beaming.

'Ah sure, Mags, you know me. They didn't want me going looking for him with the jeep, said it was too dangerous, but I'm a hard man to refuse.' He is grinning from ear to ear.

Klara suddenly breaks away from her husband and comes running over to Jerome. 'Volodymyr...you find him, drive into Ukraine...over border, very dangerous...to get him. I...' She kisses his cheek, while Dora looks like thunder. So this was the reason for all those mysterious delays that had her so worried.

'You're welcome.' The big man blushes, waving away the young woman's thanks, and Klara turns and rushes back to her husband and mother, who is progressing slowly in our direction, leaning on her crutches.

'I don't think Mammy will be letting you go as far as Limerick on your own ever again,' Delia jokes.

'That suits me, girl,' Jerome says, with a grin and a glance at Dora, who sniffs loudly.

Klara is back again, with her husband and mother this time. 'Sergeant Munroe, this is Volodymyr Shevchenko, my husband, and Olena Koval, my mother.' She says something to them in Ukrainian, and I catch the word 'Munroe', so I assume she's telling them who I am.

Olena kisses my cheek and wipes her tears, and Volodymyr extends his large unbandaged hand and grasps mine. 'Thank you, Sergeant, for minding my wife and daughter,' he says in heavily accented English. 'I am glad to meet you.'

'Welcome to Ireland,' I say.

# CHAPTER 28

'You OK?' I glance over at Kieran as we sit in the car, parked outside a fancy castle hotel in West Clare called Castle Dysert.

He nods. I can tell he's nervous. Oilibhéar has chosen the venue; apparently, he is friendly with the owner or something and comes here often. It looks like a place celebrities would stay all right, five-star, grounds like billiard tables, the flowerbeds a riot of colour. There is a stone fountain trickling away outside the main door, which is a big, black, medieval-looking thing, up a flight of steps worn with centuries of feet.

If I'd known this place was going to be as fancy as it is, I would have dressed up more, but I'm here now and I hope we all look all right. I'm in jeans and a black jacket, with a scarlet silk shirt under-neath, and high-heeled black boots. Sharon has assured me I am dressed perfectly for meeting my husband's long-lost brother who looks just like him; we had an awkward laugh at the incongruity of it all.

Kieran, who normally couldn't care less about his clothes, changed his shirt four times this morning before we left the house. I eventually had to just herd him into the car. At least he isn't in his dark-green

Aran sweater that he's owned for twenty years and that looks every day of it. He is wearing jeans, but the shirt he's selected – or rather the one I dragged him out of the house wearing before he could change it again – is a nice dark-blue open-necked one. He looks handsome.

Nora and Kevin are in their car beside ours, both looking like rabbits in the headlights. Nora had been taken by her daughters and dressed. Her hair was shampooed and set and her make-up done, so she looks well, if absolutely petrified. Kevin is in a charcoal suit and looks like he might vomit at any minute.

It's just the four of us today, Kevin and Nora and myself and Kieran. We all thought it best not to overwhelm the poor man with the whole family on the first meeting. I wasn't going to go, but all three Munroes nearly had a fit when I suggested I let them at it. And so here I am. Though what on earth I'm supposed to do to make this less awkward, I've no idea. I suppose I'm just going to have to jolly everyone along.

'Right.' Kieran exhales. 'Let's do it.'

'OK, let's.' I get out of the car, then help Nora out of hers, and she gives me a small smile.

'It's going to be fine,' I say loudly as the four of us line up in front of the imposing old castle. 'We know that he's nice. He's had a great life and he holds no bad feelings, so let's all just try to relax, all right?'

Kevin swallows and manages a nod but no words. I really hope he'll actually speak when he meets his son, but with Kevin, you never know. I'd heard more out of him in the last few weeks than in the decades before, but if this is a permanent feature of the new Kevin Munroe, it remains to be seen. At least he and Nora are back on cordial terms again, so that's something.

Nora takes her husband's arm and I take Kieran's, and we mount the steps.

In the vast lobby is a large oak-carved reception desk where a very tiny but beautiful woman in her thirties sits at a computer. She has short blond hair cut in a pixie, high cheekbones and emerald-green eyes. I head towards her, leaving Kieran with his parents standing together nervously under a vast potted palm.

235

'Hello, welcome to Castle Dysert.' Her English is slightly accented, and I see from her badge that her name is Anastasia.

'Hi, my name is Mags Munroe, and we have an appointment to meet Oilibhéar MacElroy here this morning?'

'Ah yes, of course, welcome. I'm afraid Oilibhéar is delayed, but my husband, Conor, will be here in just a minute. Let me just call him.'

She goes into the office behind the reception, and moments later a tall, muscular man with expertly cut silver hair and sapphire-blue eyes approaches. He could be aged anywhere between fifty and sixty, and as my mother always says, 'You'd stand up to look at him.' His dark suit and light-blue shirt and tie look like they've been made especially for him. I will have to bring Sharon down here to have an ogle at him; he is like an Irish George Clooney.

'Mrs Munroe?' he asks with a smile, and I instantly warm to him.

'That's right,' I say, inwardly laughing at how starstruck I am feeling, today of all days. As well as being incredibly handsome and tanned, this man is madly charismatic.

'Conor O'Shea, lovely to meet you.' He shakes my hand warmly and firmly. He is from Cork, I can tell; the slight southern sing-song accent is there.

'Oilibhéar is a friend of mine, and he just rang to say they had a flat tyre on the way here, and the spare turned out to be flat as well, so they had to have another car sent. He asked me to apologise profusely, and to tell you he and his wife, Muireann, will be here within the next twenty minutes.'

'That's fine, thank you.' I have to tear myself away from his presence; I need to relay this information to the three panicked-looking Munroes still standing by the huge palm. Conor walks with me, and after I've explained the situation, he steps in and greets Kieran and his parents warmly.

'So if you like, I can show you into the library,' he says, 'where you can relax. I'll have some coffees or teas or drinks, whatever you'd like, brought in while you wait? It's closed to the public, so you'll have it to yourselves.'

Something about the way he says this makes me realise he knows the reason for the visit.

'That would be lovely, thanks,' I say. 'Coffee would be great, and my mother-in-law will have tea.'

'And I'll have a brandy,' says Kevin, ignoring a frown from Nora in a way he would never have done in the past.

'Not a bother.' He calls over a smiling young man in his teens dressed in a dark suit too, with a name badge that says Joe.

'This is my son Joe. He'll show you to the library and take care of everything you need. And I'll let Oilibhéar know you've arrived. As I say, he won't be long.'

'Thanks very much,' Kieran manages at last. It's so strange to see him so rattled.

Conor smiles reassuringly at him. 'He's as nervous as you, Kieran, if it's any consolation, but he's a lovely man and I'm sure you'll get on great. Just call if you need anything.'

'Thanks, Conor.' I watch as he heads back to his office behind the reception, and even Nora casts him a glance of admiration as he strolls away.

In the library, my in-laws take a seat in armchairs on either side of the large fireplace, in which are crackling some aromatic logs. I and Kieran perch side by side on a delicate brocade sofa with gilt legs. We all of us wait, saying nothing. The walls are lined with books, and the flag floors are covered with rugs. It is such a beautiful room, and the warmth of the fire is welcoming; summer is nearly here, but it is a cool day out. I distract myself by trying to calculate how much it must cost to heat this old castle. A fortune, I decide weakly.

The door opens and we all sit up straight, but it is Conor's son Joe, wheeling a trolley with a large coffeepot, a small teapot, a glass of brandy and a plate piled with little cakes.

'Here ye go. That's cow's milk, but if ye need almond or oat or something, we have that too?' He looks like his mother in his colouring, blond and green eyes, but he has his father's build.

'Cow's milk is fine, thanks very much,' Kieran says gratefully, pouring himself a coffee, just to have something to do, I think.

'Not a problem. Pull that rope there' – he indicates a large scarlet rope hanging from the ceiling beside the fire – 'if ye need anything else.'

'We will. I'm sure you're busy. We'll be fine.'

'Ah, it's quiet today actually. We had a big group for the last few days, so it's nice to get a minute.'

'So it's a family business, is it, this place? It's amazing.' I gaze out through the French windows at the beautiful grounds.

'Yeah, well, us and loads of other people work here. My mam and dad own it, and I work here, just in the school holidays. So does my granda. My twin, Artie, isn't into it, so he's up in Dublin doing some kind of a summer school, studying hard maths or something bewildering, don't ask me. I think he's mental to waste the summer doing schoolwork.' He smiles around at us all, and Nora actually blushes. 'And my little sister, Lily, is the baby of the family, and she's too small to work.'

'Was it always in your family?' Kieran asks, glad to have something to take his mind off things.

'Castle Dysert?' The lad laughs. 'Not a bit of it. My dad is from Cork. He grew up without a shilling. And then as an adult, he was a mechanic and then he was a tour bus driver. He met my mam when she was working as a waitress in a hotel in Kerry years ago, and then a really rich American left my dad a pile of money, for no reason really except that he's a nice fella, I suppose, and so he bought this place.'

'That's incredible.' I find myself intrigued.

'Ah sure, you'd be here all day if I told you the full story of this place, floods, ghosts, fires. My dad rescued my brother and me from the eastern tower one time when this headcase set fire to it. We were only small, and he had to throw us out the window.' His smile is mesmerising; he is a chip off the old block. 'Films have been made here. The gardens are designed by the most famous garden designer in the world. We even had a famous kidnapper stay here. Matchmaking, murders, love stories, long-lost families – ye'll have to come back for a holiday and we'll tell ye the whole story.'

A pager beeps on his belt. He takes it and presses a button.

'I'm being summoned, so I better go. Enjoy the cakes. The new pastry chef is something else – everyone is suddenly finding reasons to do their jobs via the kitchen.' And he's gone.

We pour the drinks, adding sugar and milk to cups of coffee and tea we have no interest in drinking, but it fills the time. Though Kevin swallows his brandy in one gulp.

Eventually, after what seems like forever, Conor appears again, and he ushers into the room a slightly older version of Kieran and a tall dark-haired woman in a long green coat.

'Right, I'll let ye to the introductions. Call if ye need anything at all.' He withdraws, leaving Oilibhéar MacElroy and the woman, who I assume is his wife, Muireann, standing in the middle of the carpet. The four of us all get to our feet and just stand there as well.

Nothing happens.

Nora stares and stares, and so does Oilibhéar, his eyes never leaving hers. Kieran is pale, and his father looks like he's going to be sick. I wonder should I say something, and I decide I should.

'Oilibhéar, Muireann, I'm Mags, and this is my husband, Kieran, and my parents-in-law, Nora and Kevin Munroe.'

I hope I've pronounced his name correctly. The Irish for Oliver isn't that common a name, so I've been practising – 'Olly-vayer'.

Muireann takes my cue and comes forward, grasping my hand. 'Lovely to meet you, Mags.'

Then without anyone saying anything else, Oilibhéar moves towards Nora. He stands before her, tall like Kieran, and she is dwarfed by him. He opens his arms. She takes a step closer. He draws her into a hug. Long seconds pass before he releases her, and when he does, I can see she is crying.

'I'm so sorry, Oliver, so sorry. I should have…'

He wipes her tears with his thumbs, a gesture so intimate it feels almost wrong to be watching.

'Nothing to be sorry for, absolutely nothing. I have had a wonderful life, and now, meeting you, well, all the bits of the puzzle are falling into place.'

Kevin steps forward then. 'Hello, Oilibhéar. I'm Kevin, your father.'

He looks shy, but he's clearly well able to speak for himself. It seems like he's found his voice for good these days.

'Hi, Kevin, it's lovely to meet you.' They shake hands, and both men are beaming, friends already. And finally Oilibhéar turns to Kieran.

'I never met someone who looks exactly like me before.' He smiles.

'Me neither.' My husband chuckles. 'My...our' – he corrects himself – 'other brother, Gearoid, he looks nothing like me, so it feels strange, doesn't it?'

'Good strange, though,' Oilibhéar replies.

'So who would like a drink?' I pull the scarlet rope, and Joe appears, and I order more coffee and tea and another brandy for Kevin. Oilibhéar orders one too, and that seems to break the ice, and soon I am standing where I should be, on the periphery of things, Muireann MacElroy beside me, smiling fondly, both of us watching as the Munroes talk and talk and talk. The conversation is light and easy and lacking the awkwardness you might expect. Nora keeps touching her son's hand like she can't believe he exists, and Kevin puts his arm around his wife's shoulders and squeezes her as she laughs at something her long lost son has just said. He really is so like Kieran it's uncanny.

'I feel like I can exhale now.' Muireann murmurs beside me.

'I know what you mean.' I smile in reply. 'It's been quite a journey hasn't it?'

Kieran is telling Oilibhéar something about the Irish soccer team, and his brother rests his hand on his shoulder. The gesture is intimate but easy, and I see Kieran has lost all the tension he had coming in here.

Oilibhéar will fit in just perfectly to the family.

It's all going to be fine.

## The End

I sincerely hope that you enjoyed this latest visit to Ballycarrick and Mags. If you did I would greatly appreciate a review wherever you purchased the book.

If you'd like to join my readers club just pop over to www.jean grainger.com and sign up, I'll send you a free ebook novel as a welcome gift. My readers club is 100% free and always will be and you can leave at any time.

If you'd like to get a taste of another of my books, please read on to sample the first book in my Kilteegan Bridge Series.

* * *

**The Trouble With Secrets - The Killteegan Bridge Series - Book 1**
**Chapter 1**

*KILTEEGAN BRIDGE, CO CORK, 1948*

'Don't leave me, Paudie. Don't leave me. I'll die. I swear, I'll walk into the sea and I'll die.'

'Maria, why are you saying this?' Daddy's voice was strange – it was broken and sad. He was normally stronger sounding or something. 'Of course I'll never leave you.'

'I've seen the way Hannah Berger looks at you, Paudie. *Everyone* sees the way she looks at you, right there in the church in front of the whole parish, in front of her own husband. She wants you for herself. She's heart-set on having you.'

Lena kept very still in her special hiding place behind the carved and painted settle beside the fire. Her brother and sister were in bed, but she'd come down to fetch her doll. She was small for seven, and most days she liked it here behind this long wooden seat with the high back, which could fold down into a bed for visitors. You could hear things, and it was warm near the fire, and nobody gave you a job to do. But now she was listening to things she'd rather not hear, even if she didn't understand any of it. Mrs Berger couldn't have Daddy all to herself, even if she did find him useful around the estate. Daddy belonged to Mammy, and to her, and to Emily and Jack.

'This is all in your mind. I love you, Maria...'

'Then stop going to see her!'

241

'If we could afford for me to stop working up there, you know I would.'

A wild sob and a crash of crockery. Mammy had thrown something down from the dresser. Lena prayed it wasn't her favourite bowl, the one with the bluebells painted on it that Daddy had brought her from the fair in Bandon. He'd brought Emily a green velvet ribbon at the same time, to tie up her long blond hair. Emily was beautiful, tall like Mammy, and though she was only nine, people always thought she was much older. She could be bossy sometimes, but usually she was nice. Jack was small like Lena. He was only five. Daddy had brought him a small wooden donkey, just like Ned, their donkey that pulled the cart on the farm.

'Maria, Maria, stop now, love...' Daddy's voice was firmer. He was trying to calm Mammy, soothing her like he did with Mrs Berger's stallion up at Kilteegan House when it went wild in the spring. 'I can't stop going to the Bergers'. That's half our income, building stone walls, pruning the orchard, caring for the horses. Hannah Berger's not interested in me as a man. She just needs a strong pair of hands around the place. She's had nobody to do the heavy jobs since her father died.'

'Let her own husband do the work, now he's home from the war!'

'Ah, how can he do that, Maria, and him in a wheelchair?'

'There's that man of his, the Frenchman...'

'He's neither use nor ornament, that fella. All he does is wait on his master hand and foot, and he pays no attention whatsoever to anything that needs to be done around the grounds.'

'You're a fool. You can't see it – she's trying to seduce you, Paudie, with her red hair and her green eyes. I'm scared, Paudie, and if she gets you, then her husband will kill you. He's evil, Paudie. There's something terrifying about him.'

Lena felt a pain in her tummy when Mammy spoke like that, like she believed that evil spirits were in people. She was very superstitious. Sometimes it was fun when she told Lena and Emily and Jack about fairies and things like that, but mostly it was scary because it was a sign that things could be bad for days if Daddy didn't manage to coax her out of it. Lena wanted it not to be like that for Daddy, or for her and Jack and Emily, but when Mammy got into her imaginary world, she often stayed away a long time. It didn't happen often. She hadn't had a bad spell since last summer, when she'd screamed there was a demon on the stairs. Lena had wet her knickers, she got such a fright. Daddy had to tell Lena over and over that these things weren't true, that it was only in Mammy's mind, before she could get to sleep that night.

Daddy's voice was even firmer now, more like his normal self, like a big strong tree in a storm. 'Maria, my love, calm yourself. There's nothing to worry about, honestly. I go up there and do some work, and they pay me well. That's all. I love you.'

Mammy fell silent. She was still breathing harshly, but she let Daddy lead her over to the settle. Lena felt the wood creak as he sat beside her, and she heard the whisper of cloth on cloth as he put his arm around Mammy. He told her all about the wild flower meadow that would be growing between their farmhouse and the sea in the spring, in just a few weeks, and how they'd all take a picnic and go to the seaside. Lena knew that when he used that gentle, low and rumbling voice it usually calmed her down.

Lena often thought her tall, slim mother was like a selkie, one of those magical tricky mermaids who look like seals in the water but who come to live with human men until they can't stand to be on land any longer and go back to the ocean. There was a picture of a selkie in a book at school, and she had long white hair, same as Mammy's, and it looked a bit like ropes coming down. Mammy tied her hair up most of the time, but sometimes it was loose and reached all the way down her back. She had eyes the same colour as the selkie too, pale as the sea on a summer's day, and her eyelashes and eyebrows were so light that it looked like she didn't have any.

Emily and Jack both looked like Mammy, pale-skinned and fair-haired, but everyone said Lena looked just like her father – dark silky hair, brown eyes and skin that only had to see the sun for a day before it went copper.

In the quiet, the fire crackled in the range and the night wind threw drops of rain against the window. The radio that had been on all this time in the background began playing the popular new song by Al Jolson, 'When You Were Sweet Sixteen'.

Lena's father started singing it softly under his breath. 'I loved you as I've never loved before, since first I saw you on the village green. Come to me, ere my dream of love is o'er. I love you as I loved you, when you were sweet…when you were sweet sixteen…'

And slowly her mother's breathing softened and the pain in Lena's stomach went away. Daddy swept up the bits of broken crockery in silence.

'Dance with me, Maria,' murmured her father.

Mammy still didn't answer, but she let Daddy pull her to her feet. And when Lena peeped out from behind the settle, her parents were swaying together around the kitchen table, her father's big strong farmer's arms around her tall, slim mother, Maria's head on Paudie's shoulder and both of them with their eyes closed. The broken crockery was in a pile in the corner, and it wasn't her favourite bowl – it was just that cracked yellow and green plate she'd never liked anyway.

Lena crept out of the kitchen, up the stairs of the two-story farm-house and into the bedroom she shared with her sister. Emily was fast asleep, her long blond hair spread out across the pillow. Lena snug-gled in beside her with her doll and lay on her back, gazing up at the sloped ceiling, the beams casting sharp black shadows in the moon-light. She was glad the storm had passed this time.

She hoped Mammy wouldn't spoil things between Daddy and the Bergers, because she liked going up to Kilteegan House with him. He let her bring up a basket of their farm eggs, and Mrs Berger always gave her an extra penny to keep for herself. Sometimes Daddy kept Lena busy, weeding the vegetable garden or picking up the branches he pruned from the trees in the orchard. But other times she played with Malachy, the little boy who was there when he wasn't away at boarding school. He had dark-red hair like his mother, and the same grass-green eyes. They would play hide-and-seek around the garden if it was fine, and if it rained, they'd hide in the tack house, where the saddles and bridles lived, and lay out a clean horse blanket on the stone flags and sit and play cards or draughts.

* * *

### Chapter 2 - Kilteegan Bridge 1955

Lena sat in the front pew, staring at her black shoes. Her black calico dress was too tight across her chest, threatening to pop a button. Mammy had made it for her for Hannah Berger's funeral six months before, but she was fourteen then and still growing; now that she was fifteen, it was already too tight. The priest was murmuring in Latin, swinging incense around the coffin that lay before the altar. On her left, Jack looked so pale, she thought he might faint. Lena tried to take hold of his hand, but he pulled it away. He was the man of the house now, Mammy had told him, so he thought he wasn't allowed to cry or show emotion any more. On her other side, Emily sat stiffly next to Maria; they looked like sisters, they were so alike. Both of them were in tears. Lena wished she could cry as well, but everything felt so unreal, she couldn't believe any of it was really happening.

Only three days ago, Daddy had been on his way out the door to check on the lambs and saw that the crafty old fox had stolen another one. Daddy and the fox had what he called a 'mutually respectful relationship'. The fox had a job to do, but so did he.

Daddy had trapped lots of foxes in his life. He tried not to kill things if he didn't have to, but this fox must have been especially clever if Daddy decided he needed to shoot it.

She wished he'd just trapped it.

'We're not the owners of this land, Lena,' he would say. 'Nor are we the masters of the animals and plants that live here. We're just minding it. It was minded by my father and his father before him, and now it's for us to care for, and in due time, Jack will take over.'

Daddy loved his farm.

She would never hear his voice again. Never.

Now her father was in that wooden box, and the priest was telling everyone that Paudie O'Sullivan was happier now than he had ever been because he was at the right hand of the Lord. That was a load of rubbish. Daddy would never want to be anywhere except with his family.

It was Jack who had found him. Their father had been lying in his own blood in the top field with his shotgun, which he hadn't used for ages, beside him. Doc came from the village the minute he heard, but he hadn't been able to save his friend. It was a terrible accident, Doc told them. He must have fired at the fox, and his ancient shotgun had backfired, he was killed instantly. The doctor was nearly as broken by it as the rest of them. He had been Paudie O'Sullivan's best friend since they were children, and he was Lena's godfather, and he always came to see Maria when she was in one of her dangerously low moods.

The Mass was over now, and Doc, Jack and four other men from the village stepped forward to carry the coffin. Paudie O'Sullivan had been an only child, so there were no brothers to carry him, only his son and his best friend and his neighbours. Jack was barely tall enough for the task, but the undertaker put him in the middle and made sure the older men took most of the weight.

Lena's mother rose from the pew to follow the coffin, awkwardly, because she was very pregnant, her stomach huge under her loose black dress. Lena and Emily walked just behind her, holding hands. Emily squeezed Lena's fingers, and their eyes met briefly. Lena knew what her sister was thinking. Both of them had been dreading all morning that Maria would have one of her terrible breakdowns and scream the church down with fear, or else fall into one of her near-catatonic trances of melancholy. But so far, their mother had carried herself with great dignity. Maybe, like Lena, Maria didn't believe this was really happening.

The walk to the cemetery wasn't long, up a pale stony track fringed with wild montbretia under overhanging trees. The grave-yard was on a hill overlooking the distant sea, and to Lena's surprise, the priest and coffin bearers headed towards the far corner, away from the O'Sullivan family plot where her father's parents and his two maiden aunts were buried. She touched her mother's arm. 'Is

Daddy not going to be buried with Nana and Granda?' she whispered.

Maria said sharply, 'No. That grave is full.'

Lena fell instantly silent. There was an edge to her mother's voice that frightened her.

But then Maria softened and added, 'Anyway, girls, don't you think the plot I chose for him is much nicer?'

She was right. The plot over by the graveyard wall was lovely, shaded by a spreading chestnut tree and with a wide view of the distant bay. If it weren't for the stone weight of her grief, the beauty of the spot would have lifted Lena's heart.

After the graveside prayers and the sad, heavy rattle of earth and stones onto her father's coffin, Lena finally felt the tears come, and wanting to be alone in her grief, she walked a small distance away from the funeral crowd, muffling her sobs and wiping her nose with a scrap of hanky.

Blinded by grief, she nearly walked into Malachy Berger, who stood facing the Fitzgerald grave. She remembered him as the red-headed boy with bright-green eyes she used to play with as a little girl. She hadn't seen him in years except very briefly at his mother's funeral six months ago, and like her, he had grown since then – a couple of inches at least – and his hair was shorter.

The magnificent Fitzgerald family plot was right next to the more modest O'Sullivan family plot, where Lena's grandparents and grand-aunts were buried. Hannah's name and dates were the latest to be carved on the massive Fitzgerald headstone.

*HANNAH BERGER née FITZGERALD*

*b. 1919 – d. 1955*

*Beloved wife and mother*

*Gone too soon*

Only thirty-six when she died, five years younger than Lena's father.

Lena stopped. It felt rude to just walk on.

Malachy dug in his pocket and handed her a clean handkerchief. 'It's tough, losing a parent, isn't it?'

She nodded, wiping her tears with his handkerchief and handing it back.

'Keep it.' He said sincerely. 'I'm so sorry for your loss.'

Lena thought the words oddly stiff for people their age, but she'd never been in this position before. Maybe the whole wretched business had its own language, where young people spoke so formally.

'Thanks,' she managed.

'I remember him kicking a football around with me, back when I was only six or seven years old. My father had only just come back from the war, and he was in a wheelchair, and my mother was lovely but useless at football. Your dad was one of the people I missed most when I went to boarding school.'

Lena smiled through her tears. It was nice to hear this boy remembering her father so fondly. 'I remember your mam as well. She was always smiling and singing. She was full of life, and she always gave me an extra penny for the eggs to keep for my own pocket.'

He looked sad at the memory. 'That's exactly how she was, full of life. She liked you too. She missed you when you and your father stopped coming, but I suppose you were busy on the farm.'

Lena sighed and nodded. 'I missed her as well.'

Still, it had been easier not to go up to the Bergers' big house these past few years. Maria had taken against any of her family having anything to do with them, forbidding her to go, something to do with not liking or trusting Hannah or her husband. Maria took sets against people for slights or insults, a few real but mostly imagined.

For a while, her father had continued going by himself – they needed the extra money. But then Emily, Jack and Lena had all got old enough to help on the farm, and Daddy bought a few more cows, and soon the O'Sullivan homestead was bringing in enough income from milk, eggs and vegetables for Paudie to stop working odd jobs at the big house altogether.

There was a sharp jerk at her elbow, and Emily hissed in her ear, 'Mammy says come back to Daddy's grave.' And Lena stuffed Malachy's hanky in her sleeve and went with her sister without a backwards glance.

The crowd was beginning to thin. Doc had arranged for tea and sandwiches at the Kilteegan Arms, and everyone was moving towards the cemetery gate. Lena and Emily linked Maria on either side, relieved the funeral had passed without their mother making any kind of scene. As they approached the gate, people maintained a respectful distance. Clearly Mrs O'Sullivan was in no fit state to make conversation. Then, Lena saw him. Auguste Berger sat in a wheelchair right beside the gate, and he appeared to be waiting for them. As they walked past, he put his hand out.

He spoke in a French accent. 'My sincere condolences. I know how difficult it is to lose your spouse, the sense of loss, of abandonment.'

Maria stiffened and glared at him, and Lena mentally braced herself. This could be the catalyst for hysterics; that tendency of her mother's was never far below the surface. The risk was made greater because she could no longer take the tablets she used to stabilise her mood for fear of damage to the babies. 'My husband did not "abandon" me,' she said stiffly. 'It was an accident. An accident.'

'Of course.' Auguste Berger tutted sympathetically as he gazed at her hugely swollen belly. 'So sad Monsieur O'Sullivan didn't live to see this child. Or I believe it is *children*? You're expecting twins, *non*? Two new lives to replace the two lives that were lost...' His voice was barely audible.

'Yes, thank you,' Lena responded, not sure what else to say. There was something unsettling about him. Everyone knew Maria was expecting twins because she had to see the doctor in Cork for her pregnancy, whereas everyone else who was expecting just went to Doc.

'Come on, Mammy.' Emily took their trembling mother by the arm and led her gently to the car the undertakers had supplied that was waiting in the autumn sunshine.

Lena glanced over her shoulder at the man in the wheelchair, who raised his hand to her with a charming smile. Auguste Berger, Malachy's father, was now the owner of Kilteegan House. His wife, Hannah, had been found dead of a heart attack in the orchard last spring. The house was her family place, not his. She'd been the

Fitzgeralds' only surviving child, one brother dying as an infant and another in a horse-riding accident years ago. So Berger, as her husband, got it all: the big old house, the extensive grounds and a fine farm.

Behind him, holding the handles of the wheelchair, was that strange stocky Frenchman with his oily slicked-back hair. He'd arrived with Berger the day he came back from the war and had not left his side since.

Lena helped her mother into the car, and she could feel the pair's eyes on her and her family as they left Paudie in his final resting place.

\* \* \*

## Chapter 3
### Kilteegan Bridge 1958

Lena took off her shoes and crept up the moonlit path in her stockinged feet. It was nearly one o'clock in the morning. She'd never been this late home in her life and didn't want to wake anyone. Not her two-year-old twin sisters, Molly and May, who would never go back to sleep, and not Jack, who had to be up in a few hours for the milking, and especially not her mother, who might be in any sort of mood – madly happy or deep in despair or, worst of all, screaming obscenities at her for being up to no good with boys at the dance.

The front of the farmhouse was in darkness, but the moonlight was enough to help her find her way. She glanced up at the bedroom that had been her parents' and was now just her mother's. The light was off. Good – that meant Mammy was getting some sleep instead of wandering the house as she often did, talking to Dad like he was still alive.

It had been a hard few years in the O'Sullivan household since her father died. Lena and Jack had to leave school to run the farm, and it was so difficult – they had been only fifteen and twelve. Luckily, Jack had taken to farming like a duck to water and had learned a lot about old farming methods that were kind to the land. The neighbouring farmers were very good to them and looked out for them; everyone had been very fond of her father. Jack read voraciously about plants and animals and asked the advice of the old Traveller men and women who camped on their land each year about the various properties of flowers and grasses. He refused to use any of the new fertilisers on the farm, sticking to the old methods of cow shed muck, and sulphate of potash. Though it was more labour-intensive, their milk, beef and lamb were always in great demand. He'd told her about the discovery in Switzerland and subsequent use all over the world of DDT – she'd forgotten the long name of it – and according to Jack, it was the worst thing ever dreamed up.

Emily would have helped more, but she had her hands full with the twins. Maria had fallen into such a deep depression after their birth that Doc sent her away to St Catherine's, a kind of nursing home up in Limerick, where she'd stayed for nearly a year. To be honest, it was easier at home without their mother, especially since Daddy wasn't there to ameliorate her moods. Even when Maria was in a happy frame of mind, it was difficult to deal with her. She might get a notion to redecorate the whole house, pushing all the furniture together in the middle of the rooms and painting all the walls lovely bright colours, until halfway through she got bored and started doing something else altogether, leaving them with half-painted walls. Another time Lena found her planting a rose garden at three o'clock in the morning, or she could decide she was going to make them all gorgeous clothes from bolt ends of cloth she'd picked up in town for next to nothing. Maria was a genius at making clothes; she'd made the dress Lena was wearing right now – a gorgeous fashionable tea dress of yellow silk, with covered buttons. She was so creative, but she hardly ever stuck to anything. Lena had finished off the dress herself because her mother had lost interest before it was complete. It was lovely, though.

That's likely why Malachy had noticed her in the Lilac Ballroom, among all the other girls.

'Malachy Berger.' She said his name in the cool night air. *Lena Berger*. It had a nice ring to it. *A ring*. She giggled. The two glasses of whiskey they'd had in his house after the dance had gone to her head.

He was lovely, though. Most other fellas around here would take advantage of a girl who'd had a drink or two, but not Malachy; he was different to other lads. He'd offered her a lift home in his car – imagine, he had his own car, an amazing dark-green Volkswagen Beetle with cream leather interior and a Bosch radio – and on the way, he'd invited her into his house, where he'd introduced her to his father, who hadn't been shocked at his son bringing a girl home at that hour. Lena hadn't seen Auguste Berger since the day of her father's funeral, and though he'd unsettled her then, she decided it was probably that she'd been so upset, because tonight he was very welcoming and friendly.

Auguste Berger was obviously a sophisticated man, and he had an exotic look about him – it was clear he'd spent his life somewhere other than Kilteegan Bridge. The way he sat in his big armchair by the fire, it wasn't obvious he had a disability. That strange manservant brought them whiskies on a silver tray and little sweet cakes called macaroons. It felt very sophisticated, drinking a whiskey and eating a French macaroon in the lovely sitting room, like something in a film. It was surely the best night of her life.

Malachy was as well-mannered as his father. She guessed it helped that he went to Larksbridge, a fancy boarding school up in Dublin, and not the tech in the next town like most of the boys from here did. He never once made any suggestive remarks or tried to grope her; he just spoke to her like she was a normal human being with her own opinions.

He was taller than when she'd last seen him, maybe five foot ten, with broad shoulders. His red hair had darkened to rich chestnut, and he wore it brushed back off his face in an actual style, on purpose, unlike most of the local lads, who looked like they were dragged backwards through a hedge. But it was his green eyes and long dark lashes that captivated her. His lashes would be the envy of any girl. He had white teeth – Lena had a thing about teeth – and a square jaw. He looked like Cary Grant, she thought with a giggle.

When he asked her up to dance in the Lilac, she could hardly believe it. All the other girls were mad jealous, but she loved it. She knew she looked lovely in the yellow silk dress teamed up with her red high heels. She'd saved up for two months to pay for the shoes, but they were worth it even if they killed her feet. Doc had joked that he'd get her wages back from her when he was treating her corns and bunions from wearing shoes like that. She'd retorted that she had no notion of paying him a penny, that working for the local doctor, especially since he was her godfather and her dad's best friend, surely must have some advantages – free corn plasters and bunion paring maybe? She giggled again, feeling silly and carefree.

As she paused on the doorstep, a pang of familiar sadness threatened her happy mood. She glanced skywards, hoping Daddy could see her now. She was sure he would approve of Malachy; he'd always liked him as a little boy. She remembered them playing football together in the orchard of Kilteegan House.

She entered through the kitchen door and hushed Thirteen, her father's beloved Border collie, before creeping up the stairs as quietly as a mouse. Jack was snoring, his bedroom door ajar. Molly and May in the next room had a little bed each but always slept together, and their door was open enough for Lena to see their tousled blonde heads and bare feet sticking out from under the blankets. Hopefully they were dreaming of puppies and kittens and ponies; at two years old they were obsessed with animals.

Lena was looking forward to bed herself. She normally shared the room with Emily, but her older sister was doing a course in bookkeeping in Cork and was in digs for the duration. She'd be home in about two months, and while Lena missed her, it was nice to have the bedroom to herself. She needed a few hours sound sleep before she had to get up and give Jack a hand with the milking and then go to her job at the surgery.

She pushed her bedroom door open, and her heart missed a beat, her mother was sitting on her bed.

'Where were you? Were you out dancing?' Her mother's pale eyes were anxious, as if dancing was a terrifying thing to do. Her long hair was loose and unkempt, and she wore her flowing sea-green dressing gown.

'Mammy, I was at the dance in the Lilac – I told you I was going,' Lena whispered, still anxious not to wake her siblings.

'There might have been bad spirits there, evil people, who would do you harm! You can't see them – you're like your father, too trusting. You haven't the ability to see them for what they are...'

'No evil spirits, just normal lads and girls like myself, Mam.' Lena kept her voice low and even; she would not react to this line of conversation. She placed her new shoes in the base of the wardrobe, then took the Pond's cold cream from her dresser and began to clean the make-up off her face.

Mammy had been good for quite a while now, cooking and taking care of them all. When she was happy and well, she was warm and kind and talented at everything she touched. Only yesterday Mammy had been encouraging her to go dancing in her new dress and saying how pretty she was. How Lena reminded her of Maria's own Aunty Betty, who went to America. How her lovely dark hair was so healthy and shiny, and it was because she rinsed it in lemon juice. And how her petite curvy figure was the envy of the parish.

But the downturn always came, and this was clearly it.

Lena knew she should be used to it by now, but it still shocked her every time, how sudden it could be. Poor Daddy put up with it for years. They'd gone to different doctors, and they'd even tried electric shock treatment, but that made Maria so bewildered and forgetful, it was even more terrifying. And in the end, they'd had to accept there was nothing to be done except send her to St Catherine's for periods of time when she was at her worst. They were kind there, and though Maria knew what it meant when she went there, she always spoke of their kindness when she came home. Sometimes it only took a few weeks, other times months and months, but when she came back, it was like the sun had come up again and their mother was back, all the mystery and demons and darkness forgotten.

Lena often wished she could just run away from the whole confusing thing. She was seventeen now, and Doc had given her a job on reception, so if she wanted, she could get a job in one of the nice clinics in Cork, or maybe even Dublin. But she worried about abandoning Molly and May, and Jack was still only fifteen and wouldn't be able to cope by himself – he was a sensitive boy, and Maria frightened him. Lena worried a lot about what their mother's illness had done to her little brother's sweet nature. He was a good-looking boy, fair-haired and tall, the image of his mother, and he had such a gentle disposition. But he had never got the guts up to even speak to a girl, let alone ask one out. He had no real friends – he'd left school early to run the farm, and farming was a solitary activity at the best of times.

Emily was two years older than Lena and had plans to marry Blackie Crean; the two of them planned to run his family's hardware shop in the village. It wasn't much of a dream, Lena thought, but Emily and Blackie had been together since they were in secondary school, and the prospect of a life together forever in Kilteegan Bridge seemed to make them both happy. Blackie's useless, idle, sticky-fingered father, Dick Crean, was gone, skipped to England, but he was no loss whatsoever. Mrs Crean ran the shop now, but she was crippled with arthritis so would be glad to hand it all over. Emily was sweet and would do what she could to help Jack and mind the twins, Lena knew that, but once Emily was married, she'd have the shop and then maybe her own children to look after.

'I'm tired, Mam, so I'll go to bed. Maybe you should too,' she said, trying to keep the sadness out of her voice.

'Not until you tell me who you were dancing with.' Her mother's voice rose a little – anxious, suspicious, angry.

Suddenly Lena felt so tired, bone-weary of it all. She pulled off her dress and slipped on her nightie. 'If you must know, I was dancing with Malachy Berger.'

Her mother paled and her jaw tightened. 'You are forbidden to be near that boy, do you hear me? Forbidden.'

Lena knew that crazed look but wasn't expecting the blow. It knocked her off her feet, and she landed painfully as she put her hand out to save herself.

The sound of her fall and the enraged scream of her mother brought Jack running, his fair hair standing on end as he gazed wild-eyed at them, wearing his pyjama bottoms and a vest. Behind came a confused and tousled May, a terrified Molly behind her.

'Lena, are you all right?' Jack ran to her and helped her up.

'I'm sorry, I'm sorry, I'm sorry...' The words came out in a sob as Maria rushed past her children, making for her own bedroom; she slammed the door so hard it shook the house.

'Awe you awright, Lena? Awe you hurted?' Molly, who couldn't pronounce her R's yet, asked fearfully, and Lena knew she needed to reassure them.

'I'm fine darling, just a little bump.'

Jack lifted her up and carried her to the bed. He was a gentle soul, always finding birds with broken wings or bottle-feeding calves and lambs that had been rejected by their mothers. He knew what that felt like.

'I'm fine, girls. I just had a tumble – it's my silly new shoes.' She tried to laugh through the pain and was rewarded by weak smiles from her little sisters. 'You too, Jack, don't worry. It was an accident. Just go back to bed.' Lena was exhausted and just needed them all to leave her alone.

IF YOU LIKE the sound of this book, it's first in a five part series. You can download the book here:

https://geni.us/TheTroublewSecretsAL

Jean x

# ABOUT THE AUTHOR

Jean Grainger is a USA Today bestselling Irish author. She writes historical and contemporary Irish fiction and her work has very flatteringly been compared to the late great Maeve Binchy.

She lives in a stone cottage in Cork with her husband Diarmuid and the youngest two of her four children. The older two come home for a break when adulting gets too exhausting. There are a variety of animals there too, all led by two cute but clueless micro-dogs called Scrappy and Scoobi.

# ALSO BY JEAN GRAINGER

**The Tour Series**

The Tour

Safe at the Edge of the World

The Story of Grenville King

The Homecoming of Bubbles O'Leary

Finding Billie Romano

Kayla's Trick

**The Carmel Sheehan Story**

Letters of Freedom

The Future's Not Ours To See

What Will Be

**The Robinswood Story**

What Once Was True

Return To Robinswood

Trials and Tribulations

**The Star and the Shamrock Series**

The Star and the Shamrock

The Emerald Horizon

The Hard Way Home

The World Starts Anew

**The Queenstown Series**

Last Port of Call

The West's Awake

The Harp and the Rose

Roaring Liberty

**Standalone Books**

So Much Owed

Shadow of a Century

Under Heaven's Shining Stars

Catriona's War

Sisters of the Southern Cross

**The Kilteegan Bridge Series**

The Trouble with Secrets

What Divides Us

More Harm Than Good

When Irish Eyes Are Lying

A Silent Understanding

**The Mags Munroe Story**

The Existential Worries of Mags Munroe

Growing Wild in the Shade

Each to Their Own

Printed in the USA
CPSIA information can be obtained
at www.ICGtesting.com
LVHW041944070823
754572LV00030B/201